ATTILA VERES

THIS'LL MAKE THINGS A LITTLE EASIER

STORIES

Translated from the Hungarian by the Author

VALANCOURT BOOKS

This'll Make Things a Little Easier by Attila Veres
First edition 2026

Copyright © 2026 by Attila Veres
Published by arrangement with Agave Könyvek Kft., Budapest

All rights reserved. In accordance with the U.S. Copyright Act of 1976, the copying, scanning, uploading, and/or electronic sharing of any part of this book without the permission of the publisher constitutes unlawful piracy and theft of the author's intellectual property. If you would like to use material from the book (other than for review purposes), prior written permission must be obtained by contacting the publisher.

Valancourt Books and the Valancourt Books logo are registered trademarks of Valancourt Books, LLC. All rights reserved.

Published by Valancourt Books, Richmond, Virginia
http://www.valancourtbooks.com

ISBN 978-1-954321-93-9 (trade hardcover)
ISBN 978-1-954321-94-6 (trade paperback)
Also available as an electronic book.

Cover by Vince Haig
Set in Bembo Book MT

Praise for Attila Veres's

THE BLACK MAYBE

'Every decade or so, a writer comes along who reconfigures the way we think about the Weird. First Thomas Ligotti, then Laird Barron, and now Attila Veres. An astonishing collection, really unlike anything out there, which suggests a new way forward.'

– Brian Evenson, author of *Song for the Unraveling of the World*

'[Veres'] world is unique, bleak, terrifying, and all his own. Whether it's urban fables of rock music, harvests that claim souls, Aickmanesque situations or an amazing take on cosmic horror, his vision is always stunning. These stories, his debut in English, will blow you away.'

– Mariana Enríquez, author of *Things We Lost in the Fire*

'A stunning parade of terrors surreal and horrors sublime. The uncanny stories in *The Black Maybe* are as originally chilling and imaginatively dangerous as anything you'll read this decade, if not your lifetime, and Attila Veres deserves the worldwide acclaim this inventive work of horror will surely bring him. His approach is genuinely fresh. No maybes about it: this book is pitch black and totally engrossing.'

– Michael Arnzen, award-winning author of *Proverbs for Monsters*

'The ten macabre tales that make up Veres's English-language debut stake their scares on their wildly unpredictable plots. All Veres's stories begin in realistically grounded settings before veering unexpectedly into territory rife with unforeseeable and surreal menaces . . . These tales wear their resistance to conventional horror tropes and formulas as a badge of honor. Readers are sure to be impressed.'

– *Publishers Weekly*

'*The Black Maybe*, by Attila Veres, is a refreshing blast of cold cellar air. The horror is insidious and surreal, slowly chewing away what you think is real until you find yourself surrounded by a nightmare. I love this book!'

– Nathan Ballingrud, award-winning author of *Wounds*

'Attila Veres is fiendishly talented. Certain images in *The Black Maybe* caused me to glance at the darkened corners of my office as I read into the wee hours.'

– Laird Barron, author of *Swift to Chase*

'These stories dwell in the in-between places of life and death, that place where nightmares wait to be harvested. These are your nightmares, or they soon will be, so settle in for an excursion to a horrific mental, emotional, and spiritual landscape like no other. A brilliant work.'

– Elizabeth Engstrom, author of *When Darkness Loves Us*

'Original, brilliant, distinctive. These masterful stories by Attila Veres are a breath of fresh air from out of the darkness.'

– Michael Cisco, award-winning author of *The Divinity Student*

Contents

'a pit full of teeth'

How should I start this? I set out to write a story, but this is not a story. This is a warning.

The offer came out of the blue. I received an email asking if I had a short story or novella that had not yet been published in a foreign language (all my stories met this criterion), and if so, would I be willing to sell the publishing rights to an anthology funded by the EU? I was excited. It wasn't the Nobel Prize, but I had been on the verge of giving up writing altogether. Writing had always been a hopeless battle against words and time, and I felt I was running short on both. Small gestures, tiny successes like this chance offer, go a long way toward keeping me on track, if you are generous enough to call the quagmire that is the Hungarian literary scene a track.

The email was sent from a generic address, info@something, signed by an editor named Hekla Karlsdottir. From the name, I assumed she was of Icelandic origin. I searched for a corresponding Facebook or LinkedIn profile, but found nothing.

I now believe that Hekla Karlsdottir never existed.

Nevertheless, I replied to her initial email. We communicated in English. I tried to maintain a friendly tone in my messages, hoping that she would prove to be my golden ticket into the international scene. I inquired whether I was the only representative of Hungary in this planned volume? If not, who else? If I was the only one, then why me of all the insignificant authors of this insignificant country?

Hekla evaded these questions as if I had never asked them.

Not that I truly cared; the possibility of being published

abroad excited me too much. I knew I could soon be posting about it on Facebook and Instagram and whatever new social media platform came along, collecting digital likes and hearts and loving hugs, and maybe a like or two would magically turn into an actual book purchase. I needed the money; I needed it badly! I had to move soon. The apartment I was renting had already deteriorated beyond acceptable condition, and the landlord was not willing to lift a finger. Money talks, but where is a writer supposed to get his money from when half the population can't even read properly and the other half refuses to buy books?

Of course I had a Plan B.

Last year I won the Zsoldos Péter Award. I didn't even know such a thing existed until they sent me my medal. It's basically the local World Fantasy Award, only for a readership of about forty people. I won it along with other semi-important people in the field: Sepi and Botond. Sepi is an author of post-humanist crime fiction that is respected in the literary scene, selling zero copies, while Botond is the author of brick-sized space operas that mount the sales charts.

After winning the award, Sepi, Botond, and I decided to turn it into cash by founding the Academy of Fantastic Writers. We realized that although there were hardly any readers left in Hungary, everyone aspired to become a published writer.

We figured we could charge two hundred thousand Hungarian forints per person for a six-month group course or the same amount for a few days of personal training. All courses would be held online via Zoom meetings, because why waste money on renting a real room?

Being published abroad would be particularly useful for our academy, as it would strengthen the credibility of our brand and make us look like authors who really knew what they were doing.

That's why I would have said yes even if they wanted to publish my story on a Russian prison wall.

Hekla went one step further than her original request and pushed me for a story that hadn't even been published in Hungarian. A complete original. I was ready to comply.

I briefly summarized the plots of some of my completed but not-yet-published stories. They were the following:

Like Father/Son: It's about a middle-aged man and his son who eat the greasy Hungarian specialty *lángos* right after the funeral of their wife/mother. It's supposed to be a contemplative story about memory, grief, and family issues. Strictly non-horror, so I could sneak my way into one of those mainstream literary magazines and gain some attention and respect. Unfortunately, I couldn't resist my nature, and the deceased woman may or may not return from her freshly dug grave in the last line of the story. This ruined my chances of becoming a literary author; but for a simple local horror story, it contained too much sour-cream-and-cheese-type soulfulness and the obligatory sentences that drag on forever without punctuation; a feature that has defined our high-end literature since the '80s. All in all, I consider this story an immense and total failure, but somewhere in a hidden part of my soul that has been bloodied by my last decade spent trying to survive as a writer in Hungary, I still hoped that the next time I opened the file and skimmed the text, I would have an epiphany and suddenly see it as a lost gem instead of the lost turd it actually is.

Anyway.

Next on the list was *Imaginary Fire*, a confusing eco-apocalyptic fantasy about a family hiking in a burning forest. I wrote it in verse form, but since I can't write poetry (apparently, at all), it didn't turn out so well. But I figured that wouldn't matter in translation (you can always blame the translator), and I was not going to publish it in Hungarian.

There was also a more straightforward story, *Primary School Class 6B Takes a Trip to the Labyrinth of the Minotaur*. The title summarizes the essence of the plot with remarkable clarity. Spoiler: Everyone dies.

Hekla, however, chose the final story, *To Dust*.

I sent her the rest only as a courtesy; I wanted her to feel like she had options – but I knew this was the only really interesting unpublished work I had, and I wanted it to be the lead story in my next collection, if there ever was one. I was also proud of it, though I was worried it would not work well in synopsis. Fortunately, it did.

Hekla wanted it for the volume.

I sent her the story as a Word document in Hungarian. Hekla informed me that she would now hand me over to the actual editor of the volume, as she was only a headhunter for authors and stories, but did not speak the language into which the story was to be translated. It was at that moment that I realized for the first time that the story was not going to be published in English, Icelandic, or any other language I'd ever heard of. The volume was to be published as part of a language preservation program. They wanted to preserve the written form of an almost extinct tribal language, or at least to make it accessible to historical memory. Hekla gave no further details as to which language it was or what tribe spoke it. She wished me good luck and promised to publish *Imaginary Fire* in Swedish. That was the last I heard from her.

Later, the actual editor and translator of the volume contacted me. His emails were never signed, and to this day I have no idea of his name, or even gender. He sent his emails in Hungarian, although I would have preferred to correspond in English, because either his knowledge of Hungarian was severely limited, or he was using the beta version of some ancient translation software. I struggled to understand the short and rude messages because every sentence was an insult to my mother tongue. I tried to figure out what they expected from me: clues to linguistic expressions or perhaps clues to the cultural context of the story? Notes about history? Notes about myself?

Having received no satisfactory answers, or any at all, I asked more specific questions about billing and payment procedures.

I was aware that I should expect €200, but I wanted to clarify the terms of publication, although I doubted we could agree on a contract when there was such a large communication barrier between us. I gave my address, tax number, and bank details and urged him to reach an agreement as soon as possible. It became increasingly difficult to communicate with this mysterious publisher, and eventually he stopped responding to my emails altogether.

Weeks, then months passed.

I would have given up hope that my short story was ever going to be published if an envelope had not landed in my mailbox. It is a miracle it arrived at all, because the local postman hardly ever delivered anything. He simply threw the contents of his bag on top of a random letterbox or onto the floor. Many a letter was lost in this chaotic mess.

This letter, however, was carefully placed in my letterbox, even though my name was faded and barely legible. The envelope bore neither the sender's name nor their address, just mine. I suspected that this would be the next chapter in my foreign publication ordeal. I hoped that the envelope contained a contract. However, when I opened it, I found not a contract, but €200 worth of crumpled and dirty euro bills and a single human tooth.

I took care of the money first. I counted it three times to make sure the two hundred euros were all there, then put the bills in a plastic bag. They felt sticky.

After sorting the money, I shook the tooth out of the envelope. It was partially covered in dried blood. I wondered if sending tiny human remains was considered an illegal activity. People try to get rid of their teeth every day; but what do they do with the extracted teeth? If the teeth did not enjoy the safe, strong embrace of the gums, I guess they might well be considered garbage.

The only question then was: why should I receive garbage along with my money? I had no doubt that the anthology editors had sent the envelope, and the money was my payment. I wrote an email to the editor and attached a photo of the tooth. I tried to strike a humorous tone: 'Is anyone missing a tooth?' I asked in the email. The mailer daemon replied that the email address no longer existed.

This was more annoying than worrying. Had the publisher ceased to exist in the meantime, their accounts frozen? Or had the publisher changed their address and deleted the old one without sending a notification? I found the hassle involved with this publication increasingly tiresome, even though at that point practically nothing was expected of me. I had done my job, which was to write a story and get it accepted. Nevertheless, the mere transfer of money raised questions that worried me. And that was before I even considered the tooth.

Instead of throwing it away, I carefully placed the tooth in a matchbox and the box in a drawer. Maybe I was afraid that sooner or later someone would ask for it back, and if I couldn't return it, they would pull one of my own teeth.

I had a hard time falling asleep that night, knowing that the matchbox and the money were in the apartment with me, as if these objects had a gravity of their own that disturbed my thoughts. I tossed and turned in bed for hours. Then, just as I was about to give up the fight against insomnia and get out of bed, I finally fell asleep.

In my dream, I was at a friend's birthday party. This event actually took place; a typical gathering of people in their late thirties, eating more than drinking. These gatherings often end up as YouTube parties with a very specific style: '90s nostalgia disco with a dash of trash. We love to have fun at the expense of the lesser-known artists of the era.

In reality, we played the 1997 song 'Ess, eső, ess' by the band G-Play. That was the moment when the basic idea of *To Dust* formed in my head. The song captures the inglorious moment in Hungarian music when artists tried to imitate American hip-hop and rap with varying degrees of success. This particular band tried to gain relevance by turning a then-recent murder case (a high school student had been killed by her drug-addict boyfriend in 1997) into a rap song.

In my dream, however, another song was playing on TV instead: the song 'To Dust' by the band Partytime. My short story revolves around this song. I didn't want to use the real song that inspired me, because then I would have had to write about the singer, and why should I drag real people into a fictional story? So in my story, the song is similar to 'Ess, eső, ess' in the sense that 'To Dust' is a G-Funk hit from the '90s that describes a real-life (fictional) murder case and its chorus is sung by an extraordinary singer.

The story of *To Dust* is about the singer of the fictional song 'To Dust'. My fictional song is exactly like the one that inspired me: the rap-based verses describe the circumstances of the murder from an external, omniscient perspective, and the chorus tells the story from the victim's point of view, or rather, it describes the victim's feelings posthumously, after the fact of her own death, as she laments her violent demise.

So in my fictional song, the singer embodies a murdered girl. Not a person who has since died but is still alive in the context and narrative of the song, but someone who is already dead at the time the song is performed. She sings about being dead; she sings about a moment of sadness, pain, and fear that stretches into eternity. Apparently, as the singer recorded her part in the studio booth, she accidentally reached out to the ghost of the murdered girl, conjuring her.

The singer thus became a gateway. A medium.

In my dream, I heard the song as if it really existed; the song seemed real, as did the accompanying music video, shot on cheap, grainy film stock. Two bald men rapped into the camera and posed in various squatting, kneeling, and leaning positions in run-down stairwells, at the counters of closed nightclubs, or in the back of a police car. The video only showed the singer when she sang the chorus.

Her long, blond hair fell around her head, and in the close-ups she stared straight ahead as if she were dead, her eyes cold and unmoving as she lip-synced the lyrics of the chorus. During the first verse, she was lying on the floor, presumably at the scene of the murder, as the video occasionally zoomed in on disturbing details: a crack in the wall, a hammer on the coffee table, a broken mirror. At the end of the verse, the singer's face was covered with a white sheet.

In the first section of the next verse the sheet was removed; the singer performed these lyrics while lying on the autopsy table.

I woke up before the third verse.

That could have been the end of the whole ordeal. Another unsuccessful escape attempt, another promise leading to nothing but a few unpleasant memories, anxious dreams, and a bitter taste in my mouth after I realized that relative success had once again eluded me. Somehow, I am sure I could have explained why it did not work out and moved on to some other, unattainable new hope. That's just human nature. We keep telling ourselves that maybe next time it will work out, until eventually we run out of options.

A few weeks later, however, I received my complimentary copy.

It was a typical university publication with a disgusting red cover and an illegible, blurry photo poorly positioned on an otherwise mundane front page. The back cover was completely blank. The paper felt like plastic, and there was no trace of the heady smell of fresh glue that's so easy to fall in love with in publishing.

And yet . . .

I could recognise my own name in the copyright notice, although the original title of the story was not included, or if it was, I could not decipher it. Apart from my own name, I understood nothing of the texts, because the language did not use the Latin, Greek, Cyrillic, or Arabic alphabets. If I didn't know that these symbols were supposed to be words, I would have thought the volume was some kind of artistic experiment, a calligraphic printing exercise, rather than an anthology of fiction. It was not aesthetically pleasing. Not at all. The randomly scattered symbols reminded me of street litter, and a cold shiver ran down my spine as I looked at the pages.

But who cares? I was actually published!

I had to make sure the translation existed, as if I could not exist without it.

My story was the fourth. My name was recognisable, albeit heavily distorted by the foreign alphabet. That didn't bother me. Of course I was happy, but in my joy I looked for a worm of sorrow and, as usual, I found it.

The title consisted of at least four or five individual words in this language, I could see this clearly. I tried to continue rejoicing, but my eyes kept falling on the gaps between the words.

These gaps posed a problem for me.

I gave the story the title *To Dust* for a reason. I like disturbingly short titles. In translation, I could have accepted a title with two or even three words. If the phrase 'from dust to dust' was not common in this ethnic group, the translator could have expanded the title to, say, 'The Woman of Dust' or 'The Singer That Came From Dust, Soon to Return to Dust,' although in the latter case the language would have to phrase it with almost poetic brevity.

Or maybe, just maybe, they completely disregarded my original intentions with the title and gave it a new one.

I wrote another email to the editor and also to Hekla to explain the situation, but received an error message back from both. I found this annoying, but not surprising.

I tried various ways to find the book on the internet, but the search was thwarted by the fact that the typeface of the volume did not match my keyboard; I could not even type in the title. In a last-ditch effort, I asked Reddit for help. I took a sample image of a random page (why lie; not just any page, but the first paragraph of my own short story) and uploaded it to a couple of groups where people from all over the world discuss languages and linguistic matters. 'What language is this?' I asked in each post and then waited patiently for someone to answer.

To my surprise, Reddit deleted all my posts on the grounds that they violated community rules and banned me from posting any more. I had always assumed it would take more than that to get kicked out of one of their communities. Shortly before my expulsion, however, I received a reply to one of my posts: 'ratun sampi'. It was a throwaway account, and minutes later my post and the comment were removed.

I typed the two words into the search bar, but the results were unsatisfactory. It brought up the Facebook page of a presumably Thai person and some irrelevant hits, but none helped solve the mystery. I started a new search and added 'Hungarian'. I was lucky. On the third search result, an article from twenty years ago popped up, mentioning a then-young linguist, Dr. András Voit-Kelemen, whose area of expertise included researching the 'Ratun languages'. Finally, a name that was easy to research; he was an associate professor at ELTE University's Institute for Language Mediation, an expert in exotic foreign languages.

I did not find much more, just a few links to his publications that didn't mean anything to me. I sent an email to his university address outlining my problem, and since I was conditioned to accept the futility of writing, I was pleasantly surprised when he actually replied and invited me to his office.

I walked over to the ELTE building. The corridors were cold because they had no money for heating. I knocked on the office door, and Dr. Voit-Kelemen's assistant, a woman in her late twenties, opened the door. She looked tired, grumpy, frail, and generally unenthusiastic about life.

The associate professor sat behind his desk. He weighed about three hundred pounds and struggled to fit into the old office chair. He wore a corduroy jacket, which he had made his own with a few signature cigarette burns. He had stubble on his face. His lungs wheezed with every breath, but on the desk was pack of Marlboros and a plastic lighter with a naked woman on it. His nails were nicotine-yellow. His voice was deep and raspy, his graying hair like wire mesh.

I introduced myself and explained my situation and my request: I wanted to compare my short story with the translation. Perhaps, I said, the professor could tell me to what extent the two texts matched in style and content. I didn't need a written translation.

I handed him the book, put a bookmark next to my short story and waited for an answer. Dr. Voit-Kelemen took the book, glanced at the page, then let the book slip from his fingers and drop onto the desk like a discarded carcass. He coughed loudly, then fished a cigarette out of the pack and signaled the assistant to open the window.

Dr. Voit-Kelemen didn't beat about the bush for long. He lit his cigarette and made it clear to me that he understood the language printed on the paper, although he couldn't imagine why anyone would want to see the Ratun-Sampi language in print. As far as he knew, no book of fiction had ever been published in this particular language. Although he refused to say a single word out loud, he said he could translate the text for me.

Needless to say, I was delighted. Ideally, my original text and the translation should be practically identical. I said that it would be enough for me if he skimmed over the Hungarian and the Ratun-Sampi version (as far as I understood, he referred to the language as Ratun-Sampi, like the Reddit user) and confirmed that they matched, so that I could continue to rejoice about the publication.

However, Dr. Voit-Kelemen wanted to cash in on his knowledge and set the fee at one and a half million forints per page. I respect people who ask for money for their hard-earned knowledge and skills, because the value lies in the price people are willing to pay for those skills. But I wasn't born an idiot to pay such an astronomical sum, and I told him that in no uncertain terms.

Then he asked me the question I didn't want to hear. Why was I interested in the contents of the translation? I had been paid. I had a copy of the book as a sign of respect, my name was more or less visible in it. The story certainly existed in Hungarian, and it was unlikely that any living person would ever read it in Ratun-Sampi. Of course, I invoked artistic integrity. Creative control must never be lost, not even when I have given away my creation. I must monitor every step of my story's journey as if it were a child that needing to be nurtured and guided into an adulthood it can never reach.

Dr. Voit-Kelemen didn't believe a word I said; maybe he refused to understand – or maybe he just didn't care.

He extinguished his cigarette, flicked the butt out of the window and, after a loud cough, indicated that his consultation was over. If I still wanted to make a business offer for the translation, he said, I could do so by email. But I couldn't leave without answers. I was ashamed of my rising anger, but angry, even furious I was.

I took out my wallet and slammed a twenty thousand bill on the desk. I hoped the sarcasm in my voice was clear when I asked how much text would this amount cover?

He touched the bill and replied without a hint of irony.

'That will be enough for the title,' he said.

I agreed to the deal. If the title matched, or at least bore a distant resemblance to my original title, I could sit back, relax and accept the entire translation as reasonably accurate.

Dr. Voit-Kelemen ran his fingers over the title a few times, whispering words under his breath, then pulled a notepad out of the drawer and scribbled something on it. He was humming to himself, which irritated me to no end.

It took a minute before I recognized the melody, or thought I recognized it, from my dream. Because while he was scribbling on his notepad, he was humming the chorus of 'To Dust'. I started to sweat, but comforted myself with the thought that it was probably due to my agitated state of mind that I could hear my song in the toneless murmur.

The professor tore off the sheet on which he had scribbled; then he took his lighter and lit it on fire. The assistant rushed into the room with a large ashtray. Dr. Voit-Kelemen put the burning ball of paper in it; shortly afterward the flames were extinguished. The professor picked up his pen and wrote something on the next sheet in large, messy letters, carefully hiding the words from me. When he had finished, he folded up the paper and handed it to me, telling me to check the translated title once I'd left the office.

A minute later, I was standing in the freezing corridor of the ELTE basement, holding the paper in my sweaty fingers. I read the words several times, hoping each time that they would change, that they would start to mean what they were supposed to mean and not what I was reading on the paper. There were five words on the paper, all lowercase and in quotation marks.

'a pit full of teeth'

I could not reconcile the two titles *To Dust* and *'a pit full of teeth'* in any way. There are no teeth or pits in my story. In my story a professional singer, while recording the chorus of 'To Dust', makes contact with the murdered girl whose murder is documented in the song. She doesn't only make contact with the ghost: the deceased girl herself sings the chorus, possessing the singer, or her vocal cords, thus linking her own death with the singer's life. It's not about pits or teeth, but about a singer starting a new career as a singing medium.

What did this title even mean?

I could hardly sleep that night. I was afraid that I would dream about the music video again, and this time I would see the third verse, in which the singer utters the lines in a state beyond her autopsy.

Eventually I fell asleep. In my dream, I was in Nyíregyháza, where I spent my childhood. I was standing in the street while a storm raged. Books were falling from the sky, their spines literally exploding, the pages flying around me like confused animals desperately searching for a home. There were paperbacks and hardcovers in equal numbers, some in Hungarian, others in English, German, Russian, Spanish, or French. Each cover had my name on it. As I stood in the whirlwind looking at these wrecks, I was overcome with sadness; I knew that these were the books I had always hoped to write, and now that they had been destroyed before my very eyes, I never would.

I awoke just as my phone lit up, indicating that an email had arrived. The melancholy of the dream lingered as I checked the message from a certain Valéria Hegyi.

She was Dr. Voit-Kelemen's assistant and asked for a meeting regarding my translation. I sat up excitedly in bed and arranged a meeting for later that day.

We met in a crowded café near Vas Street. Valéria looked even more fragile in the sunlight. Her clothes consisted of cheap secondhand rags with tears and holes everywhere. She was wearing a pair of battered ballerinas, so adored by humanities majors. Her straw-blond hair was pinned up, but strands kept coming loose. She was pale, her skin so thin that even the wind could bruise it. Her lips were chapped because she had a habit of nibbling on them when she was nervous. She wore an old Soviet watch, a Pobeda, with a red leather strap.

Her sandwich was about half eaten when we got to the heart of the conversation. I had hoped that she would compare the two texts as a selfless, helpful act, essentially in return for the sandwich and coffee I had bought her; I assumed that a teaching assistant was just like a professor, endowed with the same skills and knowledge, only in a younger edition, waiting to take her place in the long, motionless procession of college lecturers.

But that was not the case at all.

She rolled a cigarette while talking about how the professor was the only one who dealt with the Ratun languages in

Hungary and even in Central-Eastern Europe. However, since the Ratun language group was extremely marginal from the point of view of linguistic research (especially since its oral form supposedly resembled the song of certain rare birds) and many had even debated whether it was a language at all and not just a footnote to an ethnic group that might not even exist, the field lacked young and enthusiastic researchers. Valéria was not enthusiastic either, just persistent, and I realized that she didn't understand the language herself, but she knew the basics and had access to Dr. Voit-Kelemen's records because of her position. In possession of these records, she saw no reason why she could not interpret the translated text at least on a comparative level.

Of course, she would not do this for free. Rather, she was asking for an advance because she was behind on last month's rent and needed the money urgently.

This was perhaps the last moment when I could have turned back. I actually wanted to quit because I had nothing to gain but everything to lose. I needed a moment to think about it and make my final decision, to tell her no and thus live with a nagging doubt for the rest of my life.

I excused myself and hurried to the restroom to buy some time. I hate this type of hipster college café, mostly because of the uncomfortable furniture and tiny, co-ed toilets. I could barely squeeze myself into the tight space, then had to turn around to pull shut the incredibly heavy sliding oak door, the lock of which barely wanted to budge, and then had to get my body back into a suitable position to do what I'd come there to do. I didn't really pay attention to the music coming from the speakers. It wasn't until I was washing my hands that I unconsciously started humming along to the tune coming from the speakers, and it wasn't until I turned off the tap that I recognized the song.

It was my song. 'To Dust'.

As difficult as it was to close the heavy sliding door, it was of course ten times harder to open it. By the time I left the restroom, a Miles Davis song was playing. 'So What'.

Once I had extricated myself from the restroom, in the bright sunlight streaming through the café's tiny windows, I questioned whether I'd actually heard my fictional hit while stuck in this hipster den. The sliding door made of ridiculously thick Norwegian oak – obviously heavier and more expensive than all the other furniture and furnishings in the café put together – certainly did an excellent job of filtering the sound. It's possible, even likely, that I didn't hear any song at all. It annoyed me to no end that I kept referring to it as a song, when in fact 'To Dust' wasn't a song at all, just a narrative device.

Nevertheless, I hummed the chorus quietly to myself as I approached the counter, risking my impending nervous breakdown becoming imminent. I asked the barista to switch back to the previous song. The barista looked at me like I was stupid; I didn't blame him, because that's the neutral expression on the faces of all service staff in Budapest.

I asked him if he remembered the previous song, but he shook his head. He had been outside smoking a cigarette with Valéria.

I sat down next to Valéria again and told her that I was prepared to pay two hundred euros for a detailed comparison between the Hungarian and Ratun versions. Valéria's face flushed all over; I thought it was out of anger, but it turned out to be joy. Two hundred euros seemed like a lot of money to her, and I was glad to get rid of the dirty banknotes. I thought about giving her the tooth too, but I was afraid that Valéria would misunderstand the gesture.

Back at home, I tried in vain to write something meaningful. Instead, and this was surely a sign of madness, I searched the internet for hits on the keywords 'Partytime', 'To Dust', and Song, which brought up illegal song-sharing websites, South Asian dating portals and treasure troves of pornographic content – at least until I reached the third page of search results. There, in the middle of the page, I noticed an eBay listing that made my heart skip a beat.

I clicked on the link, but it only led to a dead auction page, and when I returned to the search results page, the listing had disappeared. Still, I swear it said 'EXTREMELY RARE!!! PARTYTIME TO DUST MAXI 12" PROMO VINYL (A SIDE: RADIO EDIT/B SIDE: DJ SCHUSINSKY MIX)'

I'm sure this was the headline of the listing because that's exactly how I wrote it in my story. Even though the story is about a singer, the actual protagonist and narrator of *To Dust* is a man who has recently started collecting records. In this respect, he is similar to me, because I also have a considerable record collection.

He finds this offer on eBay. He is interested in such rarities. Although he doesn't know the song or the band, he bids on the record. He begins to research the song on the Internet, which leads him to an obscure online community that discusses the song 'To Dust', its history and its impact at length. The narrator gradually gets lost in the maze of conflicting information and comes across forums that delve deeper and deeper into the occult aspects of the song, in particular the woman who sings the chorus.

Apparently, she disappeared from the music scene after the single was released. She never released another record, made no guest appearances, and never performed live again. Some claim that she disappeared not only as an artist, but also as a person. It is possible that she got married and changed her name. Some say she went to Germany or Switzerland to become a bar singer or prostitute, as often happened in the '90s. In the early 2000s many reported having seen her living on the street, begging for money.

In most occult forums, however, it was claimed that the singer had actually become a singer for the dead. Certain deceased individuals would occasionally take possession of her and express their posthumous emotions through her, using her vocal cords. There was some debate as to whether this was a profession or not. Was the woman paid for willingly allowing the dead to sing through her, or did she become arbitrarily possessed and sing death whether there was an audience or not? In the latter case, she must have been classified as insane and institutionalized.

My story was essentially about raising doubts; the narrator is drawn deeper and deeper into various conspiracies or narratives about the singer and her entanglements with the dead, particularly about the murdered girl she first came into contact with during the recording of 'To Dust', and he no longer knows what to believe. However, the subject intrigues him so much that he uses all his money to buy the 12-inch maxi record in the hope that it will help him solve the mystery. But of course, acquiring the record brings real trouble. He gets too close to the heart of the mystery and ends up trying to track down the singer himself.

I searched for the record directly, but only a few AI-generated scam sites popped up. At some point I decided I'd had enough of the whole thing, closed all the programs and sat down to watch a talent show on TV. After a few songs I turned it off, fearing that one of the contestants might accidentally sing 'To Dust'.

Just as my screen went black, Valéria's messages popped up on my phone. She informed me that she had started the work, and judging by the first few paragraphs the story was about a man who tries to steal flowers and suffers the consequences – he has to give away his own flowers as punishment. At least that's how Valéria had understood the text, but it was possible that it wasn't about flowers, but about teeth.

She promised to check again.

Flowers or teeth, I did not care. As long as it wasn't about singers, spirits of the dead, and old records, I was fucked. Of course, no one would know but me, but that was enough. I was getting tired. Everything seemed so pointless. I lay down and tried to follow the news about the Academy of Fantastic Writers.

While I was browsing, Józsi Tomasics wrote me a message. He is one of my absolute heroes, the editor of a local magazine and several volumes dedicated to fiction in honour of Lovecraft. Old H.P. was a liquid that filled the vessel of his life to the brim.

He got straight to the point. He wanted a short story for his upcoming thematic anthology on Lovecraft and Communist Hungary. He was keen on the title Cosmic Communism. He just loved alliterations.

According to the concept he enthusiastically described, the anthology would contain stories set in 1950s Communist Hungary, with a Lovecraftian cosmic horror twist, of course. Torture centres and the Great Old Ones! The 1956 revolution and Shub-Niggurath! Our own pocket-sized Stalin, Rákosi, as Chtulhu's servant! Things like that.

He was very proud of his latest volume, Horrific Holidays, which came out in the spring. I had a story in it called *The Summer I Chose to Die*, but I hoped no one would ever read it. It was too personal.

An idea came to me, and I suggested finding something Lovecraft would have loved to fear. A tribe in Europe that almost no one had heard of. That piqued his interest, and he mentioned that he belonged to secret, closed, almost occult online groups that dealt with such subjects in the deepest way. Those were his words, not mine.

Seeing no other option, I half-heartedly promised a story of communism and cosmic horrors if Józsi in return would search for the Ratun language or the Ratun tribe in these deep, occult online groups. That was the end of our conversation, and I was alone again, waiting for the embrace of sleep.

I was too tired to be scared.

In my dream, I was standing naked at the edge of a forest. I knew there were people around me, but I could not see them.

Occasionally I heard their voices imitating the chirping and singing of birds. I could easily have mistaken them for real birds, but I knew they were such perfect imitations that unless you were dreaming, you couldn't tell bird from human. One of these invisible people who sounded like a bird took my hand and led me to the entrance of a cave.

I entered the cave. As I went deeper into the darkness, pebbles cut into the soles of my feet. I looked down and saw that I was not stepping on pebbles, but on teeth scattered along the way.

I kept moving towards the absolute darkness that lay at the heart of the cave.

Neon lights lit up above me, casting cold light on the walls. A huge pit gaped at the bottom of the cave.

This pit was filled to the brim with teeth.

On the foundation of this sea of teeth stood a table cast from metal. On it lay the corpse of a woman waiting for her autopsy. She should have been covered with a sheet, as is customary for the dead, but she was not.

I wanted to escape, but the bird-sounding invisible people would not let me. The woman on the table slowly turned her head toward me, and I realized I was in the music video for 'To Dust'; it was the third verse, and the protective wall that is fiction had collapsed between me and the horror.

The body did not belong to the singer, but to the actual murder victim whose tragedy had been turned into a pop song.

I saw the girl's face and deeply regretted having written the story at all. She gaped at me, her ruined lips moving in sync with the lyrics, though the music was absent; and instead of words, only broken teeth fell from what was left of her mouth.

To avoid a comparison with the real-life murder that inspired 'Ess, eső, ess', the murder in *To Dust* was not committed with a knife.

It was done with a hammer.

I woke up screaming. I could still hear the birds chirping in the dark room, luring me back into the dream. I had the feeling that I was not alone. Startled, I switched on the light, but the room was empty.

My sheets were soaked with sweat. I felt like I would never be able to sleep again, and at that moment I decided to give up researching the translation. Who cared what the text said? It didn't matter if it was my story or not. I didn't even care if no one knew about the publication; all I wanted was not to have a dream like that again.

I went into the kitchen and made coffee. My hands were shaking because the nightmare wouldn't go away. I could see her face clearly in my mind's eye, or what was left of it. I could still feel the teeth under my feet; I could still hear the voices that sounded like birds in my ears. I waited for the sun to rise because everything seems so much safer in daylight; fictions don't seem to haunt me as much.

In the morning, I set out to run an errand, but as I walked down the street, I realized I had forgotten what I was supposed to be doing. I stopped and realized that my mind was completely blank except for the images of the dream.

I immediately sent Valéria a message and told her to stop investigating. I did not need any more details about the translation. I would pay her in full, I said, and she could even keep my complimentary copy if she wanted. It might be worth something. Otherwise, we'd just forget this ever happened.

The message remained unread, but I was confident that if she read it, my point would come across loud and clear. The case was pretty much closed as far as I was concerned.

Later, Botond informed me that he had found the first client for the Academy of Fantastic Writers. His bitterness was obvious, because the client had actually wanted me to be her personal tutor. She asked me for a private course and even transferred a deposit of 100,000 forints to the Academy's brand-new account. As a core member of the Academy of Fantastic Writers, it was my duty, Botond said, to teach Vanda, a girl who joined us from a barely existing village via Zoom, the craft of fantastic writing so that she could eventually become a fantastic writer herself.

I took note of Botond's message, but the joy I should have felt was ashen. All my earlier worries had proved unfounded; despite the lack of international promotion, I was an important person, even indispensable to the newly burgeoning life of the Academy.

Nevertheless.

Half an hour later, I received a phone call. An accusing voice came from the other end of the line. 'Why did you have to do this?' he asked.

I recognized his deep, hoarse voice; it was Dr. Voit-Kelemen. I heard the click of the lighter and imagined his Marlboro lighting up. Was Valéria there to hand him an ash-tray? At that moment, I understood why he had called. Valéria had obviously been caught red-handed translating, and Dr. Voit-Kelemen's wallet was screaming in pain because someone had agreed to do the work cheaper.

Of course I was right. Valéria had been caught; the professor knew for a fact that the girl was translating my text, or the translation of my text. Dr. Voit-Kelemen made it clear that he was holding Valéria's notes in his hand at that moment. In an appreciative tone, he mentioned that they were quite accurate, although Valéria kept using the word 'flower' instead of 'tooth'. Though she had not gotten to the end of the story, Dr. Voit-Kelemen assured me that Valéria had rendered the essence of the text to the best of her abilities.

A long pause in the conversation followed. I could hear the professor taking a deep drag on his cigarette before he spoke again.

'Do you know why my price was so high?' he asked. He didn't wait for my answer.

'That's because it's not just a language,' he said. 'It's a sensory organ. A hand that searches for another hand in the dark, and if you read and interpret that language, it allows them to make contact, to draw you to them, even to change you. You let them see you, but you can't see them! Any contact with this language is dangerous.'

He took a few more drags on his cigarette. I felt a sense of dread that paralyzed me.

'I have read the story in Valéria's translation. It's terrible,' he said. 'Horrible,' he added. 'It turns my stomach, it's so full of horrors.'

Unexpected excitement spread through me. After all, the story had appeared under my name. If I translated it back into Hungarian, I could also publish it in my mother tongue under my name; after all, the two texts would be identical.

It would be *my* story again.

'What is *"a pit full of teeth"* about?' I asked.

Dr. Voit-Kelemen coughed or laughed. It was hard to tell.

'It's about a thief who is caught stealing and is punished for it. The harshest punishment that can be meted out in a Ratun tribe.'

He coughed, or maybe laughed again, and changed the subject.

He said he wanted me to know so I would not wait in vain for Valéria to finish her work. She never would.

Dr. Voit-Kelemen announced that Valéria Hegyi had been found dead in her apartment in the early hours of the morning. Her roommate returned from a party and found her body lying on the floor. The cause of death was suspected to be carbon monoxide poisoning; perhaps the landlord had not checked the system or the boiler valve was faulty. In any case, it was most likely an accident.

My legs were numb with shock. For some reason, I thought of her Pobeda with its red strap. I imagined the watch still ticking even though its owner was dead, and that filled me with dark, bitter sadness.

'There would be nothing special about the case,' he continued. 'Accidents often happen in this sort of cheap housing. But there's one detail the police can't figure out.'

'What is it?' I asked, but my voice was flat.

'The thing is,' Dr. Voit-Kelemen said, 'that Valéria did not have a single tooth left in her mouth when she was found.'

I said nothing, and he continued.

'I will burn her translation,' he said, 'because the Ratun tribe does not understand the concept of fiction. Everything they write down or tell you actually happened. That's why it was absurd for you to think they were translating your story. They interpreted your story as real. In their culture there is no translation, only a mutual exchange. They gave a real event in exchange for what you gave them. Valéria didn't translate a piece of fiction. She translated a record. The events in *"a pit full of teeth"* really happened.'

The line went dead.

The news sites were already reporting on the tragedy, though it didn't make the front page. I opened the Messenger chat. My message to stop the investigation was still unread, and I guessed it would stay that way forever.

I cried in the street. People walked past me and no one cared.

When I finally got home, Botond's message was waiting for me in my inbox, reminding me not to forget my class appointment the next morning. He also sent a Zoom link.

I wanted to cancel, but it was easier to do it than to explain why I was not doing it. As night fell, I told myself that I had nothing to do with Valéria's death, because these kinds of tragedies often happen, especially in poorly maintained homes.

I tried to conveniently forget about the missing teeth.

When I entered the bedroom, I realized that I wouldn't be able to go to sleep. Just looking at the bed made me shiver. The blanket was a strange shape; I had the intrusive thought that someone was already in my bed waiting for me.

I quietly left the room and carefully closed the door behind me. I sat down in the living room and stared at the TV screen. When the evening news came on, I changed the channel. I watched a report on celebrities' homes, focusing mainly on their bathrooms and toilets, followed by the daily soap opera.

Finally, David Attenborough appeared on screen talking about nature. It was one of his more recent programs; he seemed to be at least a hundred years old. He was standing in a forest, talking about the Scandinavian woodpecker in his unmistakable voice.

Did you know, for example, that the Scandinavian woodpecker can lay up to a hundred eggs a year?

Unfortunately, the species has been pushed to the brink of extinction due to overhunting. They are mainly hunted by a local tribe, not for their meat, but because they are linguistic competitors for each other, as the language of this tribe can be directly related to the song and chirping of the Scandinavian woodpecker.

'Listen,' said Attenborough, standing in the forest and pricking up his ears.

Birdsong came from a distance.

'Is that a bird or a human? A human or a bird?' asked Attenborough, and I woke up on the couch. The television was switched off.

I was awake, but the birdsong didn't stop. It was as if the birds were circling in the walls. After a few rounds, they fell silent; or maybe I never heard them, they just carried me out of my dream.

At that moment I saw that I had received about half a dozen messages from Józsi Tomasics. I had slept through his attempts to communicate, so I could only follow the events passively, half an hour after they happened.

His first question was, 'You didn't accept any teeth from them, did you?'

If they drop a tooth in the mailbox and I don't throw it in the trash, does that count as acceptance? I realized that this probably counted as an exchange. After all, the tooth was still in the drawer in a matchbox, and I gave them a story.

'Man, I don't know how you got into this, but everybody keeps real quiet about the Ratuns. I used TOR and scoured the dark web for you.'

Józsi is an angel.

'Only a few dare to write about the Ratuns, mostly people who married into the tribe and then fled from them.'

Encouraging.

'After making their posts or statements, most of these people have disappeared (or died) LOL :D'

Even more encouraging.

'So the information about the Ratun is vague at best. Some say they don't even exist, they're just a weird myth or a scholarly prank. Some scientists believe they really do exist, they just shy away from the limelight. They supposedly live in the northernmost parts of Europe, but it's impossible to say where. They could be a migratory tribe, but this hasn't been proven. For a while they were classified as Lapps or Samis, but the Samis are actually hostile to the Ratuns. They're afraid of them. They think the Ratuns literally live outside this world.'

I could definitely empathize with the feeling.

'All I know is that their language is very strange. The Samis are afraid of them because they believe that the Ratun language creates reality. That's why there is no Ratun literature or theater. They believe that when they tell a story, it becomes reality.'

I understood that only too well.

'Another strange thing is that they collect teeth. When a Ratun dies, they knock out his teeth and collect them all in a common, secret place. The Ratun leaders even pull out their own teeth while they're alive and add them to the common collection of teeth, out of respect for the tribe or for some other reason. These teeth are collected communally, and they make agreements or contracts with these teeth.'

Oh, damn, I said quietly.

'These are no ordinary contracts. You don't get a document that says exactly what you give and what you get in return, but you bind yourself to this tribe. I don't quite understand it, but it seems to be treated more like a religious or spiritual matter than money.

'One thing is for sure though: the biggest sin is stealing teeth. Because teeth are sacred to them, okay? So you can't just give them to anyone. The tribe decides together who to swap teeth with.'

I was suddenly aware of every single tooth in my mouth.

'If someone gets caught stealing from the communal supply, well, listen, you'll like it . . . They tell a story about them as punishment. More specifically, the tribe members punish tooth thieves by turning them into a story. They're actually killed, but without dying. They're killed by becoming characters in a narrative. This is an eternal, hellish form of death. A nightmare that repeats itself over and over again. Cool, isn't it?'

I gasped.

'By the way, may I announce your name for the Cosmic Communism volume? Alfonz and Balázs Farkas have already signed up!'

They always sign up, but so do I.

'It's funny! Ever since I started looking for this tribal thing, birds have been invading my house. They're practically chirping out of the walls.'

I shouted at the phone as if it were Józsi himself and not an inanimate object.

'Well, there's one in the kitchen. I'll go after it, maybe you'll have checked your phone by the time I get back.'

Józsi never came back.

I wrote him several messages to warn him about the kitchen, but I was half an hour too late. My messages went unread. I also tried to call him, but the phone only rang until the call was cut off.

Maybe he just forgot about me. Maybe he got stuck in the kitchen with a beer, or maybe a visitor knocked and now he was engrossed in a conversation, about Lovecraft, no doubt.

One can always hope.

Against all expectations, I fell asleep again. Of course, I felt guilty when I woke up. My phone was vibrating. It was Botond. He reminded me that the first student at the academy was expecting me at ten o'clock.

Don't ruin it for us, he added, and I realized I was going to do just that. It was impossible for me to teach anyone how to write. Just the thought of writing made me sick. I thought fiction was a pernicious demon that crept into a writer's life to wreak havoc. The Ratuns taught me to fear fiction.

Writing is hell, and I decided to convince my ten o'clock student to give up. Writing wasn't the solution to anything, quite the opposite. Writing itself was the problem!

After drinking several cups of coffee and convincing myself of my newfound purpose, I decided to put on a record. I went to the shelf; I craved obscure, loud, upbeat music. Of course, as I should have known, among the records I found one that didn't belong to me. I didn't buy this record, I didn't get it as a gift or steal it. This record shouldn't have been here at all; it shouldn't have existed.

I was holding a 12-inch record in an antistatic sleeve. On the sticker was the name of the band in red. Partytime. Underneath it was the title in white: 'To Dust (Radio Edit)'. I knew that the B-side would announce the mix by DJ Schusinsky.

I took it out of the sleeve to check its condition. It was almost pristine, the grooves were free of dust and scratches, just as promised on the eBay listing.

I laughed as I placed the record on the turntable. I thought the record would be blank, but it wasn't. 'To Dust' began to play, just as I had heard it in my dream. How long had this record been hidden in my collection? A few days? Since I wrote the short story? Or had the record always been there?

It didn't matter anymore; I sang along to the song and thought of the singer. Where could she be? Maybe she came to exist along with the record! Maybe she'll ring my doorbell soon and sing for me, but it won't be her, not quite, because every dead person has changed her until she's no longer human, only a gateway built from the eternally screaming voices of the dead. That's how *To Dust* ends. She knocks on my protagonist's door, singing and screaming with the fury of a thousand murdered souls.

I was terrified to experience the climax of *To Dust* in real life.

I looked at my cell phone. It was ten past ten. I got up and switched on my laptop. I found the Zoom link and clicked on it. I felt it was more important than ever to convince this student to give up the idea of writing.

I tried to collect my thoughts while the software made the connection. Another room appeared on my screen. At first it was blurry, pixelated, but soon it cleared up. There was something strange about the room, but I couldn't make out what, and before I could figure it out, Vanda sat down, her face filling the frame. She waved at me, but I didn't wave back.

This woman wasn't Vanda. Valéria was sitting on the other side of the Zoom window, alive and well. I was so relieved that I burst out laughing and told her how nice it was to see her, even though we had only met twice.

Valéria, or Vanda, shrugged her shoulders and smiled.

She spoke, but not in Hungarian. She spoke in bird calls.

No, no, no, no, I kept repeating, but Valéria, or Vanda, or whoever this woman pretended to be, just kept chirping and whistling, and then I understood what was wrong with the room on the other side of the conversation.

It was my bedroom.

I took a startled step back from the computer, and the woman on the screen laughed. The speakers squealed as the laughter echoed in my apartment, and then all I heard was a screeching sound from the computer, as if Zoom itself was about to scream. I heard the woman talking behind my bedroom door, which I had closed so carefully last night, and if I hadn't known it was her, I'd have thought a bird had flown into my room.

I couldn't take my eyes off the screen. The woman grabbed the laptop and showed me around the room. My room. Then she positioned the laptop so that I could see that my bed was gone.

In place of my bed was a stainless steel autopsy table. The body was now covered with a white medical sheet. Valéria gestured toward the camera, then opened the window and jumped. At the same moment, about a dozen birds flew past my living room window. The Zoom call ended abruptly.

I knew I was alone with the girl whose face had been smashed to pulp by her drug-fiend boyfriend. But that was a lie, wasn't it? I killed her – killed her by writing *To Dust*.

I didn't dare make a single sound. I was trying to convince myself that this wasn't real when I heard her through the door; I heard her get up from the autopsy table.

I heard her teeth hit the floor.

I ran out of the apartment. I didn't even close the door. I ran out into the street to be among people, even though I was afraid that one of them might speak with the voice of a bird, or worse, that I'd find my own voice to be chirping. The thought made me scream, and I couldn't hold back any longer.

I screamed and screamed as I walked down the streets.

That's how I ended up in a bar. I had to have a drink.

In the restroom, I saw that my nails had left bloody marks on my face. I must have scratched my cheeks at some point, but I couldn't remember. Surely I did this because of my madness. My life was turning into a simple pulp story. My phone vibrated; it was Botond asking me how I'd coped with my first lesson.

I walked out of the bar and threw my phone down a manhole.

It took six glasses of the hardest palinka they had, but finally an idea came to me! An idea, out of nowhere! Isn't the life of a writer a miracle? I had to laugh, so I did, and I didn't care that more and more people turned away when I looked at them. I became the local weirdo overnight. None of these people understand how difficult writing is. You set simple goals and find it impossible to achieve them. For example, my goal was to not have a dead woman with a hammer-smashed face in my bedroom, silently mumbling the chorus of a pop song that never existed, apart from the vinyl copy I owned.

From this came the idea to write down everything that happened. I'm going to pretend it was fiction, that I made it all up.

I'm going to turn it into a story. A story that is a warning.

I found an old, battered PC in the bar. They use it to play songs over the sound system, but I used it to write my story. I finished it in a couple of hours.

I just read the story to the audience at the bar. At first they wanted to kick me out, but I bought everyone a round so they listened to the whole thing. Some of them even laughed.

Laughed!

Now that I've written it all down, I'm sure it's all made up again! Just fiction! Now I'm safe! I save the document and go home. When I get home, none of this will have happened. Valéria will be alive again. Józsi will come back from the kitchen. I'll be normal.

And most importantly, there won't be a dead woman in my room. No, my room will be mine again.

Yes, I'm going now!

Because everything will be fine!

Everything will be fine!

Everything will be fine!

Transistor

No one called her Zsuzsi anymore. In her records she was Zsuzsanna or Mrs. Kovac. At work she was listed as Transistor 47.

Zsuzsi only existed in the past.

The past was a forbidden land. Wallowing in the past is a sign of burnout, and throughout her career as a transistor she had been careful to control her thoughts. But now, as she lay on the bathroom floor, her leg screaming with hot, red pain where the bone pierced the flesh, she had to divert her thoughts from the present.

It had been an accident. She had been clumsy when she got out of the bath and fell. No, that was a lie she told herself. She wasn't clumsy. Her right shin had cracked and broke as she stood, just like that. When she hit the ground, her right elbow and pelvis broke too. The pain was extraordinary. She thought she knew pain, but this was something else entirely, a whole new landscape of searing agony that she had only barely started to map out. She couldn't move at all, only scream.

An accident in the bathroom! How humiliating, she thought, to lie on the floor for hours, screaming and going half-mad from the stabbing pain, all naked and cold. It would be quite a while before anyone came looking for her, she knew.

Then again, was there ever any other end to this? All roads led to this protracted and painful scene. She had known that from the beginning. It was her own decision.

Knowing this, after screaming her throat raw, constantly half a step away from fainting from the pain but never quite fading into the sweet oblivion of unconsciousness, she curled up on the floor as best she could and took refuge in the memories of her childhood. The memories had been calling to her for so long, and she dared not give in to them. What better time than now? She hardly dared to think back to the time before The Institute, but now she did. She thought of the day when her life had changed. The point of no return.

She was no older than eight.

If her parents had not been so brave, she would still be living in Borsod, the poorest county in Hungary. Once the industry and mines died out in the late 1980s, most of Borsod had become a collection of dead-end villages where the laws of abject poverty prevailed. Hungary had already cut its losses and left the region to rot. Those who could, fled. Those who couldn't, accepted that their lives had come to a standstill, and the generation they had fathered was born into a world without options. There would never be enough money to move out, to start a business, to learn, even to commute to work in a city. The inertia was overpowering; so they learned to live on dwindling welfare, petty crime, booze, and cheap drugs.

Had they stayed, she might have been dead by now, because in dying villages people tend to die young.

Zsuzsi's family were lucky to have been given work elsewhere, work that came with accommodation and meals twice a day. Gyuszi arranged this for them. Gyuszi was father's half-brother; he lived in a town. They rarely saw him, but he helped them when he could. He gave them a loan to cover the cost of traveling from their village to their new home: the factory.

Zsuzsi cried when they left the house because she knew they would never return. She wanted to stay so badly, even though the roof had collapsed that spring and there was no money to repair it. Her parents knew that the family would not survive another winter there.

They set off at dawn. No one in the village could ever afford a car. Wherever they had to go, they went on foot.

The journey seemed endless. Mother and Father took turns

carrying her when she was tired, although they also had to carry Mari, her little sister, and the bags containing the remnants of their former life. Her big brother Tibi walked ahead of them, like a sentinel watching over their safe journey.

They had to cross six villages before they reached the station. They no longer had enough money for the tickets; either Gyuszi had miscalculated or the prices had risen since his last visit. Father bought tickets for a closer destination on the same route so that they could at least get on the train.

'But we will not get off at that station,' he explained to the children. 'When the ticket inspector comes, we will have to pretend we have tickets for the whole route. He won't notice the trick.'

The ticket inspector did notice, of course. Zsuzsi watched from the compartment window as Father pleaded with the ticket inspector. She couldn't hear a word over the roar and screech of the train, but what she saw was enough.

Father looked as if he were about to weep. He folded his hands as if in prayer, and then, as the inspector began to write a fine, he touched the inspector's hand to beg for mercy; he bent down to kiss those hands to show the extent of his submission. The inspector took a step back in repulsion.

The inspector looked at the family gazing at the scene through the window and then shook his head in resignation. Father's trick worked and the ticket inspector tore up the fine. Tears of happiness welled up in Zsuzsi's eyes, and the sadness she had felt that morning vanished, because Father had once again proved that they were safe as long as he was with them!

In gratitude, Father touched the conductor's hand once more, but the inspector backed away with a disgusted look on his face. As an adult, Zsuzsi shuddered at the memory, but this shudder only intensified the love she felt for her dad.

They got out of the car at their destination. A pickup truck was waiting for them in a nearby parking lot. Another family had already climbed into the back. The driver had his back to the truck and was rolling a cigarette. He looked impatient and checked his watch regularly to showcase the worth of his time.

Zsuzsi knew that only people with money wore watches. The men who came to disconnect the gas in their house also wore watches. The driver's watch was made of cheap, black plastic; it was a Casio imitation. The digital numbers changed as the minutes passed. It was easy to read, as the numbers were clearly displayed. Zsuzsi knew numbers up to 9 at this point in her life, but she could not read at all.

The man matched the names on his list with the faces, then herded the family into the back of the truck. The truck rumbled through the city, but as curious as she was, sleep overcame Zsuzsi and she only woke up when they reached their destination.

'Come on, Zsuzsi, look!' Father said. 'This is our new home!'

Night had just fallen. Powerful spotlights illuminated the barracks built from prefabricated metal parts. Clothes hung on wire ropes stretched between the buildings and the smell of food wafted from the communal kitchen. Their old house in the village was densely surrounded by thick grass, unkempt rose bushes and willow trees. There were no plants here, just gravel from which electricity pylons had risen like trees. Behind the barracks loomed older, larger buildings, where the work was actually done.

The families were led to their accommodation. The workers did not have separate rooms; three families shared an open space in each barrack and slept on bunk beds.

They went straight to bed, exhausted from the journey. Zsuzsi crawled between Father and Mother for a sense of security, so she could sleep.

'Are you sure this was a good idea?' Mother whispered to Father.

'I'm sure,' Father whispered back, and Zsuzsi fell asleep.

The next morning, a supervising manager came to them, armed with a pile of papers. His physique was different from theirs. He had more substance. According to Father, these people ate more and better food. The family fled the village so that Zsuzsi, Tibi and Mari could grow as big and strong as these people.

The man signaled them to leave the barracks and showed them the way to the communal showers. He did not introduce himself.

'Remember . . .' said the supervisor, '. . . under no circumstances are you allowed to shower during or after your shift. You will only shower if you get permission, okay?'

Father and Mother nodded. The supervisor looked at Zsuzsi.

'Do you understand?' he asked her slowly and loudly, as if he were talking to a moron.

He was wearing a short-sleeved, checked shirt, carefully tucked into his jeans. His clothes were clean, no holes or cigarette burns anywhere. He wore a watch with actual hands. Zsuzsi could not read the position of the hands, but Father explained to her that someone with such a watch was wealthier than those whose watch displayed the numbers digitally. That changed with smart watches, but that came much later.

Her father was fascinated by watches. When they had to hurry somewhere, or later when his shift started, he would tap his wrist with his index finger as if he were tapping a watch, though he never had one.

Zsuzsi nodded to show that she understood. No bathing. She hated bathing anyway.

'You can shower after you sign the contract. In fact, I insist that you do. If you have lice or fleas, you will be kicked out of here, do you understand?'

Father bowed deeply to the man and assured him that there would be no problems.

'We have a barber shop in operation, right in this building. I would suggest a haircut for everyone. Remove all hair. All over.'

'Because of the lice?' asked Mother.

'Because of the work. We measure by the gram. If you do

not want to earn money, you can leave your hair long. But I would not recommend it.'

The supervisor prepared the contracts and laid out pens for Father and Mother to use. He even indicated the dotted line for them to sign. Her parents looked at each other as if they were waiting for the other to sign the papers first. Zsuzsi sensed their uncertainty but could not understand it. They had left everything behind. They had already made the decision, had no money to return – even if they did, there was no home to return to.

Father must have realized this too, because he picked up the pen and signed all the papers without reading them. Mother did the same.

'Can the children work too?' asked Mother.

The manager smiled.

'Of course!' he said.

Even as an adult, Zsuzsi was not against child labor. Children like her needed work. Without work, they would grow up to be lazy beasts and lose all hope of a better future. However, Zsuzsi was aware that her opinion might be skewed. She had to remind herself that she was special. Special people see their past differently; they see it as a journey, a procession whose every step, no matter how hard or bitter, has only brought them closer to their destiny, until they stop for a miraculous moment of revelation that they've already made it. Then they can look back and marvel at the incredible journey they made from down there to up here. Those who are not particularly gifted may not see their life as such a journey. They may see it as a static posture, a never-ending shift in the factory.

They shaved their heads, just as the manager had suggested. Zsuzsi cried a lot about it. Her hair had never been cut before; it flowed long, like a river of beautiful silk. Now it was gone, and her head looked like a ball with a face on it.

Liberal journalists often compare the photos taken in the factory with pictures of concentration camp victims, but

Zsuzsi always found this comparison cheap and uninspired. The removal of all body hair served a practical purpose and was of great benefit to the workers. Cutting hair was a choice; you could keep it, but then you would lose money. You could get at least a quarter of an ounce of The Blue from the scalp alone.

They missed breakfast, and Zsuzsi realized that she hadn't eaten for a day. It wasn't the first time in her life.

Father told her it was all right. They would eat soon. They would eat all day long.

The shift started at eight o'clock. They were led into an old, crumbling building. It might once have been a stable. The windows were smeared with soap, neon lights illuminated the unpainted walls inside. There were no machines, just a collection of flimsy tables and chairs scattered around the three large rooms where the work was to be done. The place was musty and reeked of people. When Zsuzsi and her family started, about forty people worked each shift. Later there were up to a hundred.

A tall, incredibly thin man showed them around. He was in charge of the shift. He was missing a few teeth in the front.

'This is the factory,' said the shift leader, who Zsuzsi could clearly see he was just like them; his body was wiry without any bulk. Tobacco phlegm had accumulated in his lungs, his voice sounded like a creaky sofa. He explained the rules to them dispassionately.

'Sit where you like. You will eat here, in this room. You must eat the designated portion. You go to the window there, say your name and your portion will be given to you. When you are finished, you will bring the container back. I will be watching you, so no cheating, no throwing away, no hiding in your pants instead of eating. If you cheat, I will make sure you fucking regret it! Do you all understand that?'

Father and Mother nodded, so Zsuzsi and Tibi nodded too. Mari stayed in the shack with two other children who were still too young to take on this task.

'No washing yourself! No pissing, no shitting, no throwing up, no crying during your shift. You get water, but it's just for drinking. It's rationed. We tell you when you drink and how much. No hand washing, no face washing. No spitting, no fighting, or I'll have you thrown out! Have I made myself clear?'

The family nodded in unison. When the warden left, Father turned to Zsuzsi and Tibi.

'Be grateful,' Father said to the children. 'Not everyone is as lucky as we are. We have a job now. We work hard, and in time you will have everything!'

A new emotion fluttered in Zsuzsi's chest like a bird, and she felt like her heart might burst from this new, intense feeling. She could not put her finger on it, but she knew it meant that she loved Father more than anything else in the world.

'Are the kids going to be okay?' Mother asked.

'Sure,' replied Father. 'They need to study and work!'

Mother and Father marched to the window and told the clerk their names. In no time at all, metal containers appeared, two of them child-sized. Mother and Father carried the containers to their table.

They didn't receive any utensils. The workers, especially those of such low social status as Zsuzsi's family, could easily have mistaken work for a meal. When Zsuzsi later attended the factory school to learn to read, she was slapped if she tried to eat her food with her hands. The message was clear: we work with our hands, we eat with forks and spoons.

Gyuszi told them that all they'd have to do was eat. Even as a child, she thought it would be easy, and the portions for children weren't that big anyway. But now, as she stared at these containers filled to the brim with a dark, murky substance, it didn't seem so easy.

Father dipped his hand into the substance and took a handful. Zsuzsi followed Father's example and dipped her hands into her own, smaller portion. The substance was cold. The consistency was dense, as if wet sand had been pressed into a thick mass. She felt as if the substance were trembling in the palm of her hand, like a wind-up toy ready to go. An absurd thought crossed her mind: that the thing was actually alive.

'Don't think about it! Just do it! That's the secret!' Father said and took the first bite.

Later, the whole family adopted the nickname that everyone used: Mud. It was a fitting name. When Father took the first bite of Mud, Zsuzsi saw that he was trying to fight back a wave of shock. He was the same when he received news of his own father's death. His body trembled slightly, almost imperceptibly, and his gaze was blank. He looked ahead, into nothingness, and his face reflected this outer emptiness instead of mirroring what was happening inside him

'Are you sure?' Mother whispered. Mother's eyes were round, big windows, and Zsuzsi read fear and uncertainty in them. It made her anxious and sad again, like when they'd left home, and instead of letting the fear take her over, she decided to stop the growing panic before it overwhelmed her and took a bite of the slush herself.

A dark, metallic taste spread across her tongue, followed by a sour, earthy smell. She chewed vigorously, but the mud remained hard and freezing. She swallowed and felt an icy cold spread through her throat and stomach. It felt as if she had eaten something that was alive and not alive at the same time; like roadkill that was stiff but not yet dead.

Her stomach turned and she knew that disgust was written all over her face. She looked at her portion again; there was still too much in the pot, but then she noticed that Father and Mother had so much more.

'Not bad at all!' Father said as he took another strained bite. 'Not bad at all, is it?'

Tibi looked anxiously at Zsuzsi, then at his parents, and Zsuzsi knew he was overcome with the same kind of panic she had almost experienced a few seconds ago. Even though he was the oldest child, Zsuzsi knew he needed help and encouragement right now, so she took another bite.

She shuddered and goosebumps covered her body. The second bite was even worse than the first, but Zsuzsi shoved a third portion into her mouth because she knew she couldn't stop. Now Mother began to eat too; she moaned painfully after the first bite, but continued to eat doggedly. Father was now shoveling the sludge into his mouth like a machine, and Tibi finally accepted reality and took a bite.

'This is shit,' Tibi declared, but no one responded to his cry of outrage. They just kept working, kept eating. Tibi looked desperately at his parents. Father nodded and indicated that he should continue eating, while Mother lowered her eyes and began to cry, even though it was forbidden. She cried and she ate; she swallowed the mud and her tears.

For many, their very first shift is also their longest. The day seems endless, and no matter how much you eat, you never get full, because Mud isn't food. In your stomach it dissolves into pure emptiness, leaving a gnawing void, and the more you eat, the bigger the void becomes.

That day, despite all the hardships, there was only one event that Zsuzsi could describe as truly traumatic. It would haunt her for years to come, although she later considered it a necessary and ultimately positive experience.

During a break, Zsuzsi walked through the building. In a narrow, deserted room, a tap was sticking out of the wall. She thought it was funny because they never had running water at home. For as long as she could remember, they had fetched water from a well. She turned on the tap and pipes rumbled beyond the walls, as if a monster was moving towards her from behind the tiles, until finally water ran between Zsuzsi's fingers onto the floor. She stuck her head under the tap and enjoyed the cold on her skin.

'You little bitch!' shouted the shift supervisor behind her. Zsuzsi jumped back and only then realized that she had done something forbidden. The proof was all over her hands and face and she didn't have time to wipe it off.

There were just the two of them in the room. The shift supervisor grabbed Zsuzsi by the neck and squeezed hard. Zsuzsi cried out in pain, but then chose to remain silent as the man tightened his grip even more.

'All right, then. So this is the thanks we get for giving your family a decent job? Even though you are all scum? The lowest scum you can find. I should kick you out so you can go back to whoring with your whore mother. Is that what you want, scum? Do you want to be kicked out?'

'No! No, please don't!' Zsuzsi's voice was thin and she knew she was about to cry, but she also knew she wasn't allowed to. It was forbidden and she could not make another mistake.

'Are you going to wash your hands again during working hours?' the shift supervisor shouted in her face.

'No! No! No, I won't!' wailed Zsuzsi.

'I'll slap you three times to make you remember,' the shift supervisor suddenly said, all too calmly. 'Or would you rather go back home?'

'No! Please! I don't . . .' Zsuzsi shouted.

'You'll get five then.'

Zsuzsi would have gladly accepted a dozen, a hundred slaps, if that meant she was forgiven and they could stay.

Zsuzsi thought later that the shift supervisor had done exactly the right thing. You can't expect a snotty brat from such a disadvantaged background to understand anything but this kind of violence. He even acted kindly compared to others, who used harsher methods. Broken bones, open wounds that needed stitches, permanent marks from belt blows were not uncommon. The shift supervisors had almost free rein as long as they kept the employees in check, and these employees, as they were, only understood punishment. Who knows what would have happened to Zsuzsi if her supervisor had not set clear boundaries early on? She could never bring herself to love the shift supervisor, but she was grateful to him for setting her on the path to becoming a better person.

When she returned to her family, her face was red and bruised. Father and Mother looked at her. Mother covered her mouth in shock. Father looked at her sternly.

'Did you deserve that?' he asked.

Zsuzsi nodded.

'Then eat before I give you a few slaps myself,' said Father, and this hurt Zsuzsi more than the blows. She sat down again and looked at her hands. They seemed clean, but they were stained with guilt. She needed those hands dirty again. She reached deep into her container and stuffed Mud into her mouth; then she reached again for another helping and another.

The substance did not stay in her stomach, but it would not leave either. When Zsuzsi touched her stomach, it did not bulge from the incredible amount of Mud she had consumed; on the contrary. She felt as if she had been fasting all day, and yet she sensed that somehow the stuff was still inside and had drained all the energy from her body.

When the shift was over, Tibi cried a little. Mother had to lean against the wall as she got up from her chair. Zsuzsi later learned that workers were often ridiculed outside the factory. They were made fun of because they only had to eat. 'Anyone can eat! Stuffing yourself with food is not work,' the outsiders often said.

They didn't know any better.

Almost a third of the factory workers dropped out within the first six months. They could not bear the difficulties associated with the work. Zsuzsi's family also faced the challenges that first night, and then night after night.

Their skin burned. They could not sleep at all. They wanted to scratch themselves, but they did not dare, because that was also forbidden. They tossed and turned in the bunk beds. They cried out from time to time, but they were quickly silenced by the others in the barrack. Later, of course, they got used to the burning sensation as best they could and learned to sleep despite the itching.

Zsuzsi clawed at her pillow to keep from scratching; her skin was already a landscape of discomfort, each pore a little flame of its own. Even her throat, her tongue, her rectum itched. She was thirsty, but did not dare to drink. She was sick, but even the first night she knew it would never go away.

This sickness was the work itself.

The next morning, the itching had partially subsided, or rather, it changed its nature. The sensation no longer came from underneath the skin.

When Zsuzsi saw her parents for the first time that morning, she gasped because she thought they had died. Their faces were gray. Zsuzsi's horror was mirrored by her parents when they saw their children for the first time in the morning light. Then, after the first moments of horror, they understood that this was the expected fruit of their labor. During the night, they sweated a gray, powdery substance, and that was a good thing.

When journalists and human rights activists speak ill of the factory, they justify it by saying that the second shift is humiliating and unbearable, even dehumanizing. Zsuzsi never agreed with this assessment, either as a child or as an adult. Eating the Mud and the night that followed were hard, cruel, and humiliating phases; the second shift was always a time of relief.

Another shift leader led them to the Sweatshop, which was located in a newly constructed complex and guarded by armed security personnel at every door. The workers were undressed and their clothes put into bags before entering the sweatshop. It was a heavily heated and humidified room, like a sauna, only less pleasant.

Zsuzsi was surprised by the aggressive chemical smell when she entered. Over time, she learned to love the smell, but the first time she smelled it, it brought tears to her eyes. The room was even more cramped than the room where they ate the Mud.

All the workers are naked during this part of the process. It feels strange at first, but you get used to it. There is hardly any talking; forming words is as difficult as lifting heavy weights in the hot, humid room. You try to breathe sparingly because your lungs often itch from the chemicals in the air. Children, especially if they are too young for the work, tend to cry a lot. You quickly become frustrated and impatient because you know there is no way out of this heated room; not until the work is done.

Unfortunately, there have been several child murders in the Sweatshop, but Zsuzsi felt that one shouldn't project individual crimes onto the whole system.

In about four to five hours, the substance on the skin reaches the desired consistency, and the factory technicians lead the workers in groups of ten to the harvesting room, which is just one door away from the Sweatshop but is the exact opposite of it, as the harvesting room is refrigerated.

When Zsuzsi was first taken to be harvested, she was grateful for the sudden cold, only to start shivering a few minutes later.

She was separated from her parents. They liked to separate family members, probably because it made settling any possible financial disputes at the end of the harvest easier.

She was led to her assigned workbench, a metal structure that resembles a bed you can't sleep on. It allows the worker to assume the necessary kneeling, squatting and lying positions to help the technicians with the harvest.

Since then, curtains have been attached to each workbench to give the workers a sense of privacy. In Zsuzsi's day, there were no curtains, and privacy was just a buzzword whose meaning was lost in the naked heat of Sweatshop hours.

The newly introduced curtains, the journalists said, provided opportunities for various kinds of exploitation. If the exploitation was sexual, for example, it could take place without eyewitnesses. It would be the word of one worker against that of two highly qualified technicians.

Zsuzsi did not know what to make of it, so she preferred not to think about it at all.

She had never experienced any form of sexual abuse at the factory, either as a child or as a teenager.

When Zsuzsi started out, she was harvested exclusively by men. Nowadays, about one in five technicians is female.

After her skin had been cleaned, the technicians also had to scrape the substance out of her orifices. The most unpleasant part was the scratching in her nose and throat; over time, she learned to control her gagging.

The harvested substance was nicknamed 'The Blue' by the workers, and the word was now widely used. The substance turned a bluish color when scraped from the skin, hence the name. The workers did not know what this material was used for or what value it actually had. The journalists had no idea either.

By the time Zsuzsi reached adulthood, she knew.

When they found her, the sun was already falling into night. This was her favorite time of day. She loved the way the golden hue lay heavy on the windows. As they forced the door open, Zsuzsi knew that the paramedics were about to witness a beauty they were not used to. A naked woman lying on the floor, bathed in the golden light of the sun, like in a Renaissance painting depicting the birth of a minor but beautiful Greek goddess.

They laid her on the stretcher and started the first infusion. They gave her the good stuff and the pain disappeared. She hoped unconsciousness would swallow her up, but instead her mind wandered away from the bright lights and noise of the ambulance and straight into a dream about her childhood, about her first time in the harvest room. On the floor of the bathroom, she was haunting her past; now it haunted her.

At the hospital, the doctors examined her broken parts thoroughly. Zsuzsi regarded her doctors from under a heavy blanket of painkillers. They were the best-paid professionals because the Institute supplied only the best for its transistors. Zsuzsi knew she mustn't lose hope. These doctors could do anything. They were specialists.

Zsuzsi was already anxious to get back to work. Who would replace her now that she was bedridden?

Mrs. Fábián visited her in the afternoon. She was the office worker at the Institute; having coffees with her was the closest thing Zsuzsi had to a friendship.

'Do not worry about work,' Mrs. Fábián said, smiling encouragingly. 'The doctors say you need a few operations. They can fix your elbow. Your leg too, but there's still a long way to go.'

Zsuzsi felt as if the woman's face had been remade overnight; or perhaps her view of it was. Was the skin always so wrinkled? Was the smile so sad?

'When can I go back?' Zsuzsi asked, but it sounded like a plea. 'Who's replacing me?'

Even through the drug curtain, she could feel the panic in her own voice.

'The new boy. You met him a few weeks ago . . .'

'I am not burned out yet, am I? I can do it from a wheelchair if . . .' said Zsuzsi. 'Just until I can walk again. And I will not fall. Not again, I am not going to . . .'

Mrs. Fábián took Zsuzsi's hand and squeezed it gently.

'You know how important you are to the Institute. For us. Do not think about work now. Concentrate on healing. We will not let you down, no matter what. I promise . . .'

Zsuzsi wanted to say something else, but the thoughts fell out of her head like poorly secured panes of glass from a window frame.

There was a television in her room. She switched it on, but quickly became tired of it. Sometimes she woke up from sleep because the smell of the factory was in the room and she thought about the past again, like a real burnout.

She thought about all those Sundays.

At the factory, every day was roughly the same. They worked six days a week; three of them were spent eating Mud, three of them harvesting The Blue. The seventh day was Sunday. On Sundays, the factory stood still.

These days had a peculiar atmosphere. There was not much to do. The adults often met to play cards or watch TV in the room next to the communal kitchen. There was no pub, but if someone smuggled in a bottle or two, security turned a blind eye.

The holidays were observed, of course. Those were the days of magic. You did not have to work for a whole day, you could just live. So the workers packed as much life as they could into these days off.

On public holidays, the young workers turned the gravel road into a dance floor. They switched on a portable radio. On very special days, someone would start singing a song, and others would pick it up and sing it together, and someone in the crowd would beat the rhythm on a chair or an aluminium pitcher.

They drank too, but never at the beginning of the dance, for they had just rediscovered for a brief moment that they were not only workers, but also human beings; and this rediscovery transformed them into things of a beauty that made one's heart grow heavy. They were bald angels dancing in the dirt. The girls often wore scarves, and if they spun fast enough, it looked like they had long, flowing hair. The boys stomped their feet in a hard rhythm; none of them knew how to dance, so they recreated the idea of it to their liking. It was fierce and fast, but also full of tender moments, so Zsuzsi knew that even their violence was full of love.

Sweaty makeshift couples clung to each other, and when dusk fell and the flames of desire were ignited, the couples often disappeared into the darkness behind the barracks. It was only a few years after they moved in when Tibi became one of the dancers. He also often disappeared with a girl.

At this time, another person began to emerge in Zsuzsi; someone who was no longer a child, but not yet an adult either. Her bones became more elongated, her face lost its childish softness, and the wrinkle between her eyes, which had made Zsuzsi look so serious all her adult life, started to show. She felt the change not only in her body, but also in herself. She knew that she would soon be joining the dancers.

This thought made her melancholy and sad. As a child, she had believed that growing up was not a process, but a solid wall, with childhood safely on one side and adulthood on the other. Now she saw that the reality was much more bitter than that. She felt like the victim of an inevitable accident that tore her apart in slow motion, only to reassemble her haphazardly as an adult. She feared this process, but in a strange, painful way, she also longed for it. She longed to dance, even if she would lose something the first time; something vital that she could not measure or name, but that she knew would be gone forever.

After the dance was over, the adults often fought, but only in secret. There was rarely a reason for the fights, perhaps only despair, hopelessness, boredom, lack of prospects. Father never fought. He always paid attention to what was good for his family and everything was subordinated to that. Maybe that's why Zsuzsi's fate was sealed; maybe Father wanted his biggest dream to come true so badly that he willed it into being.

One morning an aluminium spoon stuck to Zsuzsi's hand. It was the weirdest sensation. The more she tried to shake it off, the more it stuck to her skin. The spoon felt like a crawling animal. She was scared at first, but later she just laughed about it. Soon this turned into a regular thing. Every now and then a metallic object would stick to her hand for a short time. The shift supervisor reassured everyone that this often happened, especially at this age, and there was nothing to worry about. It was just a side effect of eating Mud.

Nevertheless, the adults were now paying close attention

to Zsuzsi. She constantly felt their stares, she felt their hope. Their suspicion.

Their envy.

Maybe she was talented, they all thought. The company took talented children from the factories, and if Zsuzsi turned out to be talented, then she would have a big, bright future ahead of her.

A much better and brighter future than the family could ever have imagined.

Still, it took almost a year for her talent to manifest itself. By this time, Zsuzsi's allotted portion of Mud had almost reached adult size. The taste no longer bothered her and she had become accustomed to the process of harvesting. She no longer had to gag when her throat and nose were scratched out. Her body was also growing towards womanhood. If there was ever abuse during the harvesting phase, it started at this age or soon after. Zsuzsi heard older girls whisper that the technicians lingered too long in the orifices or moved their probes suggestively in them, though Zsuzsi did not understand what they meant at the time.

Not many of the girls saw this as harassment. Many even saw it as a compliment. Rumours circulated about older girls and women providing sexual services to the technicians in exchange for money and goods. Now that the workers are separated by curtains, it is obvious that this kind of exploitation or exchange, if it really exists, must be in full swing.

For Zsuzsi, it seemed to be the natural order of things. These girls (and supposedly some younger boys too) could not hope for a life of inviting opportunities to suddenly open up to them. Most of them did not learn to read, or not enough to actually understand what they were reading. It was not in the factory's interest to train intellectuals. Higher education was therefore out of the question. If you started eating Mud at a young age, there was a good chance that you would spend the rest of your life in the care of the factory. Life was what you saw around you, day in and day out, and if you were sexually exploited, so what? The little bit of extra money, the little things the technicians smuggled in for you, the little bit of attention you got before you withered away, made all the difference in the great monotony of things.

Zsuzsi had already been preparing herself for such a life, even if she did not admit it to herself.

Only it was not the life she was meant to have.

One night she woke up and realized that her parents were looking at her with fear in their eyes. Zsuzsi realized that she was lying on the floor, but had no memory of how she got there. She was cold and her skin felt bruised. Everyone in the barracks was wide awake and staring at her. Some with envy, others with fear.

An hour later, the factory manager arrived. He listened to her father's report, and it was only by overhearing this conversation that she learned what had happened.

The barracks had woken up because Zsuzsi was talking in her sleep. She was either speaking gibberish or a foreign language, because they could not understand a word. Despite their many shouts and pleas, even threats, she did not shut up. Someone finally switched on the light.

They saw that Zsuzsi's eyes were rolled back as she spoke. Father tried to shake her awake, but without success. She just kept talking, looking inward, her body limp.

They were wondering whether to call the company doctor when suddenly they felt it.

The air pressure dropped. Everyone shivered from the sudden cold. Some swear they even heard the roll of thunder; some felt nauseous – one girl even threw up.

Then it was among them.

An invisible force yanked Zsuzsi out of bed. She lay in its grip like a rag doll. She was thrown against the wall, but was stopped just a few centimeters before impact. Zsuzsi remained in her trance state and never once stopped her recital in that strange language. She was still speaking even as she began to rise towards the ceiling.

After playing with her body in the air for a few minutes, the force gently set Zsuzsi back down on the floor. At that moment, she woke up. For the next week, every metallic object stuck to her hands.

In the morning, experts came to examine her. They took her to the factory doctor's office.

Until then she had been like a wild animal, always moving along with the herd without considering herself separate from the whole. Now Zsuzsi was separated from her herd, and while she waited alone in the treatment room for the experts to arrive, a realization dawned on her: she was an independent person. She could be separated from her parents, her siblings, her home. She could have solitary experiences, good or bad, that were uniquely her own, and with that she felt the first premonition of a great loneliness.

The experts measured every inch of her, attached wires to her skin, took blood and skin samples, asked her stupid questions and showed her colourful pictures from a book. She had to describe what she saw on them, even if the pictures were just meaningless blobs. She did not have to undress, but she felt much more exposed than during the harvest. By the time the experts had finished, she was drenched in sweat and had a slight tremor in her hand. They left her alone in the room and told her to wait.

She needed to go to the toilet urgently. She had no way of measuring the time, but she knew it was passing slowly.

No knocking. The door opened and in walked the tallest woman Zsuzsi had ever seen. She was wearing a long black skirt, blue gloves and a blouse buttoned up to her neck. She had a silk scarf wrapped around her head, although she had her own hair. She leaned on a black walking stick and walked with a noticeable limp. She was ageless; Zsuzsi saw her as an old woman, but her face had no wrinkles. It was her eyes that were old.

She closed the door and stared at Zsuzsi. The girl's heart was beating violently. She had a premonition that she would be punished, but she knew that this punishment would be different from the previous ones. It would cause serious damage that would leave a permanent scar.

The woman held her gaze for what felt like an eternity. Perhaps because she sensed something about her own fate in that endless moment.

The woman took off her gloves and walked towards Zsuzsi. She placed her walking stick against a hospital bed. Zsuzsi felt as if the woman was sucking the last bit of air out of the room; she could barely breathe.

'Relax,' the woman said. Her voice was hoarse and deep, and Zsuzsi caught the scent of a recently smoked cigarette.

'Once I was like you,' the woman continued. 'Now the question is: do you want to be like me?'

Zsuzsi could not answer.

'How old are you?'

Zsuzsi had the feeling that ants were running on her tongue, paralyzing her.

'I asked you a question!' the woman snarled.

'Twelve!' said Zsuzsi.

'Have you ever thought about the future? What will you be doing in five, ten, fifteen years?'

Zsuzsi shook her head, because such time spans meant nothing to her. What would she be doing in ten years? The same thing she had always done.

'If you are really talented,' the woman continued, 'you could start a new life. Would you like to?'

Zsuzsi was on the verge of breaking. She did not know what to say because she did not know the expected answer. In the factory, everyone knew the answers that the shift supervisors and managers liked because they always wanted to hear the same things; now her bladder was burning with tension because she had to think for herself.

'We are going to make a new, better person out of you. It's

hidden underneath the filthy creature you are now. Is that what you want? Do you want to be like us?'

'I do not know what you are,' Zsuzsi hesitated.

The woman grinned.

'Of course you do not know. But you have a sense of it, don't you? When I came in through the door, you felt it. I can feel it in you too. I once sat where you are sitting now. I was just as scared as you are. The fear will pass. We will free you from it. It will roll off like mud from a shoe. But you have to hold on. Rebirth is not easy. It's painful, just like it was painful to be born in the first place.'

Zsuzsi rolled the words back and forth in her head.

'But we do not remember that,' she whispered. 'We don't remember our birth. So we don't remember the pain.'

The woman looked at her for a few moments before speaking. 'I do like you. If only you didn't stink so much,' the woman said to Zsuzsi. 'Open your mouth!'

Zsuzsi opened her mouth and the woman reached in and grabbed the girl's tongue. Her grip was fierce. In her fright, Zsuzsi even forgot to scream. She could no longer close her mouth. The woman pulled, so Zsuzsi had to bend forward to prevent her tongue from being torn out of her.

'Stay calm,' the woman said, and Zsuzsi let out a sound of despair that she didn't know existed inside her. She had never felt so alone, so punished. Not even when she was beaten or when she was locked up, because others were beaten or locked up too. It was a natural part of life, a communion she shared with people who were like her in almost every way. But this, this was something else, the first moment of a different life tailored just for her. The woman let go of Zsuzsi's tongue, then lifted her fingers to her mouth and licked Zsuzsi's saliva.

'Yes,' said the woman. 'I sense talent.'

She gave Zsuzsi a faint smile.

'See you on the other side, kid.'

Satisfied, she grabbed her cane and staggered out of the

room. Zsuzsi was left alone with her terror and confusion, and not knowing when she could leave, if ever, she squatted against the wall and urinated on the floor.

Late that evening she was allowed to go. She hurried back to the barracks and cuddled up to her parents. They hugged her tightly. Tibi and Mari looked at her with shining eyes that threatened to burst into tears.

'You'll rise, Zsuzsi,' Father whispered in her ear. 'Do not think about us anymore! Just rise up high! As high as you can!'

Zsuzsi cried only then.

The next morning, a man from another sphere descended to Zsuzsi's barrack. He was high management – even a shareholder. The likes of him were rarely seen in the factories, only when a talent was discovered.

Those who were not on duty admired the man, who was cut from a completely different cloth than they were. His manicure and hair were perfect. A single piece of his clothing cost more than the workers had ever earned in their lives. The dust that stubbornly settled on everything seemed to give the man a wide berth. And that car! They had never seen anything like it, only in pictures. A Porsche.

As he sat down with Mother and Father, Zsuzsi looked at the watch on his wrist and saw immeasurable wealth. Even its clasp was made of gold.

He said his name was Zoltan. That was all they ever learned about him.

'Your daughter has talent,' he said by way of introduction. Mother and Father beamed with endless happiness.

'That's why,' he continued, 'we want to take Zsuzsanna out of the factory line. To give her a special education. So that her talents can develop.'

Zsuzsi shuddered. Her name sounded overly serious when pronounced like that. Father squeezed Mother's hand.

'Of course,' Father said. 'We only want what's best for her.'

Zoltan smiled kindly.

'Well then. Listen, we can take Zsuzsanna from here to an institute where she will study and receive an education. If she studies well and abides by our rules, she will have a secure job in the future. A job that is well respected, in demand, and very well paid. All you have to do is sign this, so that she can come into our care.'

He placed the memo and the transfer contract on the dirty table in front of her parents. Zsuzsi had never seen so much paper. They must have felled a small forest for it.

Father looked at her and smiled sadly. Zsuzsi understood that he would sign it. Either that, or Zsuzsi would stay in the factory and eke out her existence as a worker with no chance of social advancement. This was the family's only chance of success. Father looked at the man again.

'Will she be all right . . . ?' he asked.

Zoltan gave Father his friendliest look.

'We will cherish her. Because she is indeed a treasure for us!'

Zsuzsi was taken that very afternoon. She would not see her family for years.

After the second operation, a nurse came to check on her. Her eyebrows were thick bushes over her eyes. She shook her head disapprovingly as she changed the bedpan.

'Just say what you think,' Zsuzsi said. Her voice was hoarse. The nurse lowered her eyes as she began to change the sheets.

'I do not understand why you are all doing this,' she said, although she had probably meant the statement as a question. 'You know this is what happens. You do it anyway. What do you gain from it?'

Zsuzsi stared at the nurse for a long time.

'Gain?' she asked back.

'I've seen people like you before. They'll stitch you up, but you'll end up back here in no time, only worse. And even worse after that. And yet you don't want to stop! There must be something in it for you, right? A win!'

'Why are you a nurse?' she asked the woman. The woman shrugged her shoulders.

'It pays the bills. But it does not kill me, as you can see.'

Zsuzsi chuckled dryly.

'If we live, we die,' she said. The nurse shrugged again.

'At least my bones don't pierce my lungs when I turn on my side.'

Zsuzsi said nothing in response. Only when the head physician came in to inquire and they were left alone did she say anything.

'There's a nurse here. She has thick eyebrows . . .'

The doctor nodded.

'Nurse Helmeczy. She has excellent qualifications.'

'Dismiss her,' Zsuzsi said. The physician's face expressed astonishment.

'I'm sorry, but I'm the chief physician here! And you are my patient, you do not tell me what I . . .'

'You know who I am,' said Zsuzsi. 'You know what I am. By this evening, that woman will be unemployed! Not even a job in another hospital! She's finished! Do you understand that?'

He nodded, then he examined Zsuzsi's bones and all further questions concerned her personal well-being. Zsuzsi never saw the nurse again.

But her question stayed with Zsuzsi, and now her dreams and memories revolved around the time after the factory.

The first few months at the Institute for Gifted Children were so traumatic that she could only remember them as a blur. Her memories were blurred and confused not only because of the trauma, but also because memories are somehow wonderfully connected to the idea of the human face. It is through the face that we understand other people and the world, and our memories emerge from the processes of understanding. But the Institute was faceless.

Perhaps there were other gifted children at the Institute, but Zsuzsi was isolated from them and vice versa. She now had her own room, with an adjoining bathroom and a gym. She lived practically alone in the cold, clean, and functional building. Only her teachers and supervisors visited her.

They all wore silk masks decorated with a golden triangle, the symbol of the Institute. They wore wide robes to conceal their gender, their voices were distorted and inhuman.

During the lessons, the learning material was mainly presented in video form, but there were no people on the videos and a machine voice read out the text. The teachers never touched Zsuzsi, except when she was being punished. They rarely explained the reasons for the punishment. They expected her to figure it out for herself, and she eventually figured out that the punishments were given at random.

And so it went for a year.

One morning she discovered that a window in the corridor was open. Zsuzsi stood at the window for minutes, wondering whether the jump would kill her or not. Her will to live proved stronger than her desire to escape that life, and when she decided not to jump, she chose to be strong enough to endure anything. If not for herself, then for Father.

She would even endure the music.

The music came with the first human features. Her name was Kata; she had a beautiful, heart-shaped face with warm, loving eyes. Zsuzsi could hardly breathe for joy when Kata entered the music room for the first time, though she feared a terrible moment when Kata would remove her face to reveal another mask underneath.

She visited Zsuzsi once a week. Every time she saw Kata's face, Zsuzsi felt how efficiently they had killed a piece of her soul so that it could be reconstructed later. She longed for that reconstruction now. She was ready to be a different person.

Ready to please the Institute.

'Do you want to listen to music?' Kata asked every time she visited her. If Zsuzsi said no, Kata left the room immediately and did not come back until a week later.

So Zsuzsi learned to say 'yes' every time Kata asked this question. Kata then put on a record that sounded like a soundtrack for boredom. At the factory, everyone listened to songs driven by hard rhythms and simple melodies; songs about love, longing, money, and hard partying. These were the themes that resonated with the workers. People knew the lyrics to these songs and could sing along with them.

But these new songs were endless, the melodies almost indistinguishable. The first few times Zsuzsi didn't even hear music, just noise. Still, she associated the music with the human face, and the human face now stood for emotional dependence.

Kata rarely spoke while they listened; sometimes her eyes were even closed, but her face played along with the music, expressing an alternation of emotions to guide Zsuzsi; at other times she simply watched Zsuzsi and smiled at her kindly, observing the girl's reactions.

Sometimes she would announce what was playing.

'This is Mahler,' she would say, as if Zsuzsi should know what a Mahler was. Other names followed week after week: Bach, Beethoven, Penderecki, Strauss, Wagner, Chopin, and so on, but none of the names meant anything to Zsuzsi.

Nevertheless, she lived for these afternoons, because when Kata came to her, Zsuzsi felt a little more human again. Kata never punished her, except by her absence. Kata was always nice to her, and Zsuzsi listened to the music for Kata's sake.

Eventually she discovered melodies that broke away from the noise and rose to crescendos; she marvelled at the silences between certain notes, where perhaps the soul of the music was born. Soon she understood the music.

As her understanding developed, and once she had mastered the art of numbers and comprehensive reading, her studies took a new turn. She was now given books and had to interpret them in writing. She felt that she was expected to form her own opinion, even though she had been brought up not to have one.

'When you interpret . . . ,' Kata said when Zsuzsi asked what to do, 'you take raw material, in this case a book, and turn your understanding of it into pure information.'

Zsuzsi thought about it for a moment and then looked at Kata. 'Like when I ate Mud? And turned it into The Blue?'

Kata nodded.

'The difference,' says Kata, 'is that it's not your body that does the work. It's your mind. Your mind is as much a part of you as your body. You just have to learn to use it.'

Seeing it like this made it easier. She saw learning as Mud and knowledge as The Blue. With this new way of thinking, she managed much better. Her punishments became less frequent and less severe. Eventually new teachers were introduced to her; they wore no masks.

Now she considered the Institute her home. By now, she could read and write fluently, even spoke English and Abaddonian, had a solid understanding of math and the mysteries of the human body, the planet's ecosystem, and the nature of parallel worlds and shadow biospheres.

As an adult, she understood that normal children learned nothing about these things. For them, the world was singular and indivisible. However, Zsuzsi knew nothing about the world when she arrived at the Institute; she only knew the factory and the people who worked there. The realization that human beings are made up of cells, tiny units of life with their own little goals, joys, and tragedies, was shocking. Accepting that there are other forms of existence besides our own seemed like a no-brainer compared to the ideas of human biology.

The Institute celebrated her fourteenth birthday with the gift of showing her a future to aspire to. They took her to the Transistors.

That morning, she looked at herself in the mirror. She was wearing blue dungarees with Velcro pockets. She had grown a lot in the last few years, and her dark blond hair had turned light brown. She let it grow to shoulder length. It was as if a stranger was looking back at her from the mirror, and Zsuzsi liked this stranger. This stranger was clean and well groomed, she read and understood books easily, listened to good music. This girl was talented. They had actually washed the dirt off her and revealed this other person underneath, and she was grateful for it.

'Remember one thing,' said Zoltan, 'whatever you see, you must never talk about it! Not to anyone! You've been told that, haven't you?'

It was the first time he had visited Zsuzsi since he took her out of the factory. He was wearing a different watch now, but it was no less expensive. His car was still a Porsche, just a newer model. The man hadn't aged at all; he even seemed to have gotten younger.

'But of course! You can trust me!' said Zsuzsi. 'I won't talk about anything I see.'

The man nodded in agreement, knowing that she couldn't talk to anyone anyway.

They drove her to the place in a minibus. All the windows were covered. When she got off the bus, she was blindfolded. Zoltan didn't take the blindfold off until they were inside.

They entered a waiting hall with safety notices on the wall. 'No talking while the transistors are in operation.' 'Sleeping during transistor operation is strictly prohibited.' 'The use of watches, telephones, and electrical devices outside this door is prohibited.'

Zsuzsi signed a confidentiality agreement. She leafed through the papers but didn't read them. She trusted the Institute, because if she couldn't trust the facility, who could she trust? She signed them all. She had developed her own signature at her teachers' request. She thought her signature was elegant and mature.

The man took the papers from her and led her into the transistor room.

Four transistors were working that day, three women and one man. This was an accurate indication of the gender ratio:

on average, only a quarter of the transistors were male. It was difficult to determine whether the girls were more talented or whether the boys couldn't cope with the Institute's strict depersonalization process.

The transistors didn't care that Zsuzsi and the man were watching them; however, one of the women glanced at Zsuzsi as if to say something, but then averted her eyes. The transistors were all stark naked.

Each was holding something that looked like candy or a tiny piece of bread, although it couldn't be bread because it was blue. Then Zsuzsi understood, and now she thought she could smell it from afar – the smell she knew so well from the workbench.

'Is that The Blue?' she whispered to Zoltan.

'Yes!' he replied. 'We use it to switch them on.'

The transistors dropped the candy-sized Blue into their mouths and closed their eyes. Their silence was absolute. Minutes passed.

A hum filled the room. Zsuzsi looked around anxiously, thinking there might be a beehive somewhere and the insects might attack her, but then she realized that the source of the sound was the four transistors.

They were moving now. Their limbs twisted, their faces took on a new, disturbing expression every second, but these expressions were not signs of emotion. The bodies and minds of these four transistors were seeking positions of resonance with the other, parallel transistors. That was the process of making contact, she later learned. But now she just watched and marvelled.

Zsuzsi thought back to the holidays in the factory, to the young workers preparing for the dance, searching for the right rhythm, the right movements that would set them on the right path. Perhaps the dance at the factory and what was happening now meant the same thing, only the power behind the transistors was real. The dance is just a symbolic gesture; what was happening here was not protected by metaphorical or symbolic layers.

It was not a gesture, but an action.

At last they found what they were looking for, both within and in worlds other than their own. Zsuzsi did not participate in the communion of The Blue, but she clearly felt the moment when they reached their destination. She felt a force hit her stomach from the inside out, as if it was trying to escape her body through her navel. She felt her bones vibrate beneath her flesh, like magnets responding to the call of a powerful force. Her teeth ached and her hair stood on end. She had an irrational fear that her body would fall upwards, into the sky.

She kept an eye on the transistors, who were now all assuming the same posture: heads tilted to one side, fingers like claws, faces contorted, eyes rolled back, chests puffed out.

They rose from the ground in this posture.

At the moment of their ascent, Zsuzsi's head was filled with strange thoughts that she knew were not her own. The transistors reached the height of contact and the transmission began. Zsuzsi's consciousness could no longer keep up, and the thoughts became such a strong noise that she was momentarily lost in them.

She watched the transistors hovering high above, and suddenly, as if lightning had struck her heart, she realized that she wanted to be up there with them.

She watched them for hours, even though the transistors simply hovered motionless above her; yet Zsuzsi sensed that something real and important was happening at that moment, invisible to the naked eye.

At the end of the session, the transistors descended from the air. They lay on the floor like dancers after a strenuous performance, all sweaty and panting. They were still beautiful, perhaps even more beautiful than before.

Zoltan accompanied Zsuzsi back to the waiting room and left her alone to take care of some minor formalities. That's when Zsuzsi made the biggest mistake of her youth. She had been ashamed of it all her life, even as an adult.

Zoltan had taken off his watch, following the rules, and placed it on the table before entering the transistor room. It was still there now. She had never owned a watch before, and now that she was alone with one, and such an obviously valuable one at that, the temptation was too great. She had no intention of stealing; stealing the watch would ruin her life.

No, she just wanted to try it on.

The metal was cold in her hand; she let her fingers glide over the crystal glass. It was a beautiful piece. Patek Philippe, the dial claimed. Zsuzsi put the watch on her wrist. The weight on her hand gave her a serious, if not entirely unpleasant, feeling. She looked for a reflective surface, but could only see her distorted image above the steaming coffee on the smooth plastic surface of a coffee machine. She came to the conclusion that the watch suited her quite well. Then she took it off and put it back on the table.

Only the watch had already stopped.

The man came back a few minutes later and picked up the watch. He looked at the motionless hands, then at Zsuzsi. His gaze was so icy that Zsuzsi's insides filled with fear. She knew she must have broken a taboo, a rule so strict and firm that it would cost her the future she had just accepted for herself.

'Did you touch it?'

Zsuzsi was too frightened to speak, and she realized she was gasping for air as if she were choking.

'I just wanted to . . . it looked so beautiful,' Zsuzsi stuttered. The man looked at his watch, then back at the girl.

'Only ten of these watches were made. Do you know how rare that is? How valuable?'

The old instincts kicked in. She wanted to cry, yet she knew she mustn't, even if it was all over, forever! Forever! She would eat Mud again, or worse, she would be thrown out into a world she no longer knew, or had never really known, but it was better that way, because then she wouldn't have to see Father's disappointment.

The man stepped closer to her. Zsuzsi backed away, her muscles so tense they ached. Her whole body was trembling.

'It will never work again.' Anger resonated in the man's voice. 'You have ruined it. Do you understand that? You have ruined it forever!'

'I'm sorry! I'm sorry! I'm so sorry,' Zsuzsi whimpered and involuntarily slapped her hands together as if she were praying, just as she had seen her father do on the train ages ago. Later, she was ashamed of her pathetic behaviour. She should have waited in dignified silence for her punishment, as she had learned at the Institute.

The man was very close now; he was two heads taller than Zsuzsi, broader and stockier. Zsuzsi closed her eyes, preparing herself for slaps, for the blow of a closed fist, for solitary confinement, for flogging, for any punishment harsh enough to redeem her and give her the new life she had just been promised.

The man grabbed Zsuzsi's hand; the girl flinched. She felt the cold metal on her skin as the man fastened the watch to her wrist.

'You wanted it and now it's yours,' Zoltan said. 'Because you are important. This watch meant a lot to me. A lot. But you mean even more.'

That was the final blow; she fell to her knees and her hand sought out Zoltan's shiny leather shoe to stroke it, even kiss it, just so that he would forgive her.

'Stand up! You're not in the scum anymore!' the man barked.

Zsuzsi cried the whole way home, both out of relief and great sadness. The watch remained on her wrist, and although it was already worthless and beyond repair, she never took it off. It would always remind her of the mistakes she had made and how forgiving the Institution was. Whenever she read an article criticizing the factory or the Institution, she looked at the watch, because the watch was grace itself.

That summer, she was finally allowed to visit her family, only to find that she could never go home again.

The barracks seemed to have shrunk. The smell that had once felt like home now felt foul: the stench of unwashed bodies, rotten food, rotten teeth, badly dried clothes, all mixed together. Her stomach growled. Father offered her a seat, a formality reserved for a guest. But she could hardly bring herself to sit down on the dirty, broken chair. The occupants of the barracks looked at her insistently. She felt disgust and pity for her former roommates, and she could feel their envy. She was the girl who had made it! In their eyes, she was already rich.

They looked at her broken watch, the ultimate proof of her wealth and immense success.

It became clear that she was now speaking a different language. She had refined herself too much in the Institute, and her carefully chosen words were sharpened blades that hurt the workers' self-esteem.

Father smiled at her. He was already an old man. The skin on his face was sagging, most of his teeth had fallen out, and a lump was growing on his neck. His nails were black, and his stubble was shockingly white.

Mari entered the barracks. It was like meeting a stranger. Her eyes were the same, but the way she looked at Zsuzsi was different. Mari was wearing a headscarf, a T-shirt with the sleeves cut off, and sweatpants. She had the beauty of youth, but Zsuzsi saw that this beauty would wither before it could fully blossom. Mari stared at Zsuzsi for a long time.

'So the wind blew you home?' she asked coldly.

'I was granted leave,' Zsuzsi said.

'Did you bring anything?'

'What should I have brought?'

'A present or something.'

'I do not have anything.'

Mari laughed mockingly and nodded in the direction of Zsuzsi's watch.

'A nice piece of nothing, huh?'

Zsuzsi covered the face of the watch with her palm.

'I'm going to visit Mom in the infirmary,' Mari said, turning her back to her sister. Father buried his face in his palm as if he was ashamed.

'What's wrong with Mom?' Zsuzsi asked. 'And where is Tibi? Can I see him?'

Father looked at her with such hopelessness that Zsuzsi understood there was not an ounce of protective power left in him. His children were on their own now. Perhaps they always had been, and this realization filled her with horror. Father's voice was hoarse, weak and shaky, especially when he told her that Tibi was in prison.

Tibi had had a relationship with a girl. He had got her pregnant, and although Tibi was only seventeen, he had decided to start anew, so that his child would not be born on the factory floor. At the factory, the worst possible crime was stealing The Blue. Security caught Tibi and his partner in the act.

Tibi escaped; they caught him at the city limits with 30 grams of The Blue in his pocket. The black market price was estimated at 130,000 forints per gram. The workers were paid 180 forints per gram for producing The Blue.

The girl was killed on the spot. The security service claimed it was just a stray warning shot. The bullet shattered her spine and exited through her stomach. When the paramedics arrived, they pronounced both her and her unborn child dead.

She was still a minor.

Tibi was sentenced to eight to twelve years in prison for grand larceny, distribution of a controlled substance, and criminal conspiracy. He was permanently banned from the factory premises.

When Zsuzsi heard the news, she sat down on the dirty chair, trembling.

'I thought they'd told you,' Father said. 'Of course they didn't want to disturb your studies. But he still owes you his life. You saved your brother.'

'How could I have saved him?' Zsuzsi asked. 'I didn't even know about it.'

'You're gifted. If it hadn't been for you, they'd have shot Tibi too. Don't you think they caught the girl alive? Of course they did. But they had to make an example of her. They'd have made an example of your brother, too, if it hadn't been for you.'

Zsuzsi didn't know what to feel, so she suppressed all emotion until her heart was a cool, sterile space.

'There's something else!' Father said, forcing himself to smile. 'You have another little brother now.'

'What?'

'Born last year. In August.'

Excited, Zsuzsi rose from her seat. She felt betrayed and overjoyed at the same time.

'Can I meet him?'

'Of course!' Father said. 'Yes, of course. Let's go and see him. He's in the nursery. With the others . . .'

'Others?'

Father let out a long, sad sigh.

'Your little brother isn't like you or your sister. He was born different.'

Zsuzsi frowned. She didn't understand a word of what Father was saying. Later, of course, she read up. There was no medical consensus on how or why it happened. The star lawyers at the factory and the Institute had, of course, spoken out on the subject. You couldn't prove with one hundred percent certainty that these children were born this way because their parents were exposed to Mud, although only people who ate Mud gave birth to such children. Therefore, the factory wasn't held responsible. The law works in mysterious ways.

According to the factory's reports, only one percent of children born on the factory premises were affected by the disease; journalists and researchers estimate the percentage to be closer to twenty-five to thirty-five percent.

'His name is Petike,' Father said as they approached the nursery.

The smell of decay filled the hallway. The plaster had peeled off and the raw concrete floor was bare. A few light bulbs provided dim, dirty light. The windows were covered with newspapers to filter out the sunlight.

The children cried a lot when the sun shone.

'Don't be afraid of him,' Father said and opened the door to the children's room. The smell grew stronger and Zsuzsi had to hold her nose. Father entered the room and signalled Zsuzsi to follow him.

Inside, the babies were screaming.

They were crammed into a concrete trough. Six of the babies were rolling around in the straw-lined pool; at first Zsuzsi couldn't make out their shapes in the dim light. They were all tar-black. It was only when Father bent down and picked one of them up (Petike, Zsuzsi thought, they called him Petike) that she saw what a Mud Baby looked like.

A scream choked in Zsuzsi's throat, like a nightmare. She felt the baby's gaze on her, even though the thing in Father's hands had no eyes.

'Be careful with its legs,' Father said. 'They break off easily. But don't worry about it. They'll grow back quickly.'

Zsuzsi took a step back when Father offered her the baby.

'Come on, take him! It's just your little brother,' said Father.

The thing wriggled in Father's hand. The many appendages, which Father called legs, kicked lazily in the air. Petike whimpered in his father's hands. Father left her no other choice. With a firm gesture, he handed the baby over to his daughter.

Zsuzsi held the tiny, deformed body. It was hot, its skin dry. The glands in the eye sockets were constantly producing an unpleasant, stinking discharge, as if Petike had been crying all his life.

The baby opened its mouth and Zsuzsi saw its teeth.

She couldn't remember how she had escaped from the nursery. Perhaps she'd still had the strength to push Petike back onto Father, or perhaps she had simply dropped the baby.

Later, she had a recurring dream. In the dream, she tried to throw the baby away, but it clung to her hands like the spoons of her childhood and wrapped its legs around her wrist like a black, festering bracelet. In her dreams, the baby could even speak in a terrible, whiny voice, repeating a single sentence over and over again.

'Zsuzsi, don't go away! Zsuzsi, don't go away!'

Outside the nursery, Zsuzsi tried to throw up, but nothing came out. Mari stood next to her.

'So, you met him?' Mari asked. 'Lovely, isn't he? I had to feed him when Mom couldn't. You were sure a great help then, as always . . .'

'I didn't know. . .' Zsuzsi said.

'Of course you didn't know,' Mari replied. Her voice took on the shrill, metallic tone that was peculiar to factory workers. 'They shove a silver spoon under your sweet little pussy, and it's like we don't even exist, right? Just because you got lucky.'

Zsuzsi turned away from her sister. Mari said exactly what she herself was thinking. She preferred to look at the factory buildings rather than her sister's accusing eyes: she knew her sister would understand nothing of the hardships she endured at the Institute. They both had their own truths, and those truths were irreconcilable, because this world here no longer belonged to Zsuzsi, and she didn't belong to it.

'Where's Mom?' she asked. Mari picked up a cigarette that seemed too big for her and lit it.

'At the hospital. Petike wanted to suck on her tits. But he often confuses the breast with the face, and then he bites. You have seen his teeth, haven't you?'

Zsuzsi and Mari did not meet again until a few years later, at Mother's funeral. Cancer. Father couldn't come, he was working his shift. Mari was still a minor, but she held two children in her arms. Zsuzsi was already working as a transistor. They only talked about money. Mari needed a loan, even though Zsuzsi had been providing for the family regularly since she started working. Zsuzsi gave her the loan and did not expect the money back.

When she returned to the Institute from her first and last family visit, she made it clear to Kata and her teachers that she never wanted to go back, ever. She wanted to be with the transistors.

Her actual training began the following week.

At the hospital, Zsuzsi learned to walk again, and her arm worked better than expected. She had to be careful not to overexert herself, but that was it. One winter morning Mrs. Fábián appeared at her bedside with a cheerful smile on her face, another bouquet of flowers and a box of Austrian chocolates in her hand, and announced that Zsuzsi could return to the Institute.

Zsuzsi sat up in bed, careful with her movements now.

'Can I go back to work?' she asked.

Mrs. Fábián put down the flowers and sat down by the bed.

'Of course you can go back if you want to,' she replied. 'But we're also offering you a job as a teacher at the Institute for Gifted Children. Full-time. And then this . . . thing that's happening to you will progress slower.'

'Slower?' Zsuzsi asked back, but even she could hear the reproach in her voice, as if Mrs. Fábián was responsible for the nature of this profession.

'You know what I am talking about . . .' said Mrs. Fábián. 'If you go back to work, the same thing will happen again in six to eight months. The doctor's opinion. It could be even worse next time. The deterioration accelerates from this point onwards with every contact . . .'

'Deterioration,' Zsuzsi whispered.

'If you teach, you will have a few more good years. How does that sound?'

A few good years at the Institute. Half the days with a

mask over her face and a voice distorter on her neck, the other half spent in the staff room, smoking and drinking with the rest of the burnouts. She could teach all those gifted kids and watch them blossom into transistors, knowing she had already betrayed her true purpose. She wasn't a good teacher anyway; her patience was wearing thin with age.

'No!' she said. 'I want to keep working.'

Mrs. Fábián nodded.

'Most of you decide that way,' she said, patting Zsuzsi's hand, tears glistening in her eyes. Zsuzsi looked away, because she didn't want to see this woman cry. No one should cry for her. Instead, she focused on her joy at being able to return to work again. After such a long absence, it would be like the first time. No, she corrected herself. It could never be like the first time again.

Before the first contact you are lost, but afterwards you have a firm place in the grand scheme of things.

You enter Contact as a talent, but you return as a Transistor.

As she was preparing for her very first Contact, she thought about Father and Mother and Tibi and Mari. She held a piece of The Blue in her hand and knew it came from them, just like she did. The Blue and she were siblings, and they would become inseparable when Zsuzsi put it in her mouth. Her life had come full circle.

Her first time was her final exam. If she was incapable of being a Transistor, it would show now. Just as a match can only be tested by its flame, Zsuzsi now had to prove that she could indeed become what she had been promised to be.

The Blue dissolved in her. She closed her eyes, as she had learned to do. She had used a great variety of psychoactive substances during her studies to practice controlling her thoughts in altered states of consciousness, but nothing prepares you for The Blue because The Blue is not a drug; it is raw power. It is the power of mind over matter; the key to the unfolding of the universe. Time and energy flow through you like music, you just need to know how to listen – and then conduct. You transcend the material body, now only a tool that transforms and directs the energy flowing between worlds.

When her feet left the ground, she was no longer aware of herself. She became a riverbed through which a great current of water rushed. The entity once known as Zsuzsi dissolved, not only in this world, but in millions of others. As if looking into a mirror, she saw herself floating in a thousand, even a million versions of the same space; in places discretely separated and inaccessible to each other, if not for the act of Contact.

Her bones shook with the resonance of these worlds; messages of gods passed through her from one plane of existence to another, businesses conducted transactions between different realities, scientists exchanged information and knowledge. Zsuzsi was now the bridge between them, and she always wanted more, more; if she had her way, she would never return to the ground, into this frail body, into this empty, filthy world.

Hours later, The Blue receded from her body and the trance came to an end. She descended from the air, and as she lay on the floor, gasping and trembling, her consciousness flooded her body again. That's when she felt how tired she was. She was sweaty, her muscles ached, her heart was pounding, and her head was throbbing. But the strangest feeling was in her bones; she felt as if thousands of ants were running through her medullary canals. She felt no pain, just a strange itch deep within her body.

Zoltan was waiting for her at the exit. He smiled and greeted her. It had been years since they had last seen each other, but the man had not changed at all. A warmth spread through Zsuzsi's stomach. When she thought of her father, Zoltan's face often appeared in her mind's eye, and now she knew that she made him proud.

'You've done an excellent job,' Zoltan said. 'You're one of our best.'

Zsuzsi smiled.

'Come upstairs with me,' the man said. 'Your contract is there. We'll make your status as a Transistor official, then we'll celebrate.'

He led her to a room that looked more like a luxurious hotel room than an office. It even had a minibar, a fridge, and a double bed. A bottle of champagne was waiting for them on ice. It was the first time Zsuzsi had tasted champagne, and the drink quickly went to her head. Her contract was on the table, and Zsuzsi knew she would sign it no matter what the terms were. Nothing in life could compare to what had just happened to her.

Her bones no longer tingled; instead her skin was hot. It was a pleasant feeling. She couldn't touch anything metallic. After Contact, all metal objects stuck to her hand.

'I brought you a present,' the man said and took a small, black box out of one of the drawers. He placed it on the table next to her contract. It was a delicate movement, like a slow, tender kiss.

He opened the box for her. Inside was a watch, the kind only rich people wore. A Rolex. Zsuzsi smiled, but deep inside her, like a fire under the leaves, guilt rose for the other watch that still lay among her belongings.

This watch, too, was beautiful, and Zsuzsi's heart clenched, knowing that her touch would ruin it instantly, the way it ruined cell phones and computers.

'Thank you,' Zsuzsi said.

'Come here,' the man replied. Zsuzsi stepped closer to the man.

'Closer,' said the man. Zsuzsi hesitated, but went closer.

'Transistors look their best just after contact,' said the man. 'They still have that special glow. That immense energy is still within you. You don't even realize it, but I see it. So much energy that will be wasted if we let it.'

Zsuzsi didn't know what to say, so she just smiled. The man

took the champagne glass from her hand and put it on the counter.

'But why would we do that?' he asked, reaching for Zsuzsi's neck and stroking it; then his hand wandered down, under the bathrobe Zsuzsi had put on after her shift.

Zsuzsi turned her eyes away from the man. The older girls from the factory came to her mind. The rumours about those favours. It was as if the man sensed her thoughts too.

'I can help your family,' he said. 'A little extra money always comes in handy, doesn't it?'

'Comes in handy . . .' Zsuzsi said in the ghost of her own voice. She let her bathrobe fall to the floor.

Such services were common among the Transistors, even if they never spoke about it. The Transistors knew who belonged to which company executive or board member and they did not bother each other about it. Everyone needed the little favours.

The Transistors aged, yet the executives only grew younger.

Afterwards, they lay in bed, her blood still on her thigh. Zsuzsi read the contract she had signed an hour ago. She read and understood everything except one thing.

'It says here,' Zsuzsi said, 'that the Institution will have control over my body after my death.'

Zoltan nodded.

'That's right,' he replied. 'Your body has great value to us. When you die, we will cremate you ourselves, with special care. But don't worry about that now. That's still a long way off.'

'Yes, but that my . . . my bones can be used freely by the Institute in the event of death or loss of limbs . . .'

Zoltan snorted.

'Yes,' he said and then repeated after a short pause, 'yes . . .'

'Why?' Zsuzsi asked. The man turned over in bed and put his hand under Zsuzsi's chin.

'Why do you want to know everything?' he asked. 'Why aren't you just happy?'

'I am happy.'

'Then why don't you enjoy the silence a little?'

'Because these are my bones.'

Zoltan laughed.

'Not anymore,' he said. 'They are our bones now. After you die, whenever that may be, we will take them out of your body. Because even in death, you will remain valuable to us. Your bones are important.'

Zsuzsi curled up in bed, suddenly hyper-aware of her body, her bones, her muscles.

'Why?'

'Because your bones preserve everything. Your memories are in your bones. The experience of Contact is in there, in raw form.'

Zoltan pushed the contract to the floor and nestled himself between the girl's legs.

'Why don't you shut up for a moment. Come on, let's celebrate.'

When she first started, she worked a shift almost every day. In her first year, Zoltan visited after every contact. Zsuzsi did not mind. She considered these favours part of her job. A few years later, he sought out a younger transistor; the younger ones radiated a stronger energy to feed his youth. When Zsuzsi no longer had to do favours for him, she finally learned to enjoy what he had taught her. Transistors normally coupled with each other to relieve tension. They rarely entered into a relationship and could never conceive children of their own.

The years passed quickly, the tingling in her bones grew stronger. By now she knew the risks that the Institute had strategically failed to warn her about. She had witnessed many accidents; a simple fall, an unfortunate step, even a landing at the end of Contact could lead to broken bones. It was always the older Transistors. It was an open secret. After a while, it wasn't a secret at all.

Would she have decided differently had she known?

She didn't lie to herself. She would have signed the contracts anyway because she was young. Fifteen or twenty years sounded like such a long time. That was the average lifespan of a transistor after first Contact. The energy entering their bodies weakened their bones, and in time their skeletons would collapse.

Fifteen years. Twenty, if you were lucky. That still sounded like a good deal. In fifteen years, you could live a full life. Maybe even twenty.

Leaving the hospital, she was handed a black cane; it might have been the same one the woman had used that day.

Don't dwell on the past. The past leads to burnout.

And yet . . .

Zsuzsi saw her father one last time. Although her consciousness always dissolved during contact, this one time she felt the universe with its billions of worlds fade into the background to allow her own self to emerge.

She was in the back yard of her old house, her home before the factory. Dusk was falling; she could barely make out anything in the semi-darkness. Weeds had overrun the yard, the rose bushes were overgrown. The trees were distant giants, and behind them the darkness of night loomed.

Father stood by the bushes. He looked around anxiously; he seemed confused, lost, as if this place had not been his home before. He looked younger and healthier than the last time Zsuzsi had seen him. And yet he looked so sad and broken. Zsuzsi tried to call out to him, but hardly any sound came out. She tried again and struggled until she finally managed a faint whisper.

'Dad!'

Father looked up; up, because Zsuzsi was hovering over him like a bird that would never have to touch the ground again. Father smiled and waved at Zsuzsi, and a dam burst inside her, flooding her heart with all the feelings she had held back for years. She missed Father, she missed Mother, and she loved them so much. Had she ever told them? Did they know? She could have said it now, but her vocal cords refused to obey, as if her muscles had turned to taut rubber.

'I know!' said Papa, but Zsuzsi could only lip-read the word, for in this place the only sound was the deafening whisper of the trees and rose bushes. Father waved to Zsuzsi, and Zsuzsi waved back. Father pointed to his wrist as if he were wearing a watch to signal the start of the shift. He turned and entered between the trees, into the dark of the night.

Zsuzsi came to on the floor. She was crying; she was crying even before she regained consciousness. If father had not died at the moment Zsuzsi was on shift, they would never have met.

After the funeral, Zsuzsi worked even harder; she took on more shifts. Not because of the money; she could hardly do anything with it anyway. She had never lived outside; when she walked in the city, people crossed the street to avoid her. The cash registers often broke in her presence, so she could rarely pay. The Institute managed her money and saved it for her older days. Older days. She had to laugh about it. The oldest Transistor was forty-six years old. He had rolled over in his sleep and broken his cervical vertebra. By then, every one of his joints had been padded, because the slightest jolt caused his bones to break. Transistors almost never lived past forty. Of course, they did not know that at first. And even if they did know, the time they were given seemed so long.

She returned to her apartment. She still lived at the Institute, in a building reserved for active Transistors. The apartment was comfortable – even luxurious. What more could she ask for? She instructed the Institute to give her money to what remained of her family so that Mari's children could study in the city. If they did not drop out of college, they might get a good job somewhere to break the cycle.

Zsuzsi received birthday presents from the Institute as a token of appreciation. A new watch every year.

Omega, Cartier, Blancpain, IWC, Breitling, Hublot, and who knows how many other brands. They were still in her drawer now. None of them worked. She knew she would break them, but she put them on anyway, so that at least for a second before the watch stopped forever, she could feel rich.

She lay in bed and searched her memories for the last time she was happy, but she stopped herself. You should not wallow in the past. When a Transistor thinks about the past, it's a sign of burnout.

The next day, she returned to work.

When she entered the room of Contact, she saw them on the other side of the room. A young talent; a girl with raven hair. Maybe fourteen. She was wearing the Institute's uniform. Zoltan stood behind her. He was getting younger by the year.

She watched the girl. She could call out to her, warn her of the dangers to come. But what should she warn her about? There were so many things she should tell her, but right then none came to mind, only empty, meaningless phrases, and when she looked beyond these possible warnings, she saw nothing but the dull, coarse stuff of everyday life. How could one life be better than another? Even if the girl listened to her and decided to betray her destiny, what was to become of her? After all, one had to live one's life to the full, and life is nothing but a series of shifts in some factory or another.

The girl looked at her, and she looked at the girl. Zsuzsi waved at her, she waved back.

Another Transistor touched her shoulder. The shift was about to start. She took The Blue and thought of her family that she no longer had. But she knew there were other realities, and in some they must still be together. Maybe there was one, just one among the infinite, where they were truly happy.

But here, in this world, she was born into a life without options.

She waited for the power of The Blue to fill her; she longed to ascend again – and this time, perhaps, if she rose high enough, she would finally reach the place where she ended and the world began.

The Designated Contact Individual

Broc Life Drinks has been distributing its products in two dozen countries for nearly three decades and is aggressively expanding into new markets. Our flagship product is Broc Cola, a soft drink that is best consumed cold. It is particularly popular with young, environmentally conscious urbanites, but is also enjoyed in large quantities by older people, as the drink contains the essence of more than thirteen medicinal herbs. The drink's unique, sweet taste is complemented by a distinctive, pleasantly refreshing aroma that is characteristic only of Broc Cola; a characteristic that numerous competitors have tried unsuccessfully to imitate. The recipe is a strict trade secret. Broc Cola is available in Cola, Lemon, Caramel, Coffee, Coffee Caramel, Blueberry, and Tutti-Frutti flavors. The most popular packaging for consumers is the reusable glass bottle, but it is also available in larger plastic bottles for wholesalers and in syrup form for retail outlets.

As you will see, Broc Cola is my life.

I decided to leave Hungary after graduating from college and a few failed career attempts, and at the time the job offer from Broc Life Drinks Ltd was a lifeline that I clung to with all my might. I wasn't going to admit that I wanted to flee my country, but I did. I had the feeling that Hungary was closing in on me, pinning me to the ground and preparing to deliver a deathblow unless I tore myself from its grip by force. Leaving my semi-established life wasn't that difficult. It was a life whose every aspect was a rental: my apartment, my car, my computer, my relationship. It lacked substance, and that lack was intentional. If I'd had a life with mortgages, a family, and an ever-growing stress ulcer, escaping Hungary would have been much more difficult, if not impossible. I was actually afraid of solidifying into what I thought of as a typical Hungarian who wore failures as a badge of pride, who reacted to progress and the idea of compassion with hostility, who was always several steps behind the rest of the world, until the world outside Hungary, and to some extent inside Hungary, seemed like an alien landscape whose inhabitants were a force always ready for some undefined invasion. My nationality was fixed from birth; I had to wear my Hungarian-ness as if it were a stigma, but I could aspire to be something better – a Broc Cola sales manager.

The only painful part was leaving my parents behind. I feared they would soon need my help when old age finally caught up with them. They remained like fine hooks on my heart, tying me painfully to my home. Nevertheless, I decided not to make my own fate dependent on the future needs of my parents. I did not want to wither away with them and, ultimately, with Hungary. No matter how I looked at things, it became increasingly clear that the eternally promised new golden age for this country would not come. There had never been a previous one anyway.

Still, the guilt stayed with me, despite my occasional visits home, which became less and less frequent as I prepared for a career of sorts.

Broc Life Drinks was looking for staff to expand into the Central and Eastern European market, and my skills, especially my fierce determination to succeed, and fluency in several languages, were a perfect fit for the job. Three years of hard work brought me halfway up the career ladder to a middle management position, although I spent very little time at the Vienna headquarters and in my rented room near the city center.

My life was lived on the road. I visited a multitude of grocery stores, pubs, restaurants, and hotels all over Slovakia, Poland, Romania, and Slovenia to promote our products, and soon, in line with my climb up the career ladder, I was assigned to negotiate with local retail chains and eventually with multinational companies. My sales figures were good, even exemplary. Every time upper management praised my work, I told them that I was doing so well because I genuinely loved Broc Cola. I felt an emotional swelling inside when I said it, because I meant every word, even though management always thought I was being sarcastic.

They got a good laugh out of it every time, and I was expected to laugh along with them.

In my fourth year at the company, I was offered a new opportunity.

Eight people were selected to be interviewed for this new position. They would choose one of us. It was supposedly about expanding and introducing the brand to a new, distant market. The management kept the details under wraps. They were looking for a fearless person who could handle unexpected situations. They also needed someone with no family and no established relationships, so all the candidates were single.

I was called last. The others must have left the meeting room through another exit, because I did not see anyone leave.

The interview, conducted by the HR staff, was fairly routine except for the final test. I was given a small cardboard box not unlike a matchbox. When I held the box in my hand, it felt empty. I shook it gently, but nothing stirred inside. I was asked to open it and describe what I saw. I assumed there would be a random picture or message printed on the inside of the box.

When I opened it, I found a wasp waiting in its cardboard prison.

The wasp twitched its wings furiously, but made no attempt to fly. Not yet. My hand was shaking, but I did not dare throw the box away.

I am deathly allergic to wasps. All it would take is one sting and my airways would close in a race to suffocate me before my heart gave up the ghost. I would have ten minutes to live at most.

All my life I've lived in terror of these insects.

'There's a wasp in there,' I said as calmly as I could.

I had already heard hallway gossip that the company's growth was stagnating. Redundancies were expected at my management level. All eight people selected were Eastern European workers, and I feared that some of us were indeed slated for layoff.

I could feel cold sweat dripping under my shirt. I had to concentrate on my hands to keep them from shaking. I closed the box quietly, expecting the wasp to break out at any moment and fly at my neck. How could I have thought the box was empty? The wiry legs scratched on the box as the insect moved.

My mouth was dry as plaster. The box was already closed, but my horror remained. What if my colleagues had opened their boxes with the same contents before me? What if there were seven other wasps hiding somewhere in this room? What if one of them was crawling up my back unnoticed? I felt the urge to get up and shake the invisible insects off. I did not allow my fear to show, but I could barely suppress a pitiful whimper.

I really needed this job.

I put the box on the table.

Finally, the HR staff thanked me warmly for the interview and an assistant escorted me out of the room.

A week passed before I received a cheerful email from Management. I had been selected as the contact individual. I had no idea what the job description of a contact individual was, but I assumed it was essentially customer service and sales, a job I knew all too well.

The other applicants received letters of termination but were never seen in the office again after their interviews. I learned about the letters from a secretary.

The HR department told me that my job would start the

following Monday and that it would involve extended travel. I was only allowed to take one handbag with me on the trip, which could only contain product samples and a single spare shirt for emergencies. Strictly light blue of course, the chosen corporate color of Broc Life Drinks Ltd, with a Broc Cola logo sewn onto the chest.

I was not allowed to carry any cash, credit cards, or personal documents, nor was I allowed to carry a phone or any other electronic device. The HR department said I would receive new clothes and other necessities at my destination. Of course I found these conditions worrying, but I also thought about my seven axed colleagues and how lucky I was still to have my job. I knew that this journey also offered a great reward. Several steps up the career ladder, perhaps even to heights that had previously seemed unattainable for me. I thought about the security that the job offered. Security was not just money, but also independence from Hungary. If I had lost my job, I would have been forced to go back to regroup, and I knew the inertia of my country. I would not leave again. So I accepted the job, and the next Monday I started my journey.

I must emphasize that nowhere during the briefing was it mentioned that I wasn't allowed to take my watch with me.

I had recently saved up for a vintage, but well-preserved and reliable, Omega Constellation. I could hardly afford it, but if you wanted to be successful in the business world, it was advisable to wear a watch. And not just any watch, but the right one. It is a sign of trustworthiness, and a well-chosen watch is a sign of success. I was very careful in my choice, and to be honest, the Omega grew on me. It suited me well and represented my style, personality, and life goals. It gave me an air of sophistication without masking my masculine appeal. I liked the watch and thought that wearing it during my upcoming assignment would increase my chances of success. So I put it on my wrist on Monday morning, just before I left my hotel room.

Rumours circulated around the office that the trip was quite expensive, so expensive that even the company could not afford it. Fortunately, the potential new business partner covered the cost of travel and accommodation.

A travel agent was hired to guide me through the process of the trip. He was waiting for me in the hotel lobby. He was wearing a black jacket with a gold name tag. The tag reflected two things: the distorted image of my own face and the man's name: Csabi.

As a small courtesy, I had been assigned a Hungarian guide to accompany me. We shook hands and he escorted me to the parking lot. He was driving an Audi, fresh off the assembly line, exuding that wonderful new car smell of leather and wealth. We drove down the highway towards the place where my journey would begin.

'Have you ever traveled using this method before?' asked Csabi. He spoke Hungarian with a slight accent, as if he were trying to get rid of his mother tongue.

I shook my head.

'Not with your company,' I said.

I had no idea of the nature of the journey ahead, nor of my destination country, but I was determined not to let Csabi know that. I reckoned I would end up on a plane at some point.

'They are expecting you eagerly,' Csabi said. 'We have exchanged communication with them. They are well prepared for your arrival. You'll be an honored guest.'

'Can I call from there?' I asked, probably because my mother always emphasized that I should call to assure her of my well-being in foreign places. I had not even told my parents about the assignment. Why should they worry? I already had enough to worry about.

After two hours on the sun-bleached highway and half an hour on eerily empty country roads, we stopped on the outskirts of a nameless town at a bunker-like building made of metal plates. Freshly built, it was not yet weathered; the roof sparkled in the deepest blue, the walls gleamed in brilliant white. I felt momentarily dazzled just looking at it. The building was brand new, but it already felt abandoned.

Csabi parked the car and signaled me to follow him.

The air conditioning hummed dreamily in the building. It felt like a budget airport. A real non-place that only exists so that you can pass through it. It was even odorless; all I could smell was Csabi's cologne.

Csabi led me into a waiting room: a sofa stood against the wall, with a heavy-looking table in front of it. In the corner there was a row of vending machines to satisfy the customers' needs: Coffee, pre-packaged sandwiches, chips in various flavours, and a vending machine that sold clean sheets of pure white paper. I made a mental note that this place was ripe for a Broc Cola vending machine.

There were warning notices on the walls: 'Talking is prohibited when transistors are in operation.' 'Sleeping is forbidden when transistors are in operation!' 'Reading is forbidden while transistors are in operation!' At the other end of the room was a soundproof door. A sign on the door read: 'Transmission room! No entry without permission! No entry without a guide! The use of watches, telephones, and electrical devices beyond this door is prohibited! Have a safe journey!'

'I'm not allowed to bring my watch with me?' I asked anxiously, pointing to the sign that expressly forbade this, and not just with words, but by way of a pictogram depicting a watch slashed with a red line.

It was an irrational thought, but at that moment I felt that the watch was my only support to help me overcome the unknown challenges of the journey ahead.

'No, you can't!' said Csabi. 'Weren't you informed? It's in the brochure we gave you. Watches are dangerous. Even if you had been lucky and no malfunction had occurred during transportation, the watch would inevitably be damaged beyond repair.'

What fucking brochure, I thought, but I just nodded. By now I could admit to myself how weary I was of this journey. My body felt like a magnet, pushing me away from what awaited me in the next room.

I longed for my hometown: Nyíregyháza. I longed for the back yard of my parents' house. That was what I longed for more than anything else: a green plastic chair under the fir tree in the garden. A few of hours of staring blankly ahead across the wide space of a lazy summer afternoon, emptying my mind in the absolute safety of my childhood home.

Of course, I was aware of the contradictory feelings. The place I was fleeing was the same place I thought was safe and longed to return to in stressful moments. In my mind, however, Nyíregyháza was not the same as Hungary. Nyíregyháza was a cozy, warm nest; Hungary was an animal that fed on carcasses because it was too slow, old, and stupid to hunt.

Now I felt a particularly strong desire to return home. My stomach growled at the thought of having to sit huddled for hours in a bizarre plane, train, or other experimental vehicle, only to arrive in a country God knows where, without money, documents, or a phone, and entrust myself to the benevolence of strangers I couldn't really trust.

I agreed to all that when I accepted the job, yes. But now they were taking my watch away too? That was just one insult too many. Nevertheless, I had to keep my composure. Composure is what sets us apart from animals.

'Can't you keep it for me until I get back? Or will you send it to my parents? I can leave their address . . .'

Csabi looked at me with a wide, open gaze and pursed his lips.

'I'm so terribly sorry. We cannot take responsibility for personal belongings. It's company policy, you see. We have to dispose of every item left behind.'

I looked down at the Omega on my wrist. I had saved for months to buy it! It was a perfect watch in every way, kept accurate time, was relatively scratch-free, exuded history and class without being ostentatious or distractingly luxurious, and elevated my persona to a whole new level where I could make an instant impression on the people that mattered. I wore it on an alligator-leather bracelet, another careful choice.

After a quiet, bitter moment, I took the watch off my wrist and placed it on the table.

A red light lit up on the wall.

'Just a few more minutes,' Csabi said. 'The transistors are warming up.'

I nodded and felt my heart pounding in my throat. I glanced at the clock again. The second-hand was circling around hurriedly, like a confused dog wondering why its owner was abandoning it.

Csabi looked at me; his features exuded a neutral, superficial friendliness. I often used this expression myself in my line of work.

'You know . . .' he glanced around in case anyone in the empty room was listening. '. . . I truly regret that we cannot keep the watch for you. You will understand later why that's impossible. And I want to say it openly and directly: I will take your watch with me instead of disposing of it. But you and I, we will not see each other again.'

Csabi looked at me with wide, unblinking eyes.

'I'd like your permission. So that I can use the watch without guilt or regret. I will use it either way, but I'd prefer to use it with your blessing.'

I opted for the illusion of choice, though I considered another option: destroying the watch. I even looked around for a heavy object that I could use to crush the Omega and turn it into a rubble of bent metal and broken glass. If it couldn't be mine, it shouldn't be anyone's. Unfortunately, I could not find an object that would satisfy my needs.

'Okay,' I said, forcing myself to keep a friendly expression on my face. 'Use it in good health.'

Csabi mirrored my expression back to me. It was a blank expression, devoid of any meaning.

'Thank you,' he said. 'I want to thank you for your kindness. In order to travel, you must be blindfolded. I will blindfold you myself just before we go through that door. But to make it up to you, I will look away while we are inside. Pretend not to notice that you are peeking out from under the blindfold. It's safe as long as neither of us admits it happened.'

My mouth was dry and I found it hard to swallow.

'Why would I peek from under the blindfold?' I asked.

Csabi smiled. It was a conspiratorial smile. He looked like he was about to tell a dirty joke that might go a little too far, but he trusted me to laugh along.

'What you might witness is out of the ordinary. In more ways than one. You see, those who commissioned your transport paid for the best and most powerful transistors to ensure your safe arrival. Young, fresh transistors . . .'

He gave me a knowing wink.

I was confused, but I did not show it. I nodded, knowing he had lied. He would keep an eye on me, not to make sure the blindfold was securely over my eyes, but to make sure I took it off. I had to live up to Csabi's expectations. Over the course of this journey, which started right here, I had to exude calm, masculine strength. Male jokes, teasing, and verbal conspiracies of a sexual nature are an essential part of the business world, even if I don't necessarily like that fact.

The light turned green.

As promised, Csabi blindfolded me with a black sack before we walked through the door. I think I was blindfolded because we were being watched by security cameras, although I hadn't seen any obvious surveillance devices in the waiting area.

I heard the double doors open. Csabi took me by the arm and led me inside. After a few steps, I heard a strange buzzing sound and fear gripped me. Some fears are too deep-seated in people, and when I hear a buzzing, I can only think of stings.

As a precaution, I used to listen to the sounds of different wasps and bees through headphones so that I could distinguish them even from a distance. Now I was sure that I was hearing a beehive. My allergy to individual bee stings is not as severe as with wasps, but with enough bees it can be fatal. My fear of bees, especially in an enclosed space, is just as overwhelming as my fear of wasps. This fear welled up inside me and I had to run away, even if it cost me my job and a certain amount of self-respect.

I stopped, ripped off the sack, and scanned the room for my escape route. Before I could make a fool of myself, I saw the source of the humming. I hoped Csabi attributed my brief hesitation to excitement and not panic.

Panic is the worst advisor in any business situation.

The room was lit with a few spotlights as if it were a stage. The floor was pure gray concrete. The walls of the room were shrouded in a pervasive darkness; only the center was flooded with light, illuminating five people hovering meters above the floor. They were the source of the noise that had almost made me flee. I nearly laughed with relief, but I managed to control myself. My heart was pounding hard, even though the panic was receding. Now a different kind of excitement took its place.

Csabi squeezed my arm briefly, perhaps as a sign of appreciation that I had taken off the hood, but he also gently pushed me on towards the floating figures. I felt my hair stand up to answer the call of an electric charge that filled the air. The fillings in my teeth resonated with a distant pain. Now I understood Csabi's earlier smile, which radiated male complicity. Of the five floating figures, four were women; perhaps it's an exaggeration to call them women. They were barely out of their teens, lean, muscular bodies frozen in ecstatic poses of rapture. The fifth figure was a boy; he too possessed the same striking beauty as the girls around him. An energy surrounded them, perhaps even magnifying this sight to an otherworldliness not often encountered on business trips.

Of course, Csabi's complicit smile was not meant to signal

our shared vision of beauty, but a vision of raw nakedness. It was the smile of a teenager finding a hole to peer into the secrets of a girl's dressing room. These young and undoubtedly more-than-attractive girls could now be seen and observed shamelessly, while they could not see and observe us.

The floating figures were there and not there, as if in a trance in mid-air, with their eyes rolled back, showing only the whites. The humming came from inside their bodies. At a height of about three meters, they were frozen in various contorted poses, their skin glistening with sweat. No cables held them in position, at least I could not see any. My body was suffused with an energy that these people radiated, a feeling so raw that it encompassed not only the possibility but also the fact of such a defiance of gravity.

I found their nakedness, which left nothing to the imagination, both uncomfortable and exciting. I forgot about the watch and my distress and instead was fully present in this extraordinary moment.

The humming changed register.

Csabi nudged me, signaling that the show was over. I took one last look at the five floating bodies, then pulled the blindfold over my eyes. Csabi grabbed my arm again and led me on. The humming became louder. I felt a slight dizziness, not unlike the feeling I associate with the take-off of an airplane. The noise became too much; it drowned out all other sounds and I feared permanent hearing damage.

Csabi let go of my arm and left me in a state of confusion. What should I do now? I was sure that this was just a preparation for the actual journey, a preparation that was quickly growing unpleasant.

Nevertheless, I persisted. I let the calmness of an executive manager wash over me. The foremost corporate rule is that nothing must be questioned. Standing still, blindfolded in the overwhelming noise for what felt like an uncomfortably long time, was a sign of my ultimate corporate confidence.

I felt Csabi grab me again. I followed him as he led me by the arm. I heard us moving away from the source of the hum, and I thought that what was supposed to happen was not happening, or was happening but was of no consequence to me, and I longed to catch another glimpse of the floating figures. I took off the blindfold and looked up. The five figures were still in the air as they had been a few moments ago. But something had changed, and for a few seconds I could not tell what it was. Then I realized. The man holding my arm was not Csabi, but another person. We looked into each other's eyes before I pulled the blindfold back into place, hoping that my new companion would choose to ignore the breach of rules that I had committed.

Although my companion certainly noticed the offence, he said nothing. We left the room and my companion removed my blindfold, restoring my sight.

I was standing in the same waiting room where I had started. The sofa and table were the same color, the vending machines sold the same products. But the inscriptions on the walls were different; they may have meant the same thing, but the words, even the letters, were foreign to me. If I had not known that these inscriptions had a meaning, I might have seen them only as decoration and not as warnings.

The man flashed a smile at me. His teeth were so white that they seemed to shine in contrast to his dark, bushy beard. He wore baggy camouflage pants and metal-rimmed glasses. He looked like both an intellectual and an urban soldier. I guessed he was from the Middle East, but he did not tell me where he was born.

He spoke English.

'Welcome!' the man said. 'My name is Jufus, and I will accompany you during your stay!'

We shook hands. His grip was firm.

'Have I arrived yet?' I asked.

'Of course!' said Jufus. 'Fantastic, is it not? Transistors really do redefine travel, don't they? First time?'

I nodded.

A watch lay on the table, almost exactly where I'd left mine earlier. I stepped closer to examine it, hoping my Omega had been forwarded to me despite the rules.

'A traveler didn't pay close enough attention to the travel brochures,' Jufus said. 'Unfortunately, he had to leave the watch behind.'

I nodded and fell quiet. I turned my attention to the watch. It took me a few seconds to realize that the dial was not divided into twelve hours, but fifteen.

'You can take it with you if you want,' Jufus said. 'I'd have to throw it away, which would be a shame. It's company policy, you know. It's a coveted brand.'

I pocketed the watch as if it were my own and let Jufus lead me out of the waiting room and out of the building into the shock of the glaring sunlight and burning heat. My nose was filled with a variety of strange smells that I associated with leather, dried fruit, spices you'll never taste, and sex. I later learned that this smell follows you around here wherever you go.

'Come,' said Jufus. 'I will take you to your accommodation, then we'll dine.'

In the heat, my stomach felt heavy and unbearably tight. Eating was out of the question now, but traveling is as much diplomacy as pleasure, maybe even more, so I knew I had to make an effort.

I climbed into his massive SUV's passenger seat. It was a brand I'd never encountered before, I assumed locally made.

I put my luggage in the back seat.

We drove off. Around us stretched an endless desert with a single road cutting right through it.

He stepped on the gas pedal and the car raced into the heat. The world glowed aggressively in a pale golden hue, and I felt overcome by a sudden fatigue.

'Was your trip pleasant?' Jufus asked. The answer should

have been simple, but the words melted in the desert heat, becoming useless clay figures that signified nothing.

'Of course,' I finally said, feeling a certain pride that I had managed to say these simple words out loud, and I realized that I was about to fall asleep, completely drained by this new way of traveling. I wanted to fight the urge, to stay alert, as I had only just begun my journey in a strange world, with a stranger by my side who I couldn't trust, but then again, was there ever a time when I could trust anything or anyone, apart from Broc Life Drinks Ltd?

When we arrived at my hotel, night had already fallen. It was another building freshly assembled from metal plates, standing lonely in the desert and looking more like a prison than anything else. Jufus's vehicle was the only one in the parking lot. The desert wind at night felt bitterly cold. There were no other buildings nearby. No town or other human settlement as far as the eye could see; just an endless repetition of dunes that turned the color of bones in the moonlight. I was sick of it already.

Jufus signaled me to follow him. My life had become a series of scenes of following men into anonymous prefabricated buildings.

Inside the hotel, the metal walls were covered in plaster, so you almost had the impression you were in a real brick building. A few armchairs made an effort to make the lobby look inviting. There were even a few plastic flowers thrown in for good measure, which made the whole thing seem even sadder. I had the eerie feeling that this place had never seen a guest before me. It even smelled like freshly assembled furniture and freshly laid carpet. The reception desk was deserted; two keycards lay on the counter. Jufus picked one up and handed it to me.

The other remained on the counter.

The hotel only had one floor, and it seemed to be completely empty. The building creaked softly under the pressure of the desert wind.

My room was spacious and well equipped. I had a double

bed all to myself, a desk with a matching colored chair, a tiny fridge, several floor lamps, an LCD TV on the wall, a kettle, a basket of coffee and tea, and a trash can.

The bathroom was huge, perhaps even bigger than the actual hotel room. I found everything I needed: toiletries in tiny cellophane packets, an electric razor and hairdryer in the cupboard under the tap, clean, fresh towels on a rack. There was a row of identical shirts in the closet, three pairs of matching pants with matching jackets, identical underwear and socks and a new pair of shoes, all in my size.

A large picture frame hung on the wall, but they had forgotten to put a picture in it.

Before dinner, I had only one task left: to put the product samples in the fridge, because Broc Cola tastes best when you drink it ice-cold. I had brought the samples with me in 220-mL aluminum cans, packaging that is produced exclusively for showcasing. When I took the cans out of my luggage, I sensed that something was wrong. The cans felt heavier than they should, or rather, the weight distribution inside did not seem right. I shook one of the cans. No liquid sloshed inside.

I had brought a sample of each flavor with me. I chose the Tutti Frutti can. It was one of the least popular products, and I assumed that we would soon be taking it out of circulation.

I opened the can and poured the contents into a glass. My fears were confirmed. The soft drink had spoiled in a way that was new to me and had turned into a thick, viscous substance with an odor that I found unsettling. I did not even think about tasting it, as it was obvious that the drink had become unfit for human consumption.

I let out a long-drawn-out curse, which we Hungarians are so proud of. How could I have believed that this trip would go without a hitch? That nothing would go wrong? That I could escape wearing my failures as a badge of pride like every other Hungarian?

I went down to reception. Jufus was waiting with a smile as usual.

'I think we should have dinner here. So you can rest and relax. Tomorrow we will explore the city.'

I was grateful for the care. I would have loved to lie down in my double bed and kill myself.

The guest area of the restaurant was not a communal space. The tables were divided into tiny spaces that you could barely fit into. Jufus showed the way to ours. A purple candle was lit on our table. The room was so cramped that Jufus and I often touched our knees. I found the situation absurd, but what could I do? I assumed it was a local custom, and local customs must be respected.

The food had already been served when we arrived; it was waiting for us, kept warm by dish covers.

Jufus signaled for me to start.

I lifted the cover and was overcome with horror. Wasps were piled up on my plate. They looked alive in the flickering candlelight, but after a brief shock I realized that they were dead. They had probably been steamed in cognac or some other alcoholic drink, because their smell was strong and sweet. I touched this pile of horror with a silver fork to see what else was on the plate.

'I am allergic to wasps,' I said, but Jufus had already started on his plate. Wasps crackled under his teeth. He shook his head as if he did not want to believe what I had just said.

'No need to worry,' Jufus said. 'The poison is cooked. It won't hurt you. It's a local specialty. People used to catch wasps in the desert, by hand. Today, of course, there are wasp farms. They really are among the most dangerous creatures. A single sting can deliver enough venom to kill six people.'

Jufus grinned and popped another wasp into his mouth. I looked down at my plate. My stomach was grumbling with revulsion and I knew I would be going without dinner that night.

We talked briefly about work. I learned that Jufus used to work in tourism, mainly as a tour guide, but changed jobs after an accident at work. It was only a small leap from there to his current job as an assistant executive. When I felt the conversation had reached the right point, I asked the real questions.

'Where exactly am I?'

Jufus shook his head before answering.

'Every place is relative. Because the world, like life, is constantly in motion. We move in circles, and who knows where we are in relation to others, or even to ourselves at any given time in our lives.'

I stared for a long time at Jufus, who smacked his lips happily and did not seem to notice my frustration. I wondered if he was ever able to give a clear answer to any simple question.

'What is the name of this place?'

'This place has no name,' Jufus replied. 'It's just a temporary building.'

'And the country? The city?'

Jufus nodded vigorously.

'They have wonderful names, such wonderful and powerful names that they can bring about existence. That's how the city we'll visit came to be. But I cannot put the name into words, and neither could you. Our kind has given it a name of its own, but no native resident should ever hear it, for it is a terrible insult to their ears.'

I made a mental note. The last thing I wanted to do was offend my potential business partners.

'And what is the . . . the insulting name . . . ?'

Jufus wiped the wasp juice from his lips.

'Abaddon. That's what we, the outsiders, call this place.'

If only for tourism and marketing purposes, I'm sure I would have wanted a more inviting name, but hey, I wasn't in charge. Maybe the name was well deserved. I would soon see for myself.

'If you are talking to a local, it's best to call the place The

Most Magnificent and Majestic. But do not say it out loud if you can help it. Say it in your mind . . .'

I raised an eyebrow, but decided to play dumb.

'And how do I recognize the locals?' I asked, whereupon Jufus's face contorted into an expression of religious awe, then he continued eating.

'You will!' he finally said. 'You will recognize them.'

The next morning I had breakfast at the hotel; no bizarre food this time, just scrambled eggs, toast, and a large pot of glorious black coffee. The staff were not present. Either they were hiding or Jufus himself was preparing everything for me. After breakfast, we got into Jufus's SUV and sped through the desert. After a good half hour of reckless driving, we arrived at the city, which either had no name or was called Abaddon.

It looked like the idea of a city that a child had drawn on a piece of paper that someone had picked up from the floor of the kindergarten and then decided to turn into concrete, glass, and metal. White buildings rose up in the desert, some crowded together like wild bushes in a forest, others standing alone, separated by dozens of empty garbage dumps. I hardly saw any pedestrians on the streets, and I imagined that the interiors of the huge buildings were completely empty. I imagined – and what I saw did not contradict this – that no one lived in this city.

'It's even nicer at night, you will see,' Jufus said cheerfully as he drove along the eight-lane highway that led straight into the heart of Abaddon. There was not a single vehicle on the road apart from us.

'It looks so empty,' I said. Jufus looked at me, and I could feel him appraising me.

'No,' he said. 'This city is not empty. It just has great potential for growth.'

As we approached the city center, the nature of the buildings changed. They stood just as irregularly as in the outskirts and were painted the same bright white, but here the houses leaned slightly to one side as if they were about to collapse. The closer we got to the center, the more distorted the buildings became, as if they were immortalizing the moment of collapsing, even though they all looked brand new. The human body would have to contort itself to fit comfortably between the toppling walls.

A skyscraper towered over the city center, reaching straight up into the sky without bowing to anyone or anything. It was a capitalist statement and a typical corporate headquarters: all glass, metal, and swagger mistaken for elegance. As we approached, an automatic door opened, but no one was waiting for us. The corridors were empty. We headed for the elevator. The buttons were not numbered, but Jufus pressed one of them with a manly certainty that I would love to emulate.

We spent what felt like minutes in the elevator before we arrived at our floor, maybe the 20th or 25th. I walked to the windows. As I looked down, I realized that the buildings of the city were not imitating the act of collapse, but were bending as if we were emperors and the world was bowing down to us. The whole city was built around this one skyscraper, and it was built in the image of submission.

I felt an invigorating tingle at such a display of corporate power. I enjoyed the view for a brief moment, then followed Jufus into the meeting room.

It was like entering the Ice Age. The silent air conditioning had frozen the room to temperatures that would have pleased Amundsen. It smelled of freshly assembled furniture and newly laid carpet. A lone chair faced six armchairs on the other side of a massive smoked glass table. Jufus directed me to that one chair, and I was already preparing myself for an interrogation rather than a business meeting.

I took the product samples out of my bag and placed them neatly on the table. Listening to the almost inaudible hum of the air conditioning working overtime to freeze me to death and the howl of the desert wind from outside, I was convinced that the building, just like the city itself, was completely deserted, with me and Jufus the only people around, living or dead, and now I was sitting in the exact middle of it, with cans upon cans of spoiled soft drinks. The unreality of it all threatened to unhinge me, but at that moment my potential business partners, or more accurately their representatives, entered the room, followed by their entourage.

For the most part, I managed to maintain a blank stare during their appearance.

The three representatives all wore a black veil that covered their entire bodies. They were tall and looked even taller because of the silver and gold diadems they wore on their heads. Instead of a face, they wore masks made of bone. The masks conveyed no emotions, only the purity of power.

Their hands were covered with gloves and had eight fingers per hand.

Their interpreters were led into the room on a leash, which in this culture is a sign of absolute commitment to work, as I later learned from Jufus. They both wore a piece of torn sack as a dress. Their heads were shaved and their gender, like that of the representatives, was indeterminable. The interpreters' eyes were permanently closed, their eyelids sewn shut with red thread. As the representatives walked, the interpreters crawled behind them on all fours and kissed their footprints on the brand new carpet.

This sight made me wonder, but not so much that it would prevent me from achieving my goal of introducing Broc Cola to this new market.

I greeted the representatives in English. One of them raised a hand with eight fingers, indicating that the meeting had not yet started. I nodded nervously.

The representatives placed a massive metal container on the table. It must have been stored under the table so I could not see it. One of them pulled out a small cardboard box from under his coat.

I knew it was the same box I had opened during the interview. I knew there must be a wasp inside.

They placed the cardboard box on the metal container and left it there for half a minute, then they opened the container.

There were hundreds, maybe thousands of wasps buzzing inside.

How long does it take for a person to get used to fear?

I thought of the city I saw out of the window, of the twisted buildings lying at my feet. I thought of the power and authority of the company I was dealing with, of the incontestability of the decisions made by Management. I did not move in my chair, but my shirt was soaked with sweat and I prepared myself for death.

The two interpreters climbed onto the table. They reached into the box with both hands. Even in my terror, I realized that the wasps made no attempt to fly, they just kept crawling over each other; I held on to that thought to calm myself. Wasps covered the interpreters' hands like thick gloves, and I recognised the animals from my plate last night. They were the native, deadly variety, and now I understood that this variety had been hiding in the box at my initial interview.

I was afraid that the interpreters would reach out and share their wasps with me, but instead they stuffed them in their mouths.

When they opened their mouths, I saw a gaping darkness. No tongues in there. Their mouths were just empty craters into which wasps were now crawling to form a new organ. The insects excitedly pushed against each other in tight rows until they were no longer individual wasps, but a tongue made of them.

When the interpreters pointed out to their masters that a tongue had been formed in their mouths, the representatives closed the container, locking the remaining wasps in. None of the insects escaped to wander around the table, although again I instinctively wanted to shake off the invisible creatures.

The meeting started and the negotiations ran on for what felt like forever. My biggest achievement during this session was overcoming my need to scream and run. Of course, I stumbled a few times at first as I tried to read the lay of the land, but I could will myself into focusing in pursuit of a deal. After a while, I even forgot about the wasps. They had morphed into something else and lost the original characteristic that had made me fear them.

They were now an organ and no longer insects.

I attributed the transformation to the power of this company, which was apparently able to civilize the forces of nature and turn them into a useful tool. The interpreters spoke perfect Hungarian with their new wasp organs. The Hungarian words surprised me because I thought the negotiation would be conducted in English or German as usual. I felt that my mother tongue was foreign, inappropriate, even dirty in that room. I had never conducted a negotiation for Broc Life Drinks Ltd in Hungarian before.

The representatives communicated with each other using clicks and hisses, or with silent gestures; occasionally they touched the bald heads of their interpreters, a gesture that always changed the direction of our negotiation. The interpreters spoke only Hungarian and never the language used by the representatives, which confused me about the nature of their translation work. I thought that perhaps the meaning of the words was encoded in the subliminal buzzing of the wasps and was registered by the representatives; or perhaps my partners understood Hungarian but did not know the language or were physically unable to speak it.

Nonetheless, the wasp-based communication proved to be effective, and although the organ had an unnatural undertone due to the wasps' physical characteristics, this did not hinder communication in any way.

My concern that the spoiled samples would spoil the negotiation too was apparently unfounded. They had always known

Broc Cola in this form. What I thought was a spoiled and flawed product was exactly what they wanted, which didn't make much sense to me, but I was certainly happy about it.

Still, negotiations were slow because our potential partners would not budge on one particular point: They insisted that I reveal the recipe for Broc Cola.

I can do a lot for success, but I can never share the industrial recipe for Broc Cola with anyone. I knew the recipe because it was revealed to me when we were preparing to introduce Broc Cola to the kosher markets and I had to disclose a version of the recipe in negotiations with the local religious leaders. In that case, it was satisfactory to create a fake recipe that still contained all the steps and ingredients of the actual recipe, but mixed up the order and added steps that would not result in the original and coveted taste of Broc Cola. The kosher market was happy with this method, as their goal was not to steal our product, but merely to ensure that it met their strict religious consumption standards.

In this case, however, the representatives wanted the unaltered original recipe. This seemed to make closing the deal impossible, even though the quantity requested would have quadrupled Broc Life Drink Ltd's total annual turnover.

After bringing such a deal home, not even the position of deputy CEO was out of the question upon my return.

At the end of the negotiation, and with the promise of a follow-up meeting soon, the interpreters vomited the wasps back into the container, closed it, and got down on all fours to wait for their masters to make their way out. When they finally left the room, Jufus came through the door with a broad smile.

'Congratulations!' he said. 'I hear you made a good impression!'

I raised my eyebrows in confusion.

'We still could not come to an agreement,' I said, feeling awkward speaking English again.

Jufus waved his hand.

'They were satisfied,' he said. 'They will sit down with you again soon and negotiate. In the meantime, it's my job to help you relax a little.'

Jufus became quite cheerful at the thought. His smile widened and his eyes sparkled as if my success had become his own.

'So tonight I am going to accompany you to The Club,' he continued. 'Management has put you on the guest list. This only shows how highly you are being esteemed.'

Outside, the sun was already setting. The sunsets in Abaddon are intensely red. The city, which had been blindingly white just a few hours ago, now turned crimson as it reflected the sunlight. Blood coursed through its veins as if a mummified giant had come back to life.

I could now see pedestrians on the streets, even a few cars. As I observed these new details, I noticed Jufus scrutinizing my features. He quickly averted his eyes when I looked at him, and that made me suspect that the only reason there were people on the street now was because I had noticed earlier that there weren't any.

'Can we go for a walk? Down there? In the city?' I asked.

Jufus nodded eagerly, as if he was looking forward to the opportunity to prove me wrong about what I had said earlier.

Jufus accompanied me through the narrow alleyways between the distorted buildings, watching my every move carefully.

When I spotted the signs of a subway entrance and the stairs leading down between the eternally collapsing buildings, I grew curious to see the subway system of such an exotic city. I began to descend the stairs. Unfortunately, the entrance was locked, with heavy chains securing the gates. Still, I wanted to see what the station looked like, even if it was only from beyond the bars.

Jufus ran after me and grabbed me by the arm.

'Do not go down there!' he said, panting. 'The system is not operational right now. It's under renovation, you see.'

I did not say anything, because by then I had already seen

what there was to see, the thing Jufus was trying to prevent me from seeing.

The station entrance was just a façade. There was nothing but sand behind the bars.

The Club stood on the edge of the desert. It looked more like a church than an entertainment venue. I saw two doors. The first was meant for us mere mortals.

It took me a few seconds to notice the second: a double door at least ten stories high, maybe more, because the upper part of the building was shrouded in night. At first I thought it was the wall of the building. Once it was open, you could drive an industrial crane through it.

'The gate is just for show, right?' I asked Jufus.

'Of course not!' he replied. 'The Club was built for the god Raz'hrid. When the god decides to visit the club, the gate is opened to let him in.'

I imagined that the god was a local oligarch or semi-religious leader.

'As a sign of respect?' I asked Jufus, and he burst out laughing.

'It's more practical, you see!' he shouted. 'This is his club. They mainly play Russian hard bass here! The god is known for his love of that genre. But the fact is, he wouldn't fit through any other entrance. If you had ever seen him, you'd understand that! That's the reason he opened the club! In a way, that's also why he had this whole city built. What would a club be without a city?'

A huge crowd gathered outside; the line stretched into the night, beyond the building. I noticed several middle-aged men among them, and some children too. They were all quiet; they all had their eyes on me as we passed them. They must have been envious of how easily I bypassed them as Jufus led me to the entrance. The security guards greeted him with a respectful nod, and we entered the building.

Inside, there was humid heat and neon-tinted darkness. The

loudspeakers blared out truly cruel Russian hard bass. The club was laid out like a labyrinth with the dance floor, now crawling with a mass of sweating, ecstatic people, as its center. Above the dance floor was a throne almost as big as the building itself. You had to be twenty or thirty meters tall to sit on it; you also needed a particularly bizarre, contorted anatomy to enjoy its comfort. The armrests melted down to the floor, and instead of a headrest, the backrest ended in a long, winding, padded spiral.

When Jufus showed me a drawing of Raz'hrid later that night, the anatomy of the throne suddenly made sense. Apparently, the seat was indeed tailored for the deity's maximum comfort, and when I saw the picture, I hoped that he existed only in the imagination of the locals and that I would never meet him.

Of course, my hopes were later shattered.

Jufus guided us through a maze of dark, empty corridors to the VIP area high above the dance floor. Instinctively, I looked out for a bar to see if there was an opening for some Broc Life Drinks Ltd products, but I did not see one. Drinks were brought to our table by girls who were barely wearing anything.

Other guests were seated in distant VIP areas, much like us; people like me. Business people, account managers, middle and upper management. I recognize my peers. Each of them had a local guide sitting next to them, like my own Jufus. I paid them no mind, knowing that in due course we would mingle with them to make small talk and maybe even close a few deals.

Jufus pulled a vial from his pocket. He snapped his fingers. Although I did not see anyone nearby, a moment later a waitress appeared and placed a mirror, two plastic straws and a razor blade on our table.

'Is this all right?' I asked Jufus, as I had little doubt about the contents of his vial. Jufus dismissed my question with a friendly gesture.

'It's legal,' he said. 'Legal, but pretty hard to get.'

He shook some of the white powder from the vial onto the mirror. He used the blade to loosen the substance and form thin lines. He snorted the first two lines, then applied some of the substance to his gums with his pinky. He held the mirror up to me.

Sharing drugs is a sign of trust in the business world. I had to trust my companion, my guide. As I leaned over the mirror to snort, I saw my own reflection. My eyes were cloudy, bloodshot, my face pale. In a hurry not to have to stare at myself, I quickly snorted my two lines. The first sensation was familiar: the sharpness of the substance hitting the nasal mucosa. But this substance lacked the bitter flavor of European cocaine, the distinct taste of heart medicine with which the drug is often laced. Following Jufus's example, I also applied some residue to my gums.

Jufus leaned back contentedly in his chair; at his secret signal, the waitresses brought a bottle of champagne and a bucket of ice.

'Just let it flow through you,' Jufus said between sniffles as the substance made itself felt inside me. My heart began to pound violently. The world was flooded with a rush of color, depth, and meaning. Memories swirled in my head, and I knew none of them belonged to me. Bees buzzed softly in my skull; I clearly saw myself as a little girl in a labor camp, staring at spoons stuck to my hands.

I burst out laughing. Whatever this was, it was better than cocaine. I sank into the chair.

'This is intense!' I said. 'What is it?'

Jufus opened his eyes and looked at me, and I saw the same girl in his gaze, the one with the spoons stuck to her hands.

'It's a very special substance. For a select few,' he said. 'Transistor bone. In powder form. Undiluted. You can't imagine how many worlds these bones have traveled! The many sights these bones have preserved! Now we can call them all our own!'

Jufus laughed. I laughed with him, only I did not see him, I saw the worlds beyond this world, the billions of versions of this club elsewhere, with billions of versions of ourselves sitting here, laughing just like us. I felt a synergy in my existence as I sensed my infinity spread across another, larger kind of endlessness. It felt good. It felt great.

Throughout the night, we refreshed ourselves regularly with the substance. My mood had lifted. I felt revitalized and was genuinely looking forward to everything that was to come. I longed for new experiences.

The lights changed as a variety show began on the stage in the VIP area.

At first it seemed like a magic trick. The waitresses brought eight transparent glass cubes onto the stage, each large enough to hold a person. Then they filled the glass cubes from a seemingly endless supply of aluminum buckets.

The buckets were full of scorpions. They flowed into the cubes like water.

The animals wriggled and crawled over each other, but they could not get out of the glass cubes.

When the cubes were filled, the stomach-churning beats of the dance floor hard bass stopped and a new kind of music emerged from the speakers. I glanced at the dance floor below me and saw the audience watching the action on a big screen. The sound of an exotic flute filled the club. The lights on the stage dimmed.

Something moved in the glass cubes filled with scorpions; the animals seemed to erupt from their cages like a volcano.

Eight figures rose from beneath the scorpions, their movements perfectly timed and synchronized. Scorpions fell from their limbs. The figures were backlit; the flute dramatically held its last note for a long moment. After the flute's crescendo, a Rammstein song began and light flooded the stage. Eight women stood in the eight cubes, wearing heavy make-up but nothing else.

The dancers jumped out of the cubes and performed a synchronized, dynamic choreography around the cubes to the rhythm of the song. When the metal tune morphed into a more mysterious and softer melody, the choreography changed too. The girls moved their hips sensually, and their movements as well as their gazes were directed at us, the VIP guests.

I had watched similar shows before, for aesthetic reasons of course. Still, this show had a few surprises in store when the next act of their performance began.

The girls reached into the packed scorpion cubes and excitedly let the animals crawl up their arms, over their shoulders, chests, and backs. When the glass containers were emptied, the dancers were completely covered in arachnids.

The scorpion girls then formed pairs and danced by rubbing sensually against each other; the animals moved from one body to the other as if they themselves were excited by what was happening on stage; this went so far that they held on to each other with their claws so that the dancers could weave ropes from them.

The girls began to move away from each other and intertwine the scorpions with subtle hand movements. Soon, a new umbilical cord of scorpions stretched between the dancers as they moved further apart, a rope that was three or four scorpions thick and about four meters long. At the end of the act, the girls were naked again, holding the thick scorpion ropes in their hands.

The third main act was a provocatively erotic game with the scorpion rope. The dancers stroked each other with the ends of the rope, passed it teasingly between their legs, knotted it and attached it to a metal hook to dance in the air, tied each other up and playfully whipped each other with it. The patience of the scorpions was remarkable as they endured all this without breaking the formation of the rope. Of course, I only watched the show to better understand this exotic culture, but I could not deny that I found the unique dance more exciting than expected.

At the climax, the girls each detached a scorpion from the ends of their ropes and popped the animals into their mouths. Probably under the influence of the drugs and alcohol I had consumed, I found this final act particularly arousing, and I finally admitted to myself that I desired these dancers very much. Any of them, or all. They were interchangeable in my eyes.

Darkness enveloped the VIP stage, and booming hard bass filled the dance floor again. I thought I could soon forget the performance and the strange desire it triggered in me. But after just a few minutes, the dancers appeared in the VIP area to entertain the important guests, like me. They were naked and still clutching the scorpion ropes tightly, only now they were moving alone and no longer in pairs, with the ropes cut in half. They stopped in front of the VIP tables, danced erotically and stroked the thick rope. Their eyes flirted with the guests. They danced at one table for two to three minutes and then moved to the next one.

Up close, they were even more seductive than on stage. My mouth went dry. During one of the transitions, Jufus whispered in my ear.

'You can ask for a private date with them. If you want . . .' he said, patting my shoulder encouragingly. I watched as a dancer led a VIP guest into the depths of the club, into an area that must have been even more private than this one.

My heart was pounding. I knew it was just an exciting moment full of impulses I should not act on, because I am a modern-thinking European, if only a Hungarian, and I knew that these girls must have been pushed to the margins of life by bad luck and unfair social conditions, to be used, exploited, and abused by rich or semi-wealthy men and disposed of as soon as their youth and beauty had eroded away.

I knew this was wrong, and of course I deeply condemn this sort of exploitation of women. If I could, I would free the dancers myself and lead them to a better, happier, and safer life where they didn't have to entertain audiences with scorpions between their legs.

Still.

I snorted another line of powdered bone and pointed at the girl approaching our table. She had small breasts, black hair, and big, wondering eyes. I was getting impatient, and I knew the decision had been made for me.

'I want her,' I said to Jufus.

Jufus gestured with his hand and the girl looked at me. Her posture and facial expression had changed. I recognized that look: she was surprised that I turned out to be a potential buyer. She was a professional and quickly shifted gears. She stepped closer to me. I felt the warmth of her skin. She was not touching me, but her body was only a few centimeters away from mine. Her scent was sweetened sweat; it was the scent of the city itself. She whispered something in my ear, but I did not hear it. She nodded towards the back hallways and raised her eyebrows questioningly. The message seemed pretty clear to me.

I nodded, and she smiled. She passed the scorpion rope over my neck. The animals felt cool on my skin. She pulled me up with the rope until I rose from my chair and began to follow her. There was applause and cheering from all over the VIP area and my face got hot. I wanted Jufus to reassure me that I wasn't breaking a cultural taboo and, more importantly, that there was a sufficient budget allocated for this little adventure, but the girl wouldn't let me turn back. Gently but firmly, she led me away on the scorpion rope. All I could see was her back, and it was indeed a satisfying sight to watch the muscles dance.

We entered a corridor and left the VIP area. The girl took the rope from my neck and threw it into a terrarium. The rope fell apart before it could land and the scorpions scattered around their new habitat in a frenzy.

I saw them stinging each other to death.

The girl took my hand and led me further down the corridor, which got darker and darker until I couldn't see a thing. With the darkness came absolute silence. The walls must have filtered out the noise very well. Only the sounds from our immediate surroundings reached me. Whispers, moans, deep, lustful sighs. The edges of the darkness glowed because the drug was still working in me.

The girl led me into a private room, and I could finally see. It was oppressively cramped, the walls covered in red velvet. There was a soft, double mattress on the floor, piled high with pillows. A lamp in the corner cast a crimson light.

The girl was saying something, but I couldn't understand the language she was speaking. I could barely make out her features in the dim light. I wanted to say something, but she put her finger to my lips and her finger made its way into my mouth. I licked the sweat from her skin and grinned. She made me understand that I should undress.

I followed her instructions. I placed my soaked clothes neatly next to the lamp. I was already drenched with sweat and the air felt thick.

She gestured for me to lie down on the mattress and I obeyed. She turned off the lamp and the room went almost completely dark. I could only see her blurred outline. She climbed on top of me, slowly and sensually. Her touch was hot; her tongue slid across my chest, up my neck, until it reached my lips. I wanted to kiss her, but she pulled back playfully. She whispered something in her mysterious language, which I found extremely arousing. I wanted to move to dominate her, but the girl sat on my hips and put my hands under her knees. I couldn't move, and I decided I didn't want to either. In the spirit of mutual cultural exchange, I let her do what she wanted.

I wanted to ask her about the money; how much I should pay. Could I get a bill? Or had that been agreed beforehand?

I didn't ask anything, because the girl pressed her mouth to mine. Her breath was hot and smelled of spices. My tongue sought hers.

I kept hearing her whispering, not understanding the words, but finding them sweet, inviting, irresistible. Her tongue was still in my mouth and I didn't understand how she could speak, but I didn't care. I blissfully let go of all my worries and questions. Her whisper soothed me, even if I didn't understand the words, and nothing could disturb me.

Not even the touch of a scorpion in my mouth.

At that moment, everything seemed to be all right. The girl's voice guided my thoughts, and the scorpion crawling inside me didn't bother me in the slightest. I heard the buzzing of wasps, but I wasn't afraid because the girl's whisper kept the fear at bay, and somehow I slid into the girl on top of me; or she slid into me.

As I followed the girl's voice, I stopped caring about my body and drifted into semi-consciousness, maybe even sleep.

In my dream, or vision, I was standing in a cave. Invisible people with bird voices were walking around me, chirping. In the middle of the cave was a dissecting table with a body covered in a hospital sheet.

The girl's voice also became bird-like, but I still recognised her among the other noises, and her voice led me to the table. Teeth gritted under my feet. The absurdity of it all amused me, for I knew I was only dreaming. I pulled the sheet from the dissecting table and revealed not a body, but a multitude of wasps forming a female body. She wasn't dead, although of course she wasn't even a woman, just an imitation of one. She moved, lifting her head and looking at me with wasp eyes, spreading her wasp legs, and I couldn't resist her. The need to fuck her was primal. I climbed onto the table and penetrated her. Her vagina was wet with insect venom and the wasps held my penis tightly.

I felt that I'd climax within seconds and I expected to scream because I knew that the wasps would sting me when I came. I didn't mind, so I felt a twinge of disappointment when I woke up just before my orgasm.

I sat up in the darkness. I groped around, but I could not find the girl anywhere. The lamp in the corner had gone out. I felt my way along the wall to the door, which suddenly opened and let light into the tiny room.

A cleaning lady stood in the doorway and spoke to me in an unknown language. She leaned on her mop and motioned for me to leave. I was afraid of being seen naked, but when I looked down at myself, I saw that I was dressed. My clothes were exactly as they were when I entered the room.

I quickly checked my pockets to see if I still had my valuables, only to realize that I never had any.

The next morning, the meeting with the representatives was canceled. That did not bother me. With Jufus by my side, I set off to explore the city. I felt rested, almost happy. I felt a lightness, if not physically, then in a psychological or spiritual sense. I felt purified by the private encounter with the dancer last evening. Everything felt straighter, simpler, more tangible.

Jufus had a mischievous twinkle in his eye, and at breakfast he himself suggested showing me the city's famous subway network. Surely to make up for the fiasco the day before. I gave him the benefit of the doubt. Maybe there are working lines in the city, just not the ones I stumbled across yesterday.

Jufus contradicted my expectations and we headed straight for the metro station, which was forbidden to enter just twenty-four hours ago. This time a security guard stood at the entrance and passengers were entering and leaving the station that was pure sand a day ago. That was impossible. Either my senses had failed me earlier or a station had been built overnight to sell me the image of a living, functioning city.

'Can I ride it?' I asked Jufus, certain that he would find an explanation as to why I couldn't.

'I want us to ride it. I have to show you something. At the request of Management,' replied Jufus.

Jufus greeted the guard with a slight nod, who nodded back but paid no further attention to us.

The station was deserted, despite the influx of people I had seen enter. There was something wrong with the place. The walls were made of marble and heavy stone, the benches hammered out of fine iron. The boards that were supposed to show the lines and stops were blank, as if no one had had time to plan this system, but had simply built it. On closer inspection, I saw that the benches were not scratched; no one had ever sat on them, I supposed.

The train arrived. It was a brand-new train, and its arrival caused a hot gust of wind. I eagerly boarded the first carriage. Inside it was scorching hot. I saw air conditioning units, but none of them worked. I assumed they were just props.

There were only a handful of passengers. At the back of the carriage sat an elderly couple holding hands. The man frequently wiped his forehead with a handkerchief, his shirt dark with sweat. He looked as if he could go into cardiac arrest at any moment. His partner stared blankly in front of her, sweating profusely. Her mouth twitched involuntarily.

Sitting opposite me was a woman in her early forties, dressed in black. Her sweaty hair fell into her eyes and her pale skin glistened with perspiration. She glanced at me impatiently from time to time and then immediately turned her gaze away. The subway passed through the dark tunnel without a service light or emergency exit sign flashing. That matched my image of the city. It was like a metro line that children dream up and build according to their drawings.

The woman got up from her seat and sat next to me.

'English?' she asked with a heavy accent. I nodded.

'Why did you have to do this? Why did this have to happen? Do you enjoy it?' she asked. I did not understand exactly what she meant, and she seemed to find it difficult to express herself in a foreign language. A vein stood out in her neck; I could see the beating of her heart in that vein.

'You should not have . . .' the woman continued, before Jufus clicked his tongue. She fell silent and gave Jufus an angry look. He returned her look and gave her a sign with his hand. Just then, the train braked hard. I almost fell to the floor, but Jufus caught me.

We came to a halt in a dark tunnel with no sign of a station. The nearest door swung open. The fresh, raw smell of earth filled the carriage.

Jufus gestured to the woman to get off the train. She lifted her head, smoothed her clothes, and looked at me again.

'Because of you . . .' she said bitterly and got out of the subway car. As there was no platform, she clung to the wall of the tunnel like a mountain goat. There was almost no space between her and the train.

The door closed behind her and the train moved on.

I occasionally glanced at my watch, but it was useless for telling the time. When we arrived at the next stop, the old man was panting heavily. As the doors opened, he and the woman, who I assumed was his wife, looked at the station with desperate longing; longing for fresh air and light. Apparently, this was a perk that only Jufus and I were granted. We got out, but the elderly couple remained seated in the car, looking like they were about to die. I suppose this was also part of the plan to show me the normality of the city.

The station was the exact mirror image of the station we had boarded at. A security guard sat at the exit. Maybe the twin brother of the other security guard, because they looked identical. The security guard nodded to Jufus, and Jufus nodded back, and I felt an itch to laugh.

We stepped to the surface.

There stood a single building in the distance. Prefabricated, of course, just like my hotel. A paved road led there from the subway station through a stretch of desert.

'Am I mistaken,' I said, 'or was this subway really built overnight?'

Jufus smiled.

'It was built to please you. Like so many other things.'

'To please me?'

'Management wants to please the people they do business with. It's just a small gesture. If you'd had a different disposition, we could have flown you here in a helicopter. But we realized you should enjoy a good ride on the subway. Did you?'

I thought of the woman who, if she survived the passing of the train, would have to wander through the dark endlessly, only to be crushed to death by the next train. Of the elderly couple who might die in the overheated, airless wagon. Where did they get these people from? Were they hired? Kidnapped?

'Why make me happy?'

'Because they can. It's a new business, but potent, full of new possibilities. What you think of as money is of little value to them. From your point of view, their money is infinite. But this business is about so much more than money. It's about power, you see. Such power that you can't imagine. And they indulge you and the other business partners they're meeting just to show they can. So, I'll ask you one more time. Did you enjoy the ride?'

I felt the tingle of entrepreneurial power. Now it was my turn to put on a beaming smile.

'Yes, definitely!'

When I looked at Jufus, I knew that was exactly the right answer.

We braved the heat and walked to the building on the other side of the station. Inside, more heat and the horrible smell of unwashed people awaited us. Right next to the entrance were cartons of Broc Cola. The sight of the cans filled me with a strange nostalgia. I took out a can, but I could tell by its weight that the drink inside was spoiled.

Jufus led me into a room where the combination of steam, heat, and an unsettling chemical smell was unbearable. I could barely see through the fog. Naked people stood next to bubbling barrels, stirring the contents with long wooden sticks.

They were heating spoiled Broc Cola samples and adding an unknown substance to it.

'It boils like this for hours. Look, it cools down here . . .'

Jufus led me out of the hellishly hot room and into a cooled chamber, where the concocted substance solidified in smaller pots.

'What's this for?' I asked, examining the material, most of which looked like mud that had been freshly urinated on. It was certainly not suitable for human consumption.

'It's part of a longer process. It's a new business model. So new that it had to be set in motion by the gods,' Jufus said. 'And now aggressive growth is expected.'

Aggressive growth is the most beautiful phrase ever invented in a human language.

I grinned. That's what I love about these massive companies. I don't need to understand. It's enough for me to believe in the potential for growth.

And I believed. I believed so much.

That night we went to The Club again. I took another dancer to a private engagement. Maybe the same one, I'm not sure.

The same thing happened as before.

The next day, a sandstorm swept over the city. My meeting was canceled again – but Jufus suggested we go to The Club and wait out the storm there. My room felt increasingly cramped anyway. The TV had turned out to be a mere prop, so I agreed to Jufus's suggestion.

There were only a few people on the dance floor during the day, but the scorpion dancers greeted us with invitations to private shows just as they did at night, albeit in smaller numbers.

I went straight to a private room with one of them before breakfast. I hoped I would understand more about what happened in the dark if I did it sober. I didn't. I woke from the dream of the wasp woman rested, relieved, lighter, just like the last time. I felt good.

Outside, the storm was raging. Jufus had disappeared to make a phone call, so I was more or less alone in the VIP area.

My eyes met another woman's; a sales executive, just like me.

She was in her late thirties and elegantly dressed in black. She wore her hair short and bleached. She had just chosen a dancer for a private engagement. She saw my gaze. She nodded to me and led the selected dancer into the dark.

She returned some time later. She exuded calm, just like I did when I came back from my engagements. She ordered a cocktail with the same gesture as Jufus, and I suspected that in time I would get to know these signs myself. Our eyes met again and I walked over to her table.

Her name was Alma. She represented an Austrian dairy company when she arrived here. A so-called designated contact individual, like me. We chatted briefly about business, then chatted casually about the city of Abaddon. It felt liberating to talk about the events of the last few days, especially as Alma's experiences and impressions were similar to mine. We spoke German at first, then switched to English. She was also an avid user of the substance Jufus was carrying all the time.

'When did you arrive?' I asked after we had refreshed ourselves with a few sniffs of powdered bone from the mirror.

Alma shrugged her shoulders.

'I don't know,' she said. 'Two weeks ago, tops. Maybe three. Time is different here. But I can tell you that there was nothing here at the time, except for the one corporate tower and The Club. Everything you see now was built in weeks. Even in days. Mostly at night.'

'How?' I asked.

She shrugged her shoulders and smiled. Her skin was quite tanned from the sun.

'You must understand by now that this is a corporate business on a scale that's impossible. The principles are the same, of course. But the pool of resources is of a completely different caliber. Not out of our world, or any other, if you know what I mean.'

I wasn't sure I did.

'I was offered a job at the company,' she continued. 'Out of the blue, just like that. Now I am waiting for my final contract. Then I will move on.'

'Move on? Where?' I asked, to which she shrugged her shoulders again.

'Wherever they say. And you?'

I did not know what to answer.

'I am just waiting for the negotiations to end.'

Alma shook her head knowingly.

'It's the same with me, or so I thought. But you know what? I think it's their way of recruiting. They want a deal, but they only have a faint idea of what a deal actually is. They see it as a boast. As a show of power. And so their recruitment methods are just that. A demonstration of a fragment of their power.'

'Who are they?'

She laughed.

'My parents were religious. They always worried that there was no God in corporate thinking. I guess now the gods have finally caught up with us and taken over business,' she said.

'Let me just tell you that you will be surprised by the outcome of the negotiations,' she continued. 'You will find that the company you represent and the company you're here to do business with are already the same. That's my story. And everyone's I know around here. It will be yours too.'

I quickly took a sip of my champagne to mask my discomfort. Broc Life Drink Ltd always existed in my mind as an untouchable and clearly defined entity, and it was unsettling to think that this place and the company I loved so much could become closely linked, even identical. But what would that make me? I escaped being Hungarian by becoming one with Broc Life Drinks Ltd. But what will I be when Broc Life Drinks Ltd no longer exists?

'I have seen you,' she said, 'with the girls. They're hot, huh?'

I blushed, but then remembered that I'd also seen her leaving with a dancer. I adopted as objective a tone as possible. No accusations, no shame. Just a conversation.

'I have seen you too,' I said. 'How is it for you?'

'Pleasant,' she replied.

I nodded.

'For me too,' I said, wincing uncomfortably.

'We are chosen, hence the VIP treatment up here. The dancers are just for us. I come here every day,' said Alma. 'Some evenings I visit several girls' rooms. It's a thing that gives me pleasure I didn't know existed.'

'Same here,' I said after a moment of silence. It's so easy to be honest in a situation like this, in a strange place with strangers, so I continued.

'But I never remember exactly what happens. And I do not even know who pays for them. And how much they cost . . .'

'Pay?' Alma asked back. I nodded and Alma started to laugh.

'You must be really new here,' she said, taking a sip of her drink and trying to stifle a laugh, then continued. 'That's part of the recruitment process. You're trying to do business with them. They find something you're trying to hide from them. A personal secret or a company secret. That's the first thing they take from you. That's their way in . . .'

Alma smiled.

'But you won't remember it,' she said. 'That's the best bit! You don't pay for them with money. You pay them with yourself. The more we visit them, the more they take from us. You can feel it here . . .'

She pointed to her temple.

'. . . and here.'

And to her chest.

'Things get lost. Memories. Knowledge. Emotions. It's as if they were never there. They were never yours. They're just gone.'

I thought of the relief I felt after every engagement. I thought of the secret recipe that I was supposed to know and yet, I now understood, didn't.

That was their way in. And what else did they take?

'How do you know it's not important?' I asked. 'The things they take?'

Alma shrugged her shoulders.

'If I don't remember it, how could it be important? Every thing you throw away only leaves more space for an efficient future.'

I searched my memories for missing things; I expected a gaping black hole to stare back at me, a center of horror that would show my losses. But I found nothing of the sort. Whatever was taken from me, it left no stain of pain. I sensed a blurred vision of my past, of my parents, of my years gone by. But was there anything truly worth remembering? Rented rooms, rented cars, a rented life.

Two dancers stopped in front of our table; they wiggled their hips gently in front of us and stroked each other with a scorpion.

It was easier knowing that I was the product and not them. They were using me and not the other way around.

Alma showed me the gesture she used to order the girls for the engagement. That was the first command sign I learned in Abaddon. Here, people in positions of power give orders with fingers, not with words.

We both left with the dancers, and whatever we left with them, it didn't leave a bruise.

As night fell, the atmosphere in the club heated up. Jufus saw that Alma and I had found a common ground, and he kept to the background. The evening was further enhanced by the arrival of a guest of honor.

Alma had already told me about her new job here before the guest arrived. She shouted it into my ears over the music.

'I'm going to be the social media manager for the god

Raz'hrid. You know, Insta', Face', 'Tok. It's important that he makes the right impression on his followers around the world. I have a few ideas on how to cultivate and promote his image. However, I have to completely change my way of thinking, because the whole thing is inhuman! He's coming to the party tonight and I'll discuss the details with him. Or, well, with his representatives, because he can't really talk to me. I'd sort of die, I guess.'

That explained the day-long sandstorm. Raz'hrid craved Russian hard bass tonight, so he had made his way to The Club to celebrate.

The warning horn sounded and the crowd began to riot and scream; some in ecstatic joy, others in fear. Many tried to flee, but those who rushed onto the dance floor pushed them back. On the VIP stage, the girls grabbed their scorpions and fled into the darkness. Jufus, with a vodka cocktail in his hand, watched the dance floor with a mischievous grin on his face.

'What's going to happen now?' I asked Alma, who quickly shook a large amount of bone powder onto our mirror.

'A party!' she said excitedly. 'Tonight we're celebrating with the gods!'

The gigantic gates opened; behind the shriek of the warning horn, we heard the raging cry of the desert storm and a deep rumble, an incantation of terror.

Raz'hrid was approaching. The building shook under his footsteps.

The dance floor was covered in desert sand. Some tried to push their way through to the exit, but most screamed in anticipation of the arrival of our guest of honor and the actual owner of the club, owner of the city, perhaps the entire world, and many others beyond this. Some knelt, arms outstretched in religious ecstasy towards the open gates.

Raz'hrid entered the club. He barely fit through the enormous gates. Horror rose in my throat, despite the soothing effect of the lines I had snorted.

Raz'hrid headed straight for the dance floor – the doors closed behind him. The music fell silent in awe of the god entering. I sensed the stench of million-year-old graves in the air, above the fruit-scented dry ice. The image I had seen of him earlier painted a good, rudimentary picture of the deity, but of course couldn't convey the horror and terror that surrounded him.

The god looked around the dance floor with his thousand eyes; then he raised his terrible tentacles, revealing a multitude of mouths, endless pits of despair and death – and he roared. We all trembled with fear, we were all ready to surrender to this unspeakable horror.

But the roar was not a call to fear, submission, or surrender.

It was a party roar.

The DJ took the cue and immediately put on the hardest, fastest, trashiest techno beat I'd ever heard in my life.

'My boss!' Alma shouted cheerfully. 'That's my boss!'

I feared I would faint, or I would start screaming and never stop.

The god began to dance to the rhythm of the music. Raz'hrid knew how to party properly.

I realized that the only possible human reaction in this situation was to raise your arms to the sky, screaming and shouting as if you were having the best time of your life; if you chose otherwise, you'd die. Everyone else in the VIP area did the same. We stood at the railing, jumping and dancing and screaming with joy. Jufus tore off his clothes and threw himself around to the beat of the music. I noticed the scar of a bullet wound on his body and remembered his story about an accident at work from his time as a tourist guide. But soon all coherent thought left me.

On the dance floor, Raz'hrid trampled the guests to mincemeat with his many feet. The blood splatter even reached the VIP railing. The club filled with the smell of fresh death, and I laughed, but it sounded like a shriek, because how else to enjoy the sight? Crowds of people poured onto the dance floor to replace the fallen partygoers, looking for a chance to be torn to pieces under Raz'hrid's dancing feet, while Alma and I danced in the VIP section, drinking and snorting powdered bones until finally, instead of horror, I felt that this was the best of all possible lives, and that it was all I had ever wanted.

Raz'hrid occasionally sat on his throne, resting between sets. I could barely stay on my feet. The ventilation system was working overtime to keep the smell of blood out of the halls, but with little success. Down below, the survivors continued to dance among the remains of the fallen.

'Your place or mine?' I asked Alma. She shrugged her shoulders. Her face was bloody, just like mine.

'Yours,' she said. 'Just let me talk to Raz'hrid first. Maybe he wants an Insta-story about tonight.'

The next day, I was taken to headquarters for a meeting with the company representatives. It was not until I got there that I noticed a few bloodstains on my pants. It did not bother me, although I am usually sensitive to such things. The representatives marched into the room, followed by the crawling interpreters, but all I could see was the stain. Someone else's blood, spilled in the heat of ecstacy and religious fervor. The two could not be separated. But now I had the feeling that this stain was a sign of initiation. A sign that I belonged here, at least in part.

The translators filled their mouths with wasps and the second round of negotiations began, only to inform me that they had acquired Broc Life Drinks Ltd as a business entity and had immediately ceased distribution of all their products. All drinks produced would now be transported here. That was the end of my job as an almost mid-level executive manager and soft drinks salesman.

However, I was still employed by Broc Life Drinks Ltd, so

technically I was in employment of the company I had come here to do business with.

Therefore, the negotiation was no longer a negotiation, but a job interview about whether I had a job or not.

I knew I couldn't go back home. Never. And as I sat there, I felt a stabbing pain in my chest. I missed Nyíregyháza. I missed my hometown so much that the pain it caused was physical.

I had to get rid of it.

The night before, I had brought Alma to my hotel room. She thought it was cute. She said that she had stayed in one of these hotels herself but had since got her own place in the city. I didn't understand what she meant, so I asked her if she meant living quarters, like a house?

She said no. She said she meant a neighborhood. We left it at that.

She stood at the window and looked out into the desert, then she undressed. I would have liked to paint this scene if I had a touch of artistry. Later we lay in bed and talked. She showed me the photos she had taken at the party. Posing dancers and waiters, laughing businessmen with champagne glasses in their hands, pretty girls in glittering party dresses, their faces still fresh from the blood on the dance floor.

'I have signed the contract,' she said. 'There'll never be another opportunity like this. And you?'

'Me?' I replied.

'They want to take you too. Otherwise they would not have made you the contact individual.'

Alma smiled. I shook my head.

'No. I have to go home,' I said. 'My parents don't even know I am gone.'

I'd forgotten to call my mother, and I was horrified that I could barely remember her face.

'I don't remember my own parents,' Alma said.

'Are they dead?'

Alma stretched her limbs and reached for a cigarette.

'I don't know if they are. I don't remember either of them. I'm a lot lighter that way, you know. You could be too.'

Alma stroked me, and I stroked her back.

A small cardboard box was placed on the table in front of me. The three masked representatives watched my reaction carefully. Something moved inside the box; I heard the wasp's legs scratching across the thick paper.

The interpreters spoke in unison again.

'Inside the box,' they said, 'there is a wasp. It's a desert species that can kill six adult men with a single sting.'

I was asked to open the box.

I touched the bloodstain on my pants, then grabbed the box and opened it. There was a wasp wriggling in the cramped space, just as the interpreters had promised. It was a disgusting, terrifying creature, its dark abdomen moving furiously with the fierce confidence of a creature unsurpassed in nature.

I was asked to hold the wasp in my hand.

We were lying in bed when Alma turned to me and stroked my face.

'You know my name,' she said, 'but you never told me yours.'

'Haven't I?' I asked back, and I felt a sense of unease that I couldn't place. How could I not have told her my name? I had sat down next to her in the club and we had struck up a conversation. She had introduced herself. Surely I must have introduced myself too.

'Didn't I?' I asked again and Alma shook her head.

'What's your name?' she asked.

I wanted to say my name, as I had said it so many times before. My mouth moved, my tongue moved, and my vocal cords moved, but no articulate sound came out. In place of the word, those two or three syllables that meant my name, I found only a dark abyss.

'What's your name?' Alma asked again.

'What's my name?' I wanted to ask back, but I was paralyzed.

What is my name?

I sat up in bed to check my ID or passport, but of course I didn't have any with me. Alma sneaked up behind me and kissed my shoulders.

'Don't worry,' she said, 'I don't think I'm Alma either, I just call myself that now. Because the name is the second thing they take away from you. Then eventually they'll take all the rest until all the superfluous bits are gone and we can really be ourselves.'

I buried my face in my hands, and where there should have been fear, I felt relief instead.

I had to laugh, so I laughed; I laughed until Alma laughed too. I was still laughing when Alma finally left.

I almost laughed again when I shook the venomous wasp out of the box and into my open palm. Its legs tickled my skin.

I felt no fear. I felt no panic.

I looked at my future employers.

'Do you want me to eat it?' I asked.

The masked partners looked at each other, and I knew I had a job for the rest of my life.

In the corporate world, you always have to trust unconditionally, because if you can't trust your company, you can't trust anything at all.

Jufus smiled as he waited for me at the conference room door, now greeting me as a colleague rather than a guest.

'I'm very happy that we'll work together from now on,' he said, although I still had no idea what my job would be. Nor did it matter. A few dozen more nights at the club with the girls and I'd be light enough inside to be capable of anything.

We got on the subway, which now had working air conditioning and passengers who looked like they might survive the ride, and Jufus took me to my new accommodation. I was already considered a local employee, so I was entitled to my own permanent home. Of course, it wasn't just a home. Like Alma, I got my own neighborhood in the city.

When we stepped out into the sunlight, the sight made me dizzy. At first I couldn't comprehend it at all; then, as I focused on the details, I could finally admit that the metro had actually arrived in Nyíregyháza; my hometown, even if it was a smaller version of the city. It contained only the buildings and street corners that were important to me, that gave that electrifying sense of being home. Of course, it wasn't a perfect replica – the walls of the buildings were white, and exotic plants grew on the streets instead of birch trees and shrubs. But the desert dust suited this version of Nyíregyháza well; it was exactly like the Great Hungarian Plain.

Jufus showed me the way to my mother's house; not where it had originally stood, but exactly where I felt it should be now. The house was empty, my parents not only gone but never there, and soon I won't even know that I should miss them, because to me they will never have existed.

Jufus handed me the keys and let me explore the house I had known all my life. Soon I will no longer know what this building means to me – it will be just one exotic element among many in the city, but it will be mine. Oh, how I long for the moment when I can finally free myself from the meaning of everything! Only then will I be free, truly free from myself, from my memories, from Hungary.

I went into the garden where I used to spend the summers with my parents. Instead of the huge pine tree, there was a towering palm tree, but I could accept this version too. A hole had been dug at the foot of the tree. Wasps had built their nest in the hole – they buzzed around the garden and darkened the sky in numbers that seemed infinite. Under the tree stood a garden chair made of green plastic, just as I had imagined in my fantasies.

I sat down in the chair and let the wasps buzz around me. I

leaned back and let a serene, thoughtless calm wash over me, knowing that I was turning into what I had always wanted to be. Not a Hungarian. Not a businessman. Not a corporate manager.

Not even myself.

But an individual suitable for any task.

Damage d10+7

The party had already been going on for four hours. On behalf of a destitute elven king, they set out from the tavern of D'mar E' Stvat en route to the Plain of the Unburied Dead. They had already fought their way through two dungeons, defeated the Red Demon, and obtained the Crystal Key. With this key, they were ready to return to Estrat, one of the picturesque towns of the Dolritori Empire, where most of their adventures take place. They meant to ride a griffin on the way back, but the griffins were not cooperative.

'The griffins are restless,' said Balázs, the game master. 'You can feel in the air that it's no longer safe to fly with them. What are you going to do?'

The adventurers looked at each other in confusion.

'My God, what would I do? I'd jump on one,' Noel said, positioning himself on the chair to suggest dominance, though it made him feel terribly uncomfortable. He tried to really put himself in The Ax's point of view.

The Ax was the barbarian warrior he had chosen as his avatar at the start of the party. It was his first time playing a real-time narrated role-playing game. The game they were playing now was based on D&D, but it was Balázs' own version and world, with simplified rules and an almost limitless variety of choices. He found it odd that every action was narrated verbally. In his youth, Noel had loved computer-based fantasy games like *Diablo* or *Dungeon Keeper*, so he thought he would enjoy live role-playing as well. But instead of being mesmerized by the words that narrated his adventure, he was too aware of sitting among a bunch of office workers in their late thirties or early forties, pretending to be sixteen.

'I think we need to leave. Maybe they sense some danger,' sighed Sári, in character. She played as a necromancer priestess. In reality she worked as an accountant at a company that made offset-printing blankets. A few tattoos hinted at her wilder days before she settled into the safety of monthly salaries, paid vacations, and company benefits.

'I don't want to walk back across the plains,' Dénes declared. He had organized the party and was hosting it in his kitchen, but he appeared to be the most bored of all the players. He rolled up his shirt sleeves and glanced at his character sheet, as if he were playing poker. This was the seventh time he had adventured through the Dolritori Empire under Balázs' direction, and he was getting tired of the game. He might have already been tired of it after the first or second session. Still, he kept organizing these events in his kitchen, perhaps in the hope that these occasions would serve as a kind of mortar for their friendship, welding his guests closer together in all areas of life. This also made it easier to introduce his new partner, Fruzsi, to the group. She liked role-playing.

'Get movin'! I don't care how,' Fruzsi moaned. Dénes and Fruzsi had moved in together six months ago, and Dénes still couldn't believe his luck. Fruzsi was ten years younger than him, and was at least two notches above his previous girlfriends – and at least four notches above Dénes himself – so he had to keep his patience. She would irritatingly incorporate meme English into her vocabulary, mostly expressions she picked up on Reddit and forced into Hungarian sentences. She worked as a copywriter and was able to effortlessly adopt that cold, ironic, and detached Budapest attitude that Dénes had never managed. She had a little bit of a habit, but that was natural in Budapest's corporate world. Dénes knew that the girl had just done a line of coke in the bathroom, which was difficult to reconcile with the innocence of fantasy adventures, but he kept his opinions to himself. Sometimes Fruzsi needed a line, otherwise she fell into a gloomy mood.

'All right,' said Noel. The afternoon was getting too childish for his taste; they were standing in front of some imaginary griffins, as if they really had to weigh the pros and cons of imaginary decisions. He had been drawn into the game with the promise that anything could happen in Balázs' adventures, yet he felt oddly constrained.

'I will ride the griffin,' said Noel.

'The griffin roars at you,' said Balázs. 'He looks you in the eye as if he's challenging you to a fight . . .'

Noel clicked his tongue.

'If it's a fight, let it be a fight,' he said. 'I will attack the griffin. With my fist.'

'The griffin will engage you in combat,' Balázs replied and placed the pair of ten-sided dice in the middle of the table.

They rolled the dice at the same time. The griffin had no chance; The Ax's damage value was equal to the number rolled plus seven, and the griffin's defense was three. Noel rolled a six, and the griffin rolled a five.

'Your hit the griffin in the throat,' said Balázs. 'Its leg buckles and the griffin almost falls off the rock.'

'I'll catch it!' Sári shouted.

'You reach for the griffin and grab it under the wings, pulling it back to safe ground,' continued Balázs. 'The griffin shakes itself, and now it looks at you with respect. You who have defeated and saved it. It lies down on the ground, inviting you to mount it.'

Sári's face beamed with happiness at having saved an imaginary creature.

The game continued; Balázs ran the adventure in a seemingly unemotional and matter-of-fact manner, giving the players enough freedom to make their own decisions while still keeping the action tightly controlled. But they were not teenagers anymore, and most of the group weren't even particular fans of role-playing games. They had already finished off the chips and fizzy drinks and were switching to booze; Noel was halfway through his fourth can of beer, Sári was making herself a strong spritzer, and Fruzsi was running to the bathroom to snort a line.

They were all hungry and ready for the excitement of violence.

The plot of the adventure led them back to the outskirts of Estrat, where Isla, the fairy girl, lived; she had the other half of the map they were looking for.

Dénes already knew Isla, as she had appeared in five of the previous adventures he had played with Balázs. Altogether this was Balázs' eighty-fourth adventure to feature the fairy girl. Still, this was the first time something like this had happened.

Isla responsibly handed over half of the map to the adventurers, asking them in return only to find her father's silver chalice when they reached the catacombs beneath the Plain of the Unburied Dead. This, by the way, was part of a longer storyline known only to players who had played in this world at least four or five times.

The map was received; the party should have continued to the next installment of the adventure.

'I want to fuck the girl!' said Noel.

'What?' Balázs asked.

Noel shrugged his shoulders.

'The Ax is a barbarian warrior. We've been roaming around here for what feels like years, hacking up monsters and skeletons and stuff. The Ax covets a woman after a fight. He's got enough sense not to go after his own teammates, but when he sees this hot piece of fairy pussy, he wants action.'

Fruzsi laughed.

'You stupid asshole!'

Noel grinned.

'Exactly! The quicker we get this done, the quicker we can move on. I'll make what's-her-name an offer . . . !'

'Isla,' said Sári, whereupon Noel nodded vigorously and opened his fifth beer.

'Hey! You said anything was possible in this game. We could do what we want, we could make our own decisions, and so on! Isn't it so?'

Dénes cleared his throat.

'As long as it's consistent with your character,' he said.

'I just explained to you why it is,' Noel retorted indignantly. Dénes nodded.

'Okay, good point,' Dénes said. 'The Ax is indeed not the sharpest knife in the drawer, and . . . what was the backstory? He grew up around dogs or something?'

Noel sighed theatrically.

'He was kidnapped in his childhood and trained as a gladiator. He had to fight with dogs in the . . . haven't you seen Conan the Barbarian? We're not going any further until I've fucked the girl!'

Balázs stared dumbly at nothing at all, as if trying to block out the world. He knew he had to say something, anything. So he forced himself.

'You can't do that,' he said. Noel raised an eyebrow.

'Why can't I?' Noel asked back. 'I think I could, because my decision is consistent with my character.'

He took a sip of his beer and held eye contact with Balázs to make sure the game master understood it as a challenge.

'You want to seduce Isla . . . ?' asked Balázs.

'No!' Noel said impatiently. 'I'm telling her that I'm going to fuck her!'

'Okay. Let's roll the dice on charisma.'

Balázs' palm was sweaty as he threw the dice; but when he saw the number, he relaxed a little. The persuasive power of The Ax was far surpassed by Isla's numbers.

'Unfortunately, Isla declines your offer,' Balázs said. 'She asks you to continue your journey to the catacombs and retrieve her family relic as soon as possible.'

'No!' said Noel. 'I'm going to grab the fairy and slam her on the table.'

'She slips through your fingers,' replied Balázs. 'With the magic . . . of the fairies . . .'

'That's not how it works,' said Dénes. 'Roll on it! On damage, because The Ax uses barbaric power.'

Balázs pressed his lips together. He knew Dénes was right and hated him for it. He took the ten-sided dice in his hand. Noel took his as well and pretended that this scene was no big deal. He sipped his beer and shook the die in his palm.

The two dice rolled across the table at the same time. Noel rolled an eight plus seven, Isla a four.

'Isla can't slip away from you,' Balázs said, his voice sounding strange and metallic in his ear. 'You grab the girl tightly and pull her to the table in the middle of the room. But Isla pulls out a knife hidden in the hem of her dress and attacks with it.'

Dénes leaned forward in his chair, his eyes sparkling. He was interested in the game again, now that a hint of adult danger was present.

'Roll!' Dénes commanded. Sári poured herself another glass of wine. Fruzsi grinned as she watched the rolling dice, beads of sweat glistening on her forehead.

Noel rolled an eight again. Isla rolled a three.

'She stabs you,' Balázs said, 'but the blade breaks on your armor.'

'I think it breaks on my legendary abs,' Noel remarked. 'I'm ripping her clothes off.'

'We'll roll on that, too,' said Balázs.

Sári groaned, the wine almost splashing out of her glass.

'Come on!' Sári said. 'Let him get it over with!'

Balázs looked at Sári and Fruzsi.

'You'll let him do this?' he asked the girls, then turned to Dénes. 'Aren't you going to stop him?'

Fruzsi shook her head and rubbed her nose. Her pupils were dilated, her eyes sparkled with excitement.

'No! This is the most exciting part by far.'

Sári shrugged her shoulders.

'I just want to get on with the story. Let him have his fun!'

Balázs looked at Dénes; this was their seventh adventure as game master and adventurer. The seventh!

Dénes shook his head.

'Team unity is more important than the chastity of a throw-away NPC fairy.'

Noel grinned; he was pleased with himself. He had beaten the game master, after all. He tried to cover his excitement with cynicism.

'You're tearing her dress woven from colorful spider silk,' Balázs said. 'Isla, the fairy girl stands naked before you.'

'I'll hold her and . . .'

'Wait,' said Sári. 'Shouldn't you take off your clothes too?'

Noel laughed excitedly.

'Okay. So I'll take off my pants. And I'll start . . .'

'Isla asks you not to do this to her . . .' said Balázs.

'What, should we throw again?'

'No,' said Balázs. 'You've already beaten her. She's naked and trembling with fear. She looks you in the eye and begs you not to. Have mercy on her. You don't need to roll the dice. You just have to decide. For you.'

Silence fell over the table. Noel felt confused for a moment; it was as if for a second he could see the line of his own decisions with a blinding clarity, and somehow they made no sense.

Fruzsi slammed her hand down on the table.

'Let's not dick around!' she shouted. 'Come on, just do it!'

Dénes also licked the corners of his mouth excitedly. This was the moment he looked for in every adventure. The unexpected situation that let you look deep into your own soul and see yourself there for a moment. After all, this was just fantasy. Nothing here was real. Decisions had no consequences, so they could all pretend to be demons if that fit their mood. There was nothing to be ashamed of, because this cruelty wasn't hurting any living soul.

'Fuck that bitch!' Dénes said. Sári said nothing as she fiddled with her phone. The momentary uncertainty in Noel evaporated; his violent desires were supported by the company at the table. There was no stopping The Ax.

'I'm forcing her legs open,' Noel said. 'Will she resist or will she let it happen?'

Balázs' hand clenched into a fist.

'She fights!' he said. 'She's grabbing at your eyes with her fingernails!'

'I'll hit her,' Noel said. 'Hit her hard. And I'm pinning down her arms.'

'We'll roll!'

Noel smiled.

Isla threw a one. The Ax threw a ten.

After that, The Ax did to her whatever he wanted.

The game concluded at seven in the evening. They raided the catacombs, but failed to retrieve Isla's silver cup. They didn't talk about her anymore. Best was to forget about it completely. What happened, happened; why disturb the past? They strategically decided not to return to Estrat after the catacombs were finished. They didn't want to see Isla again.

Balázs left the apartment at eight o'clock, with the character sheets, notes, and dice in his backpack. When he stepped out of the building, he began to shake uncontrollably. By the time he got to the end of the street, he was crying, but he couldn't understand why. His thoughts kept circling around the violence that had been done to Isla without ever reaching the core of the event. Even though he had narrated it, he now turned the memories of his own narration into a blank page, as if nothing had happened. But that wouldn't protect him for long.

An act of senseless violence had been committed, and there was no turning back.

*

There were many things the adventurers didn't know about their game master.

Balázs had been involved in a car accident when he was a child. His brother was driving; he had obtained his driver's license 6 months earlier. They were hosting an exchange student from the UK at the time; he was sitting in the passenger seat. Balázs took the back seat.

When the car skidded, Balázs felt like his guts were about to burst; he closed his mouth tightly as the centrifugal force threw his body out of the seat. In retrospect, it always seemed strange to him; how did his mouth instinctively know what to do?

He had no recollection of the impact – perhaps because he had lost consciousness, or maybe his mind preferred not to register it. When he regained consciousness, he felt the taste of iron in his mouth. His face was warm with blood. It was his brother's blood, splashed all over the cabin. The irony of fate: Balázs was the only passenger who had not fastened his seatbelt, and yet he was the only one to survive the crash. It was difficult to determine the cause of the accident. The most likely explanation was that the car was traveling too fast and the inexperienced driver lost control of the car, skidded, and crashed into a power pole. Due to a manufacturing flaw in the vehicle the airbags did not deploy at the moment of collision, costing the driver and his first passenger their lives.

Balázs was already fully conscious when they pulled him out of the car. The minutes he spent alone with the two bodies in the shattered interior determined the next stage of his life. When the firefighters arrived, they only glanced at the two miserable corpses in the front seats and began to free Balázs from the wreckage. He had been born by caesarean section; and he was born by caesarean section again, only this time they used metal cutters to free him from the weird, cold flesh around him. As they carried him to the ambulance, he glanced back at the car and decided, perhaps with his last rational thought for a long time, that the thing bent over the steering wheel was not his brother.

His brother used to have a face; the thing in the car had just a blur of raw meat.

He spent four months in hospital. He was operated on three times, once for internal bleeding and twice to fix the bones in his leg. Otherwise, the doctors said that apart from a few scars, no traces of the accident would remain and that Balázs could continue to live as before. Through the haze of painkillers, Balázs watched his parents grieve; he could not even attend his brother's funeral because he was confined to bed. When he was allowed to leave the hospital, he became the center of attention for the whole family; even Enikő, his sister, took care of him, although she had treated Balázs like a jerk before.

He had been home for a month when his parents decided that he needed psychiatric help after all. They thought they had been prepared for this. A psychologist at the hospital had explained to them what they could expect and how survivors process trauma. They decided to stay strong for Balázs' sake and put up with anything he said or did as long as it helped him to get back on his feet. But Balázs dealt with the trauma in a different, altogether more disturbing way than the doctors had predicted.

One morning, the household was awakened by his screams. This had happened before; they had been warned about the nightmares, the flashbacks, the guilt. Only this time, when they rushed into his room, they found him lying on the floor screaming, a pool of urine around him. He later explained what had happened. He had wanted to go out of his room, and when he opened the door a new kind of certainty was revealed to him: the certainty that there was nothing behind that door – that a wind was ready to sweep the world away, to break reality apart, and if he stepped out, he would be annihilated along with everything he knew to be his home. It was only when his parents stormed into his room that this feeling subsided; but soon it returned, and these episodes became regular.

Over time, with the help of his psychiatrist, he had learned to talk about it. He had no hallucinations. He saw the hallway, the doors to the other rooms – even the door to his brother's room, which hadn't been opened for weeks – as they were. He heard the usual noises of the house. No reason to be suspicious, really. And yet he knew that this sight, this vision of order, had come about because he was looking. He knew it was a trap: if he stepped out into the corridor, there was a possibility – and it was not a certainty, just a possibility – that the world would be torn apart with his next step and he would fall and fall and fall into a cold, primal chaos.

A crucial aspect of his delusion was that this critical failure of reality was not certain, only the probability of its happening was never zero.

The psychiatrist wanted Balázs to stop projecting the experience of the accident onto his entire life, thus turning it into one giant car crash. Balázs knew the psychiatrist was right, but he also realized that the man's steadfast insistence on the stability of the world was a lie, a form of self-deception spread by those who believe they are in control of their own lives. He understood the nature of this self-deception, but he was beyond that. He had survived the accident, although he felt it would have been better to perish, and self-deception was no longer an option. Life was governed by agents of chance, and nobody was in control. But knowing that didn't lessen his fears.

The situation worsened over time. Balázs could no longer leave the house. If he tried and forced himself to step out, he would soon fall to the ground and scream at the top of his lungs, knowing that in the next moment a powerful force would pull the ground from under his feet and smash him to pieces. Soon even his room felt dangerous.

He no longer saw people as people, but as masks driven by an unfathomable goal. These human masks could also burst open at any moment, their insides scattering to the winds like ants before an earthquake, and Balázs would be left all alone. One morning he woke up and realized that he too was just a mask, empty inside like all the others. Surely that was the reason why he had survived the accident. There was nothing inside him to die. He began to hurt himself with knives. Only the sight and taste of his own warm blood could temporarily convince him that he was actually alive.

Balázs and his parents knew that things could not go on like this. The tranquilizers and anti-anxiety medication only drew dark circles under his eyes and made him stupid and fat, but they could not change the facts of his life.

His sister Enikő fought for Balázs with everything she had. She was resilient. She had already lost one sibling and didn't want to lose another. Enikő skipped the years she could have spent as a child and pushed herself into adulthood prematurely. She no longer cared about herself and her own needs; her only task was to save Balázs from himself. This became a recurring principle in her later life as well: she helped her parents through divorce instead of enjoying her college years, she helped her first husband out of a gambling addiction instead of enjoying her adult life, and she also ushered her own children into adulthood at the cost of hollowing herself out.

When movies, sports, and other games failed to restore Balázs' faith in the world, Enikő tried role-playing games as a last resort. She equipped herself with a set of borrowed manuals for M.A.G.U.S., a Hungarian knock-off of Dungeons & Dragons, but in many ways a better functioning system. She narrated an adventure herself and did an exemplary job of sticking to the twists and turns of the pre-made adventure module. Balázs only joined in so as not to upset his sister, because even in his condition he felt that something particularly valuable had developed between them. But by the time they reached the middle of the adventure, he was able to forget that he was living in a universe that was in perpetual collapse.

After the game was over his fears returned, but he analyzed the game and his own behavior to find the key to his fleeting peace and found that it was the act of rolling the dice. In the fantasy world, skeleton warriors could leap out from behind the walls at any moment, and powerful wizards could send curses your way, but the dice somehow made chaos manageable and controllable.

In role-playing games, he found joy not in being someone else, but in the fact that the dice brought order to the world. He simply applied this principle to the world around him. So he crawled back to reality, dice roll by dice roll. In the early days, he rolled every morning against the hallway collapsing when he opened the door. Would the street collapse when he left the house? All he had to do was roll the dice. He trusted the ten-sided die; if it didn't land on the right numbers, he preferred not to leave his room. If a good number was rolled, he could live that day without fear. As he began to trust the world again, he lowered the number he had to roll against the chaos until the number was basically nothing.

Enikő continued to play with Balázs because she saw the positive effects the game had on him; however, as they played through the M.A.G.U.S. and badly translated D&D modules, Balázs found that the adventures left him unsatisfied. The games revolved around the extraordinary – you had to constantly exist as a hero in a world that offered opportunities for adventure in every pub corner and in the depths of every cave. It wasn't like real life.

So he began to create his own world. Like God, he first rolled the dice to see if the sun would rise, and when he rolled a double six, the sun rose for the first time in the world where the Dolritori Empire would later stand. He took a spiral notebook and opened it to the first page. He began to write, but only noted down what the dice allowed: The light of a new day shone on the world. A world that even he did not yet know, but with his dice he created something new every day: forests, fields, castles.

People.

When the infrastructure of the city of Estrat was suitable,

every building had to be populated; blacksmiths and bakers, soldiers and witches, whores and innkeepers, robbers and farmers were needed. When Enikő discovered her brother's obsession, she persuaded her parents to buy dozens of spiral notebooks, notepads, various folders, and office supplies so that Balázs could write down and organize everything.

Balázs did not write literature; he wrote notes. Not stories, but proof that the world was stable and expanding instead of disintegrating and falling inwards. He logged his rolls and recorded the events in Estrat. When bread was burned, when people were robbed, when a guard dropped his weapon, when a horse was stolen, Balázs recorded it. He kept an eye on everything, and although he could have considered himself a benevolent god, he did not make the actual decisions. A complicated system was developed for weighing up the roll thresholds for introducing new characters or events.

After a year of building the city of Estrat, he finally agreed to let Enikő and a close friend visit the city. He prepared the adventure for weeks. He did not narrate from a module – quite the opposite. The starting point of the adventure was provided to him by the world he created and the dice he rolled; when the players began the adventure, they entered a narrative that was already in motion and would flow even without them. The players thoroughly enjoyed the game, especially when they saw that their every action was recorded in one of Balázs' carefully kept journals, leaving a lasting impression on his world. It was as if they had a second life in which they left a more lasting mark than in the one they were actually living.

Balázs became a game master, and his life began to resemble that of a normal person. He was able to go to school, where he eventually graduated, and then to college, where he studied computer science. He was now back at school; he was the administrator of an interconnected network of three colleges. The machines and systems were at least fifteen years out of date, but that didn't bother him, especially now that he mostly worked from a home office. Balázs did not have high expectations of his career. After all, his real job remained game mastering. Every morning, before his coffee, he rolled to see if the sun would rise in Estrat. Every morning it did, and Balázs was able to start his day in peace.

Before a session with players, he would spend several consecutive mornings setting the pieces necessary for the adventure in motion. The players rarely understood this, but the adventure did not take place because Balázs was narrating it. Balázs narrated because the adventures happened independently of him. The ten-sided dice determined the path of every living creature in Estrat, and so the players also became avatars of the will of the dice. Since Balázs' imagination was also part of this universe, things in Estrat naturally happened within certain extremes. Estrat existed in a generic medieval fantasy world, the people in the town all fulfilled some kind of function, and events almost never had to do with inner processes; characters had emotions only as needed for driving the narrative. The innkeeper was often angry, the farmer was content, the soldier was stubborn. For Balázs, life was a sequence of actions, because – even if he thought about it less and less as the years went by – life was the opposite of what he had seen collapsed over the steering wheel.

Isla arrived like any other character: as a mixture of will, necessity and chance. A fairy was needed for an adventure, but at the end of the journey, Isla, the fairy girl, ended up in Estrat, where she saved the life of a nobleman's son with her healing herbs. This allowed her to stay in the city; people like Isla were otherwise not tolerated. Over the years, the inhabitants of Estrat grew to sympathize with the girl, and Isla had become an indispensable inhabitant of the city. Who else would heal the sick? Who else would help bring children into the world? Who else would protect the town from the forest witches when there were no adventurers around? Isla was a good friend to everyone. Few inquired about Isla's past; but this past was dense and dark, and Isla was a far more powerful fairy than the people of Estrat could have guessed.

It was meant to be a revelation further down the road. After a long series of adventures, in which Isla was to be only a minor character, a massive, climactic event for a choice selection of players would reveal Isla's backstory and true powers, not just to the players, but to Isla herself. She was immortal; a demigod, but she did not yet know it.

However, this series of adventures was interrupted that Sunday afternoon, and when Balázs woke up the next morning from a vague nightmare, he was no longer sure what he was trying to achieve with all this. He made a coffee and opened a notebook to jot down yesterday's adventure before he set about leading the world into the next adventure, set for Wednesday, this time in a different kitchen. Wednesday's adventure was, of course, a continuation of Sunday's, even if the players would be different.

Balázs had to keep moving to larger apartments because of the journals. The future was only safe if every element of the past was preserved. He numbered and labeled the notebooks carefully, although he rarely read them. He opened the current notebook. He only gave the notebooks a number when every page was filled; the current one was journal no. 1920. These journals filled more than two dozen IKEA bookshelves, and their number had been growing for almost thirty years. When Balázs looked at these notebooks, he felt how stable the world was. How each roll made it firm and unchanging. Even the very first notebook, opening with the description of the very first sunrise, was still on one of the shelves.

He sat down at his desk with his coffee and began to make his notes of yesterday's adventure. When he got to the part about what The Ax had done to Isla, his hand paused over the page. An uneasy feeling came over him. If he wrote it down, it would be part of this world forever. But what choice did he have? What happened, happened.

But what if it didn't? After all, only what he wrote down on these pages was part of the history of Estrat. Why should a shameful event like this have to be made real by recording it? Perhaps it was now his job to act like a god and filter what could pass from the realm of fantasy into lived reality. Something may have happened in the course of the game; Isla may have suffered, but perhaps it would be easier for her if what happened to her was made void. That way she would not have to endure the violence, because it wouldn't be made permanent.

'What violence?' Balázs asked himself, already having made his choice.

The pen finally touched the paper. Slowly, thoughtfully, he rounded the letters. 'The adventuring party continued their journey after receiving the missing half of the map from Isla. There were no further incidents in the city.'

He looked at the sentences. He liked what he had written. He flipped back through his notebook; the style remained consistent. Although he was narrating an epic fantasy, Balázs' voice was cold and detached; he recounted events in level, unembellished sentences. He liked this style because it made Estrat seem more real.

He worked a little until lunchtime, and in the afternoon he started preparing for Wednesday's adventure. Of course, he also wanted to include Isla, because her story needed to keep moving. He paused in thought – maybe he should let the fairy girl rest. But then he thought of his diary. Nothing had happened. He himself made a note of this. Why should he let Isla rest? She was completely fine.

He began to move the characters around in Estrat so that everything would be in place and under the right conditions by Wednesday's adventure. Kar'ldar's black priestesses needed to venture deep into the forests of Estrat to summon Hrav Truk'de-ra, the demon that had lain in a death-like slumber for a thousand years and which the adventurers had to defeat in the end – but they could only do so with three crystal daggers. They were able to obtain one of them from Isla.

Balázs rolled the dice to get Isla out of her house and acquire her crystal dagger from a passing wizard. According to his own weighting method, a roll of four or above with two dice was enough to accomplish this action.

The roll of two dice resulted in a three. Isla did not want to leave her house.

Balázs leaned on the table and motionlessly observed the two dice that signaled unsuccessful action. A three against a four.

He immediately translated the number in his head into an action, as he always did. But now the action was absence. A closed door. Silence behind the walls. Balázs couldn't see into Isla's house; he only muttered to himself that Isla's house would remain closed.

Closed!

He rolled again; it wasn't his habit, but he did it anyway. The threshold wasn't changed. He needed to roll a four.

Again, he only managed a three.

Balázs slammed his hand down on the table. Even he didn't understand why. Sometimes you just can't roll an event. You have to trust the dice. Maybe tomorrow.

Until now, he hadn't had to think about what Isla did in her house; she lived like everyone else when she wasn't involved in an adventure. She slept, ate, mended clothes, brewed potions. When she left the house, she gathered food, sang sad fairy songs in the tavern, and gathered herbs in the forest. Balázs rarely had to take care of these things, because they happened without his supervision.

But now Isla had become a closed door.

In the evening, he activated other characters; the black priestesses arrived in the forest, the wandering wizard took residence in the local tavern, the baker baked the bread with the magic ring inside that he had received three adventures ago. Everything went according to plan.

He didn't roll for Isla again that day, no matter how much he wanted to.

In the morning, he woke up tired. He made himself some coffee and then sat down at the table. His palm itched for a roll, but he knew he shouldn't do it. He shouldn't make it seem like this was important, like it was more important than other rolls. First he rolled the dice for the sunrise. The sun rose in Estrat without any problems. Balázs made a note of this. Then he rolled the dice for the awakening of the wandering mage and his morning activities. The mage got dressed, had breakfast, and wrote a letter to his superior. The baker baked bread at dawn; the next day, the adventurers would find the magic ring that called them to adventure. The black priestesses retreated to a cave at dawn; the light of the sun wasn't allowed to touch their skin before the ritual. Balázs kept a record of all this. Life went on at its own pace. There was no problem.

Then he rolled for Isla. The same action as yesterday; same threshold.

He rolled a three again. Balázs felt a thick drop of sweat run down his back. Isla's door would remain closed.

He picked up the dice and shook them. Something was wrong with them; maybe he'd bought a weighted die by mistake? Or the same number was printed on several sides? Yes, he thought, that could be it! The dice are defective! He would have to repeat the roll with a different set!

He had dozens of other dice, which he kept in a jar. He shook out two fresh ones and turned them over thoroughly in his palm to make sure they were flawless. He rolled them.

He rolled a two. A double one; not just a failed action, but an absolute failure of the desired action – indeed, its opposite. Balázs saw the closed door with his mind's eye, but he also knew that this was not passivity. That something was brewing behind that door. He rolled the dice again; then again. Both times he rolled double-ones.

The door remained closed, but the silence behind it grew thicker.

The situation had only gotten worse by Wednesday's game.

'What the hell!' said Árpi. He had been on at least a dozen adventures under Balázs' watch. His character, a level 20 paladin, was currently fighting a low-level spirit warrior; the outcome should not even have been in doubt. Yet he kept rolling poorly, while the ghost warrior was doing exceptionally well. This had been going on for two hours now; the warriors' rolls were extremely weak, while their opponents' were remarkably strong. Furthermore, they had run into every unfortunate twist of fate imaginable, and only a portion of the tools necessary to complete the story had reached the adventurers. They had barely made any progress; they had not even managed to enter the forests of Estrat.

'The spirit warrior avoids your sword and jumps to your side,' Balázs said. 'You were careless, the spirit dagger is wounding you.'

'Bloody hell!' Árpi banged on the table.

'Maybe we should pack it in,' Cseszi said. She was the oldest player at the table. Her arms were covered in tattoos; one of the tattoos depicted Masna, the Arzhedan Planewalker who was Cseszi's constant avatar. 'This is just not working out today.'

Balázs clenched his fist. He'd never had to end an adventure prematurely.

'Let's try something, okay?' he asked. Cseszi raised an eyebrow.

'You see a lonely house at the edge of the forest,' Balázs said. 'You've visited the house before.'

'That's where the fairy lives, isn't it?' asked Árpi. 'We've been there countless times.'

Balázs nodded and continued.

'Yes, you have had adventures with her or with her help.

The door to her house is locked. Fear is kindled in your hearts. And curiosity. What could Isla do now . . . ?'

'That's not a very elegant narrative . . . ' Cseszi remarked, but she stifled the rest of her comment when she saw the pain on Balázs' face.

'I think,' said Cseszi, 'that it is time to visit my old friend. After all, I defeated the dragon golem with her help last time. What could be up with her? I'll go to her house and knock.'

'Roll!' said Balázs. 'For charisma.'

Cseszi rolled the dice; and for the first time in this game, she managed to roll successfully.

'The door opens slowly,' said Balázs, unable to contain his excitement. 'You're stepping inside.'

Balázs leaned forward over the table.

'What do you see?'

Cseszi smiled in confusion.

'What, you're the storyteller!'

But Balázs didn't answer, instead looked at Cseszi pleadingly and repeated the question.

'What do you see?'

Árpi and Cseszi exchanged glances. Cseszi sighed impatiently; but she saw such pain in his gaze that she had to make an effort. It couldn't be that hard to tell a story; you just had to string words together that became sentences and had some meaning that would satisfy the imagination for a while.

She closed her eyes, hoping that would help her see the imagined scene better.

'I'm entering the house,' Cseszi said. After the first hesitant moment, the images came easily to her. She had the feeling that she wasn't even imagining them herself.

Balázs' nails dug into his palm, a vein throbbed at his temple, and his heartbeat felt like rusty clockwork.

'It's dark inside,' Cseszi said. 'The window panes are closed, and the windows are painted black.'

Cseszi's voice deepened as she described things she had seen instead of making them up. 'There's a strange smell. It reminds me of school! Of the ink I spilled on my notebook as a child. And there's another smell. Something is rotting here.'

Árpi sighed wearily.

'The action . . .'

'Quiet!' Balázs snapped at Árpi. 'Let her tell the story!'

Cseszi continued.

'Something's moving in there! I step closer. Marks have been carved into the floor, some kind of symbols. There are animal skulls on the walls. Some of them still fresh. The stench is terrible.'

'No, no, no, no!' Balázs whispered to himself involuntarily. His stomach clenched as if it had been falling forever.

'I hear a noise. Someone is sitting in the corner. It's too dark to see. I step closer and call out loudly. Isla? Isla?'

The kitchen fell silent. Balázs did not even notice, but his mouth twisted into a grimace, as if he was waiting for a hammer to hit his head.

Cseszi's eyes opened and she looked directly at Balázs.

'My God! What have you done to her? What have you done to her?'

Balázs pushed his chair back and knew he had to escape from there.

'What have you done to her?' Cseszi shouted at him in a rage.

'We didn't do anything!' Balázs stammered. 'Nothing has happened! Nothing! I can show you! It's in the journals!'

With trembling hands, Balázs pulled the notebook out of his backpack as evidence and searched with sweaty fingers for the page on which Isla had experienced this particular nothing.

He showed Cseszi the lines as if the fact that he had written the words down were proof. But this evasive, vague line looked more and more like a confession. Especially now: perhaps he had accidentally touched the pages with his sweaty finger. Yes, it must have been that, because Isla's name was now smudged.

It was no longer a name, just a blur of ink.

Cseszi took the notebook from him and sniffed the pages.

'Yes,' she said coldly. 'Her house smells just like this book. The smell of your ink. And that's exactly what she looks like now. After what you did to her.'

Cseszi pointed to the smudged, illegible name, that terrible stain on the white paper, then she threw the notebook at Balázs.

'Nothing happened,' Balázs repeated in a thin voice. 'Nothing.'

'Get out of here,' said Cseszi. 'Get out of here and don't come back.'

Balázs silently gathered up the rest of his belongings and quickly pulled the door shut behind him.

It was only later that he realized how absurd it all was. How could Cseszi have known what had happened in that house? What The Ax had done? Obviously she had conspired with someone. Surely Noel was trying to trick him. A practical joke.

And anyway, none of this was real. Balázs had to accept that too. No matter how seriously he took the role of game master, Estrat was fictional and the characters were all made up. They didn't really exist and therefore they could not be . . .

Nothing happened! Nothing at all!

Balázs felt the ground move beneath his feet; the pavement lifted and the concrete began to crack at its edges. Up in the sky, the clouds collapsed as if a hole had opened up in the stratosphere, sucking everything out into space until heaven and earth became nothing.

Balázs threw himself on the ground and screamed. He curled up, clutching his knees, waiting for the fall, that eternal fall that would end with a crash into the car soiled with his brother's broken teeth.

'Sir, are you all right?' a man asked. He was dressed in a conspicuously old-fashioned manner, like a relic from an earlier era, with a hat and wire-rimmed glasses. Balázs was lying in a fetal position. He looked up from between his arms, startled, and looked into the man's freshly shaven, worried face.

'Are you sick? Should I call an ambulance?' asked the man in the hat. Balázs touched the concrete. It was solid again; though he knew everything could collapse around him at any moment.

'It's all in your head,' he reminded himself. 'It's all in your head!'

The man helped him up from the sidewalk. They both tried not to notice the stain on Balázs' pants.

When he returned to his room, he had calmed down somewhat. He wished he could call Enikő; she would know what to do. The dead know everything. She had helped so many people throughout her life; it was only natural that she could not help herself. She succumbed to cancer four years ago.

He changed his pants, washed himself, then took out the journal. Rage flooded him; he was angry at Isla. Isla didn't even exist; he had imagined her, she only lived in his head. If Isla existed in some imaginary form, it was only because Balázs had created her! Isla should be grateful, she should kiss Balázs' feet with joy, and if he told her to, she should allow an entire Roman legion to ravage her body, because as a fictional character, that was her duty to her creator!

Balázs opened the notebook. Isla's name on the last page had become completely illegible; it was nothing more than a black blob of ink, which also made the surrounding words illegible. 'The adventuring party . . . Isla . . . incident . . .'

While he was reading, Balázs' fingers also became stained with ink.

'No! No! No!' he now said aloud. 'No! No! No!'

The next morning all the dice turned against him. All he could roll was absolute failure. The entire population of Estrat, including the demons and black priestesses living in the forest, the talking animals living by the lakes, and the disembodied apparitions, became not only passively but actively hostile to Balázs' goals.

Around midday, the ink began to flow from the journal. The thick ink soaked the pages, flowed across the table and onto the floor. The air was heavy with the smell.

It's just ink, he told himself.

Just ink.

He rarely dreamed of the city of Estrat. It happened occasionally, of course, especially when he had spent a lot of time preparing an adventure. But even then, he tended to dream about the living room or the kitchen where the game was to take place. He dreamed about telling an adventure, not about the adventure itself.

That night he awoke in Estrat. He saw darkness; the thick smell of ink rose to his nose. Balázs sat up.

Darkness was replaced by a faint light. There was a glow from a candle. Balázs shivered and felt the first wave of panic. He recognized the room: the bloody animal heads on the walls, the scratched markings on the floor, the black-painted windows. The walls felt cold to his touch.

There was someone else in the room; their figure was barely recognizable in the semi-darkness.

'You came,' Isla spoke from the corner.

'Forgive me!' Balázs said. 'Please, forgive me!'

Isla gurgled. Her voice was hoarse and low.

'I'll forgive,' said Isla, 'if you bring me his heart! And his cock, severed with a rusty knife!'

Balázs shook his head.

'But he's a real man!' he protested. 'He's alive! How could I do such a thing?'

Silence descended over the house. An absolute silence that stretched between life and death. A silence that turned love into hate.

'So you could inflict any insult you wanted on my body and soul because I'm not real enough to feel offense and pain?'

She moved toward him.

'Do you want to fuck me too?' she asked, then laughed. Her laugh was a dry clatter, like pebbles tapping on the roof of an abandoned house.

'No!' Balázs exclaimed. 'No, of course not . . .'

Isla got down on her hands and knees and crawled slowly towards Balázs on the floor.

'Come on! I don't even exist! You could fuck me too! If you still want me the way I am now, then do it.'

'No!' Balázs cried out again. 'No, I don't want that! I'm so sorry, I shouldn't have let him do it! I shouldn't have!'

Isla now ran on all fours, her long, silver fairy hair falling in her face. Balázs tried to retreat, but behind him there was only the wall. He had nowhere to run.

Isla touched Balázs' leg; the fairy girl's hand was cold like roadkill. Isla's fingers traveled inch by inch up Balázs' leg. She was naked. Just as beautiful as Balázs had always imagined her to be, and he couldn't control his desire. Only her face was shrouded behind that waterfall of silver hair.

'No . . . !' Balázs said. 'No!'

'You don't like me anymore, you say? I'm no longer a source of desire for you?' said Isla, as she sat on Balázs' hips. Cold, black ink flowed from between her legs. She reached between her thighs and let the ink flow into her palm.

Isla stroked Balázs' face with her cold hand. Balázs involuntarily closed his eyes so he wouldn't be blinded by the flowing ink.

'And yet I wake up to this sorry sight morning after morning. Because of you. Look at me! Look!'

When he opened his eyes again, Isla pulled back her long silver hair and her face was clear for him to behold.

Balázs wanted to scream, but the horror paralyzed even his vocal cords. Yes, he recognized the face, or rather, the absence that must now be called a face. He knew it from his childhood, from the night of his second birth.

It was his brother's face on the night of the accident, that mockery of a face Balázs had seen when he was carried to the ambulance.

'Love me! Kiss me!' Isla said, and she kissed Balázs, even though she had no jaw, no teeth, and her saliva was ink, and in that moment Balázs accepted that there was no waking up, because in Hell nightmare and reality are one.

Then Balázs realized that he was no longer asleep. He woke in his own bed, in his own room.

He was shaking, drenched in sweat.

It was only when he shuffled into the bathroom and saw in the cruel white light that both his face and his pajama bottoms were smeared with black ink that he began to scream.

In the morning, the ink overflowed the apartment. Almost two thousand journals and they all had become a black swamp. The past ceased to exist as Isla's pain devoured every word. Balázs felt himself becoming empty inside. He felt nothing but fear and shame.

He picked up a pair of dice, because that was his duty. What good was he if he couldn't even roll the dice for the sun to rise?

He threw the dice. Double zero. He rolled the dice again, and when another double zero came up, he remembered that he always used 1 to 10 dice. Now all sides of the dice showed zeroes, and Balázs knew that the sun would no longer rise in Estrat.

Somewhere on the other side of the ink, Isla was laughing.

'You have to come with me! Please, come with me!'

Noel had already heard that Balázs had become unstable, but now that the game master was standing before him, it became clear that Balázs was not just unstable. Balázs had completely lost his mind. His clothes were soiled with ink stains, his arms and neck were covered in wounds he had obviously inflicted on himself.

'Listen,' Noel said. 'I'm sure it's important, but I have work to do . . .'

'Maybe if you apologize to her . . .' Balázs interrupted, tears flowing from his eyes. Maybe it was just because they were mixing with the dirt on his face, but the teardrops looked like ink.

'Who?'

'Isla. The one you . . . raped,' Balázs replied, and at that moment Noel noticed the dungeon master's bad breath.

'I'm sorry, but I don't know what you're talking about.'

'The fuck you don't!' Balázs shouted. 'You wanted it! You caused it! And now you have to pay for it!'

Noel took a step back. It dawned on him that this situation was serious. He needed to call the police or an ambulance, and he tried to remember where his phone was. Maybe on the charger in the kitchen.

Balázs took the knife out of the back of his pants.

'She wants your heart!' he said.

'Shit!' Noel cried out and took three steps back. Still, he was surprised at his own calm. The shock might come later, he thought, as adrenaline rushed into his bloodstream.

Balázs did not move. He continued to stare at the blade in his hand.

'Come, please, come with me and apologize. She's in my apartment now. I'm not making this up anymore. And it's all your fault. Only you can make it up to her! Please, make it up to her! I don't want to kill you!'

Noel felt his mouth go dry.

'Listen to me! It's all in your head. You're just imagining it . . .'

Balázs shouted.

'Do you think I don't know that? Do you think I'm stupid?'

'No,' said Noel. 'I don't think you're stupid. But I can see that . . . you need help. And I want to help you. Come on, we can solve this together!'

Balázs cried; he cried because he wished Noel would show himself to be a monster today. He wanted to see the rapist in Noel, the heartless, hateful tyrant who only took pleasure in the pain of others. But Noel looked at him the way Enikő had long ago, with a strange mixture of pity and attention, and now, now came the worst part, perhaps even worse than seeing Isla's face.

Noel crossed the room in a few steps and embraced him, not caring that Balázs might make use of his weapon.

'I'm sorry,' Noel said. 'It was just a joke, okay? I didn't think it was really important, but I can see that it is. I'm sorry!'

That made Balázs sob even more; then he pushed Noel away and, shaking his head, began to retreat from the apartment. The knife fell from his hand.

'Go to her! Or she'll come to you!' he said.

Noel watched as Balázs turned away from him. He felt the urge to pick up the knife and go after Balázs to give it back to him, but he was afraid that would only complicate matters. He wondered who he should call as soon as the game master was a safe distance away. And then it happened.

Balázs screamed from the hallway. He staggered as if the ground beneath him were shaking, and he tried to regain his balance, even though the floor seemed as stable as ever to Noel. Balázs' scream grew louder and louder, then he threw himself on the floor and curled his legs into a fetal position.

Balázs' scream had distorted into a painful howl. His body lifted off the ground and, as if he were being pulled in a thousand directions by a thousand ropes, he was torn apart in mid-air. He burst like a balloon, his parts whirled around as if a howling wind were chasing a hundred shopping bags, and finally these parts were absorbed into themselves; they became nothing, and in a short time there was no trace of Balázs ever having existed.

Noel stood there for minutes, paralyzed; he stared at the empty hallway and thought he had gone mad. It must have been a schizophrenic fit, he thought. He clung to the door; he could feel the solidity of the wood under his fingers. This was solid. This was real.

He looked at the spot where Balázs had been lying just seconds ago. The hallway was empty now. How could one prove that a person had once lain there? That Balázs had once existed?

He decided to forget the whole thing. Balázs had never been here. They had never spoken to each other. The corridor had always been empty.

There had been no incident.

But the thought would not let him rest. Especially when he was woken up that night by an uncontrollable coughing fit.

The cough shook his body so much that he was not sure if he would be able to breathe again. Fluid flooded his lungs, a cold, thick substance.

Finally, he coughed up ink and two ten-sided dice. All the sides of the dice were black. Noel thought the numbers were covered in ink, but when he washed them off in the sink, he saw the sides were blank.

Go to her. Or she will come to you. Isn't that what the game master said? Noel looked at the blank dice, then thought about the ink stains next to his bed and the taste of ink in his mouth, and decided to go to Balázs' apartment. If nothing had happened in the hallway, then Balázs must be home now. He knew the address.

It was already past eight in the morning when he left his apartment. The streets were teeming with people, looking up at the sky in horror. Many were checking their phones, hoping that the news websites would somehow help them reconcile reality and reason.

That morning the sun failed to rise.

He reached the game master's building. In the stairwell, he

was seized by another coughing fit; this time four dice fell out of his mouth and clattered onto the tiles. Dazed by the taste of the ink, his memories of that Sunday afternoon came flooding back. Could it really all be his fault? And what about the others? After all, he was part of a group of adventurers. What one of them did was the responsibility of all. Why was he the only one to suffer the consequences?

He looked out onto the street, at the pitch-black, starless sky, the panicked townspeople, and like frost on grass, the understanding settled into his soul.

It was not just he who would pay for this sin. It was everyone.

The ink had already begun to flow down the stairs. From behind the game master's door, Noel heard the clatter of a thousand dice hitting the floor, and he knew he had no chance. His dice were all blank.

I don't deserve this, he thought.

But he knew he deserved even worse.

The Summer I Chose to Die

We were restless and excited as we waited outside on the beach for the monsters to show themselves. We, Boti and I, had a real craving for a new kind of experience. I knew that looking back on that moment a few years or even weeks later, I'd feel a remarkable sense of unreality, as if it had been part of a movie or a game, maybe just a dream or a half-remembered story I had read somewhere, and not my real life. Still, I knew I wouldn't look back years or even weeks later because hopefully I'd be dead by then. That's what made this moment so special.

Dusk fell over the beach. Boti and I hid behind some rocks that scraped my knees bloody. I tried to carefully change position, but it wasn't comfortable on those rocks. I could feel my nose running; no wonder, considering how much I had abused my mucous membranes that morning – and I knew I'd soon be overcome with the urge to snort a line of whatever Boti had on him.

The waves lapped gently against the shore; I could hardly hear the roar of the sea, so accustomed had I become to it in the last few hours. Boti wanted a place where the monsters only appeared sporadically and in smaller numbers, just a stray specimen here and there. That was why we had come here, but now I was worried that we had chosen the wrong spot.

An hour ago, Boti and I were still deep in conversation. To be honest, we'd been pretty far gone all morning. We talked compulsively about any topic that came to mind. I remember in a particularly vulnerable, emotional moment, I promised that if I had the chance and it was in the country's best interest, I would gladly eat the Hungarian Prime Minister. It was a conversation that came out of nowhere and went nowhere. Those are my favorite kind of conversations. We were completely lost in the directionless flow of the moment.

If we had been attacked from behind at that point, we wouldn't have noticed. There were numerous weapons between us, but we weren't paying attention to anything, just the aimless exchange of words. I don't know what we used that morning, maybe Boti didn't know either. When we set off on this little excursion from Hungary, he packed all his supplies, and the contents of some of his small plastic bags were opaque even to him.

If we had been attacked, it would not have bothered me if I had died. Boti was of the same opinion and said he didn't care, so he might as well die too. Still, I hoped it would be me.

Of course, dying wasn't the goal at the moment, it was just a possibility. I wouldn't have minded, because I had decided at the beginning of the summer that I would die before the end of the season.

Boti nudged me on the shoulder and said, 'There's one, look,' and I finally managed to focus my gaze a bit, and yes, the thing was there. It was crawling out of the water, just like I'd seen on the news and in random internet pictures. But I had this feeling that it was mine. A sight I could claim as my own. In the deeper water, it glided along with its limbs pressed against its sides, but as the water became shallower, its arms and legs detached from its soft, shimmering blue skin, and it crawled on all fours towards the shore.

It was ugly as fuck, to be honest. Kind of terrifying too. I mean, there's definitely something creepy about their appearance. Monsters, right? No wonder there was such a panic when they first attacked. And just look at their size! Two, two and a half meters of massive body, and they can move as fast as a lizard, even though they are not lizards, but fish-people. The one I saw now looked a bit like a Komodo dragon, and in my dazed state I thought a dragon had crawled out of the sea until it stood on two feet, like a human. It cast a long shadow as it wrapped its tail around its body. It stretched out its muscular arms, which ended in those long claws that everyone feared so much at the beginning of the invasion. I could barely see its face because the sun was blinding. Its mouth was wide open, that much was certain. On land, they always keep their mouths open. It makes them look stupid; Boti and I laughed a lot about it as we sat in front of the TV or computer screen mimicking their gaping mouths. We laughed and couldn't understand how a thing with such a stupid face could exist in our world.

The mouth was full of sharp, needle-like teeth. Their bite is dangerous. We looked at all these terrifying pictures of the wounds those teeth can cause before we got to the beach, and I can tell you they weren't pretty. So I was hoping that I would die if we were attacked. Dying wouldn't have bothered me as much as one or more of those jagged wounds. They are so inconvenient.

Boti raised his rifle and took aim at the sea creature. We bought the gun at the harbour this morning. I let him use the gun because he claimed to be a good shot. As a teenager, he had even competed and won a few medals in target shooting. At least that's what he said. The rifle was old and worn, and we hadn't tested it. If he missed, the likelihood of an attack would increase and the element of surprise would be lost. It was in the cards that we might not make it out alive.

He pulled the trigger. The sound of the shot echoed across the shore, and I flinched with considerable delay.

The bullet hit the monster in the throat. I don't know if you should call it a throat. With these fish-people, the head is completely fused with the body. It's one big, barrel-shaped body, followed by what you might call a head, because it's got this dumb mouth and a pair of pitch-black, dead eyes. Anyway, we hit it just below the mouth where the neck should have been. It was totally dramatic because it stumbled a bit, put out an arm like it was calling for help from heaven – and only then did it make a squishy, slurping sound as it tried to breathe through its own blood; or maybe I just heard that sound in my head. It was a beautiful sound. Everything was beautiful now. I was glad to be here, on this beach, because the sunset and the sea were gorgeous, and finally the rocks stopped cutting at my legs as I rose from my hiding place. The monster seemed to be a lump of soft, dark velvet by the water. It was a positive moment. I know I only felt that way because we had used a lot of drugs, but still. I took drugs to experience these positive moments; they allowed me to take pleasure in a crappy sunset or a cute bug or helped me find beauty in the fact that we just killed one of these fish-people. These are important things. You have to learn to rejoice in them, even if the joy is artificially induced. As I said, this whole scenario seemed unreal to me anyway.

We grabbed the knives and hooks and whatever else we had scavenged from the locals and ran towards the monster. Boti was wearing his Crocs, as usual. I wore water shoes, because if there's one thing I worry about in life, it's those sea urchins. If you step on one barefoot, the spines never come out. They ruin your whole vacation.

I was glad I was wearing them now because the monster's blood was gushing from his wound and dripping merrily down between the stones where it flowed into these fat little pools of blood. It was dark, although I thought fish blood was supposed to be light. Then again, we had no idea how much of this creature was fish and how much was human – or something else entirely.

It was alive, gaping open with its mouth and making snapping and coughing noises. Inside the mouth, just behind the circular rows of teeth, some kind of organ, perhaps a gill, was opening and closing at an increasingly rapid pace. I thought the monster would look more interesting up close, but it was just a fish-man like any other. It was a disappointment, to be honest. It lacked the element of the exotic. I had expected more. It was as interesting as an ordinary fish or an average human. It was both at the same time, only in a bargain-bin version. Its eyes were covered with a cataract or some kind of eyelid for the sea. For the first few hours after they crawl out of the sea, they cannot see anything on land. Their sense of smell is supposedly very keen, so they will pounce on a human because they are able to orient themselves by scent. You have to be careful with them and so on, but basically they're blind and quite clumsy.

I searched its face for something human. Maybe I wanted to feel guilty for killing it, or marvel at how much it looked like me. I wanted to hope that if this war between our species had never happened, maybe we could have had a drink or something. I'd ask the monster, 'Hey, what's up?' and it'd say, 'Yeah, not much,' and then we'd just sit at the bar in peace and sip our beers.

Boti put a hook in the fish-man's palate to open it as wide as possible. The hook dug in deep. They have soft flesh. They look like tough guys, but they don't have much substance. They're too soft for the land.

Boti said, 'What's the matter, aren't you going to help?' and my pleasant, positive mood vanished. I became focused. I grabbed another hook and pulled at the monster's mouth from the other direction. I thought it would stink like a fish or have the pungent smell of ammonia. The fish-man had a neutral smell. It smelled like nothing at all.

Boti seemed pretty professional, though it was his first time doing this. His technique got even better later. He used a large fish-fileting knife, pushed it into the monster's mouth, stabbed deep behind the teeth and cut around the mouth with a few forceful movements. This is because when you cut around behind the teeth, you can pull out all the teeth with a strong tug and rip them out along with the gums. The teeth have to be removed for safe access, but they look even stupider afterwards because their mouth is an unnaturally circular open wound.

That's when I realized what the problem was. We had forgotten that the fish-man wasn't quite dead yet. That's why the gurgling noises had intensified so much. I wanted to tell Boti, maybe suggest we kill the sorry son of a bitch first, but he wasn't interested at the moment. He was hyperfocused. He shouldn't be bothered when he's like this. He attacked the freshly cut wound with his knife. After a while, the creature stopped twitching, but I did not realize that until later. Time turned to dull metal. It didn't stop, it just became too dense for me to measure.

Boti cut the fish-man's head apart. Its bones were soft too, basically fish bones. Behind the skull was a brain, along with other organs whose functions humanity had yet to identify. Boti dug through the brain tissue, consulting his cell phone every few seconds. He did it all from pictures he had found on Reddit and on non-public forums.

Finally, he shook his head.

'No eye,' he said, and I accepted that. I was still holding onto the hook, and the black liquid was pooling under my feet, but it didn't bother me because I had my water shoes on, and I felt something deep, or I felt like I should feel something deep, which is almost the same thing. Eventually I made do with the fact that I felt nothing. Boti cut strips of flesh from the fish-man's side after consulting his phone once more.

'Let's go, do a few lines, then we'll come back later,' Boti said and collected the weapons. We left the body on the shore for the birds and made our way to our accommodation.

I think I forgot to tell you why I chose this summer to die. I use the word 'choose' as if it's a conscious act, like a suicide, which it's not. But that again makes it sound like it's some kind of consent to die, like a zen thing, a finding of inner peace and that sweet spot where everything is okay in a nothing-can-touch me way, like I'm just chilling and waiting for nirvana to happen. That's nonsense, I can tell you that.

It's just that I'd rather not be alive at the end of the summer.

I've no pain, no illnesses. I consider myself to be of sound mind. Basically, everything is really fine. I'm doing well. That's what I always tell people and they like to believe it. They don't see anything wrong.

It's hard to put my finger on the reasons why, because even to me they sound completely banal. I feel hollow and exhausted. My country has used me up, devoured me and thinned me out. And yet I'm quite a useful member of society. I pay a lot of taxes. I'm a team coordinator in a multinational company. It's a good job, I think. I never had big dreams, like, I don't know, becoming a musician or a writer or just doing something, *anything*, with real passion. I'm not capable of creating anything, I suppose. I even lack the desire for it; I just feel the void where that desire should sit. Lately I've been envious of artists because I'm sure they don't fade or hollow out like I do, or if they do, they do it in different, more exciting ways than I do.

I guess I'm just an average person. Of course, there is no such thing, because everyone is a snowflake or a raindrop or whatever; and listen, I don't mind as long as it means as long as it means what it meant in my parents' or grandparents' generation. In the past, being average paid off. You didn't have to excel to get ahead. You could build a life with a car and a house and two children out of small change. Not anymore. Year after year, I feel like I'm treading water. If I take one step forward, the world takes two steps back. Maybe even three. I live in a rented apartment that gets more expensive every year. I've long since resigned myself to the fact that I'll never be able to buy my own property. If you don't own an apartment by the time you're eighteen thanks to mom and dad, you never will. The way things are now, my generation can say goodbye to the idea of a pension too, because the system will collapse in a decade or two. How could I afford to start a family this way? And why, when I'm already so dispassionate about it all? So that I could usher a bunch of embittered children into terminal poverty?

In the years it has taken me to come to this personal conclusion, even my country has decayed around me. It has become rough, unpleasant to the touch. It is hostile to me and others, yet we cannot stand up for our rights, for our future – for ourselves. We are pathetic as people, and it is disheartening to realize that it can only get much worse before a collapse would allow Hungary to start again. And this doesn't just apply to my country. For years I have been reading in the news that the global economy is going down the drain and an inevitable financial collapse is looming, even bigger than the last one. And then there's the ever-bubbling fountain of articles about microplastics, the global warming that we can't seem to stop even though it's going to kill us all, the gleeful deforestation of the rainforests that would help us breathe, but who needs air when the earth is so hot and we're all poor anyway?

There is just no hope. We are all alone against the whole world, and we are all facing a losing battle.

So, fuck this battle.

That's where I have thinned out. I have become hollow with this hopeless struggle for things I can't afford and don't need; but I have never been smart enough to replace that struggle with a longing for something truly meaningful.

Lately, drugs have been helping me. When I take them, I am connected to myself and my real feelings. They help me get through the days and weeks. I met Boti through the drugs. We went to the same gym and got along well; he always had good stuff and often shared it. For him, drugs were a lifestyle. We often hung out together, went to parties or talked nonsense until dawn. He actually ran a family grocery store and just did a little dealing for friends on the side. He was a man who cared about the quality of his stuff, and he was always giving life advice to go with the dope. He taught me to enjoy my happy moments to the fullest, even if they were only triggered by drugs. That's a very good lesson that I still hold on to.

At the time I met Boti, I often went partying alone; mostly techno, hard bass, darkpsy. The bigger the venue, the more overwhelming the crowd and the louder the music, the more I liked it. I tried to become one with the ecstatic, sweating masses. I wanted to belong, to dissolve myself in the crowd. My transformation, however fleeting, remained a failure. It was always just me, standing in the middle of the dance floor in deafening noise.

Occasionally, I would pick someone out of the crowd and follow them around all night; I even followed them home. They never noticed me. I didn't want anything from these people, I just wanted to know that they were going somewhere, that they had their own lives apart from the small snippet I saw in the clubs, that they weren't just set-pieces in a sad comedy that would disappear once they'd played their part.

One night I was standing in the crowd, and suddenly I realized that I wasn't part of the crowd at all, to an extent I hadn't understood before; I was standing completely apart, even though I was in the middle of the dance floor with sweaty bodies swarming around me in the heat. I wasn't even really there, even though I was sharing the same space with all these other people. And yet I was standing above and apart from them; I was watching without being watched.

And then it occurred to me that I could even be dead.

Being dead would not be so dissimilar to how I was experiencing life at that moment. Being alive or dead would not have changed anything, neither for me nor for others. In this perfect superposition I pondered the situation, exploring my feelings, fears, arguments and counter-arguments while the steady bass of 4/4 techno thumped around me; until I finally decided that this summer I would give it my all. This summer I would be constantly in search of a profound experience, I would be present in my life, every single moment would become meaningful through my constant gaze. I would strive for the highest peaks possible, at all times. I wanted to see and experience extraordinary things, knowing full well that they would be unattainable in the everyday banality of my life as an ordinary person. Trading the chance of this experience for the pursuit of a secure future made me ordinary; a superfluous person, interchangeable with anyone else. I saw it now, and it filled me with dread. I knew it had to stop.

With this decision came the realization that I would die this summer; only then could I truly savour every moment of my passing existence. Without the firm boundary of finality, I might lose focus again and trade life for a future I did not want. Fuck the future, for years all I did was worry about it, paralyzed by a fear whose source I couldn't name; or could, but then the list would go on forever, starting with financial insecurity and ending with the heat death of the universe. After I made my decision I felt a weight fall from my shoulders, and I separated myself from the future and its associated fears as perfectly as I had separated myself from the crowd. There was only right now; only this one summer mattered. Then a crash would come. I knew I would be chasing such a height of experience that reaching that pinnacle would necessarily conclude my life. I felt no sadness or sense of loss at this thought, only joy.

See? I was able to turn this decision into a positive experience. In fact, anything can be considered a positive experience if you educate yourself to be positive. My life changed for the better because of this change in attitude. Later, when I shared my decision with him, Boti supported it as well.

Not long after this, the invasion of the fish-people began.

I had taken all my vacation days at work, plus a period of unpaid leave, citing family reasons. It was easier than explaining why I was quitting. I withdrew my savings and sold my meagre stock portfolio. The money I had set aside for the future was now in my hands and ready to be burned. I was calm and actively looking for positive, happy moments to experience. That's why we missed the beginning of it all; when the first reports of the invasion came in, we were completely out of it in Boti's apartment. We lost the plot even more than usual; after a three-day nonstop binge fuelled mainly by amphetamines, we switched to ketamine and hard psychedelics, which led us down a rabbit hole two days deep. So we were late to the party; after waking up from our trip, we tried to figure out if our brains were fried or if humanity had actually been attacked by a deep-sea civilization while we were out. Everything pointed to the latter scenario.

They emerged from the water and began massacring vacationers and fishermen on select beaches in Asia, South America, and Europe; later, North America and Australia were also attacked, but with far less efficiency. It was the element of surprise in the first wave that made it so successful and terrifying – tens of thousands died, their blood stained the seashores red. It took only a few hours for the initial shock of the attack to be overcome by swift military retaliation around the world. Armies were mobilized and soldiers systematically shot the attackers back into the water. The monsters are obviously not immune to well-spent ammunition. But there are so many of them, a seemingly endless supply of the monsters crawling to shore from immeasurable depths. Their waves of attack are endless, and they will not stop until our armies build a protective wall out of the invaders' corpses along the shoreline. Then, when the corpses of their fallen comrades have rotted enough, they will attack again.

Massive attacks are the most newsworthy, but it's not their only method. Sometimes the fish-people choose entirely new places to attack, or they sneak up on the shore in smaller numbers. The large crowds are easy to spot. Smaller groups or individual fish-people can easily sneak ashore without being noticed by the military.

A brief bout of paranoia marked my initial comedown as I

watched the news. It's crazy how the world turns upside down while you're on a trip, just in the blink of an eye. Knowing that this summer would be my last helped me a lot, and my anxiety and paranoia subsided for the time being. For the first time in my life, I was glad that Hungary was a landlocked country. I watched TV with a beer in my hand, trying to reach that big, immeasurable feeling I knew I was supposed to feel; after all, it was a world-changing event, a really big deal, right? Some deep-sea civilization had always lived down there, so our idea of the world was in for a serious re-evaluation, and they decided to attack us out of the blue, real drama-like. So if there was anything worth really experiencing, it was this. I needed the big emotions; a deep, cold shiver and that immense, oppressive, nameless feeling that you get when you look at the moon and know it was there long before you walked the earth, and that our ancestors, those strange, half-ape people, looked at it just as you do now, and that you too will disappear like your ancestors; but the moon will always be there. There must be a name for this feeling, something like awe, but much scarier; and I wanted it, no, I *needed* it to flow through me as I rolled myself a thick comedown joint and reached for my phone to catch up on the news, but instead I opened Tinder and this new app that had even hotter girls. I wasn't trying to hook up with anyone; I was just looking at the pictures, all the pretty faces, and I was kind of zoned out, oblivious to what was happening in the world, so this big, nameless feeling had escaped me while I was scrolling.

Boti threw an empty soda can at me; it brought me back to the reality of the invasion. My comedown joint was only half-burnt.

'Hey,' he said, looking at his cell phone and grinning from ear to ear. 'Hey,' he said again, 'listen to this.'

'Apparently it's a fact! The flesh of these fish-people ... apparently you can eat it, and it's a powerful drug!'

The television was on. The news reported that a state of war had already been declared in eight countries; there was footage of Chinese People's Army soldiers shooting at the attacking fish-people army, followed by a close-up of the bullet-riddled body of a monster lying in shallow water like a teabag – and then footage of children crying.

In the meantime, I had read up on the relevant forums and had to grin too.

We immediately set off for Croatia. Tourism was one of the pillars of the Croatian economy, so they continued to take in foreigners despite the invasion. It took a few days to sort out the details of the trip and we lived on amphetamines so we could stay awake and leave as soon as possible. By the time we left, we hadn't slept for days again. Boti was behind the wheel, doing lines of poppers and coke to stay awake while driving 180 mph on the highway, and I knew he shouldn't have been driving. I was sure he would make a misjudgment or just fall asleep at the wheel despite the stimulants he was taking. I unbuckled my seatbelt so that my body could experience the full force of the eventual crash.

That calmed me down and I fell asleep.

I only woke up again here in Croatia when the car pulled into the parking lot of our Airbnb accommodation. We've been here ever since and it's fantastic, really fantastic. The weather is great and the water is lovely, you just have to be careful if you want to swim because there is a war going on.

The best thing about this war is that it's not against real people. It's funny because it's like a video game. Nobody has a guilty conscience when they have to kill monsters. Even when we crossed the border into Croatia, the border guards encouraged us to kill all the fish-people we saw. Both the locals and the tourists actively participated in the defence against the invading forces. There was only one simple rule to follow: If you see an invader, you kill it, or if you can't, you alert someone who can. The war has now relaxed the rules so that even tourists are allowed to carry deadly weapons. This war is a good thing.

Positive. Unlike the wars before it. We are not shooting each other for a reason never properly explained only to have to face the reality later that we killed our own neighbours, encouraged to feel pride in our victory or even our defeat, advised to keep quiet about all the rape and torture, but also encouraged to feel sadness at the sheer number of people lost in the war while acknowledging that their dying was also somehow great because that's how they became true heroes or something. War in Europe has always been confusing in this way. At least until now, because this is a really good war. Humans against non-humans. It's a clear deal, and everyone is totally okay with it.

So we sat down on the shore with our weapons to hunt fish people and then feast on their flesh. Everyone on the forums said it was great stuff. Those who had tried it swore it was a special kind of experience; and the icing on the cake was that it was completely free.

Our Airbnb was very well-chosen, by the way. I would rather spend a bit more on the rental and have a comfortable, spacious and cozy place to chill out. Of course, we boarded up the panoramic windows facing the sea, just in case of a major attack. The landlords left us nice messages all over the apartment, little tips on places to visit, favourite places to swim and eat. They also left us a semi-automatic pistol. We found it in a shoebox with a bow on top. Places like this can count on my positive feedback on Tripadvisor.

Boti said the gun was old, might have been used in the war, and I had no idea what he meant until I remembered there was a war here when I was a kid. I don't think anyone still cares about it today.

We returned to our house after killing our first intruder, and instead of doing a line of whatever, we both ate from the meat Boti had cut from the corpse.

As a culinary experience, it was nothing to write home about. The meat tasted metallic and kind of coppery. It has a flavour that I can't quite put my finger on. It's not as bad as it sounds, in fact it's rather bland. I've eaten worse things in my life.

I chewed on the meat and Boti kept talking, so I listened. I only knew as much about the news in the world and the fish-people invasion as Boti told me.

Every intelligence agency and all the scientists were of course frantically trying to figure out the whys and hows of the invasion, like what's the backstory, what's their goal, where they're coming from and so on.

Every day a new piece of information came to light. While I was chewing on the meat, Boti had confirmed that what had been thought to be a legend was actually true. There had been a town or village, and the inhabitants had actually been having sex with fish or fish-like creatures for centuries. I guess the fish fucked the human girls, and the human boys fucked the fish girls, and never thought to turn the scenario into its own genre of porn. Anyway, according to the news, this was one of several possible places where this happened, but this was the first one to be confirmed. He mentioned the name of the location, and it annoys me to no end that I have forgotten it. It's something*mouth*.

Exactly what species of fish was involved in this mating, or why this mating frenzy was triggered, Boti (or the intelligence agencies now speaking through him) could not yet say, but there were already hints of a religious aspect, an alleged sect of believers of some obscure god. Presumably this sect, or cult, had been waiting for this moment, for the beginning of their own private apocalypse. The basic idea of their belief was, and I'm not making this shit up, that a very old dude was sleeping at the bottom of the oceans. This dude is an inhuman being or a god who would destroy everything upon awakening. The fish-people are in league with the old god, according to the researchers, but at this point everything was uncertain.

Boti was still reciting superfluous information when I

looked out the window and told him to shut up. Shut up, because a party had just arrived!

A motorhome and a camper van had just parked in our parking lot overlooking the beach. I had seen a power outlet earlier, I guess our landlords rented the space out for campers. Under normal circumstances I would have been a bit annoyed about this, as we wanted the place to ourselves, but I could tell at first glance that it was a party crowd, with dreadlocks and colourful clothes; tribal tattoos for the older generation, those childish dotted tattoos for the young. I also have a tattoo in the crease of my right arm. The infinity symbol – a loop that never ends. When I got it, it seemed so profound: like, this is infinity and it's on me and I am infinite or I am finite and the world is infinite, I don't know, but somehow I hoped it would connect me to something bigger. Since then, all I see is a messed-up number eight.

We still had some meat left, so we finally went out to greet the tourists with a gift. I immediately liked them and considered them our guests. They seemed like regulars at Goa parties. Not all of them were postmodern hippies; there was this guy who looked like a wholesale businessman in his twenties; and then there was this girl with eyes that seemed to be dreaming all the time. She caught my attention all right; she had that kind of air about her that just draws the eye. Later I was advised not to hit on her at all because she was after girls, and I understood and accepted that, although I never believed in such strict barriers between orientations. You follow the desire that grabs you at a certain moment, wherever that desire takes you. Flesh is flesh, not man or woman.

They did not accept our hospitable gift of the invaders' meat because they wanted to hunt their own. Obviously they were here for the same reason we were – free drugs. We laughed about it, all of us, like old friends, and I knew everything would be all right. Their group was gathering information from the same sources as Boti, but Boti went even deeper than they did, and their first time hearing about the eyes was when we told them. Of their rarity and the supposedly intense trip they induce when eaten. Well, apparently the highest intensity, because according to our limited sources, so far no one had survived the trip. Boti didn't mention this information to our guests. Why freak them out, right?

We shared a beer and rolled a cigarette, and I was about to tell them in horrible, broken English that I was planning to die when the invader's meat hit my system. Somehow I had already forgotten consuming it, so the slide down into the trip was a surprise.

I moaned and said 'oh no', like in a movie, and I said it in Hungarian, one of those moments that no one understands. I started to ripple, and the world rippled too, and we continued to ripple together. I felt my limbs grow cold. I felt a sense of alienation from myself, as if I were wearing someone else's body and not my own, and I had thoughts that were clearly not my own. I felt fear, the presence of a huge, alien being that was beyond my own grasp of existence.

I had taken more aggressive psychedelic substances before, so I forced myself to come out of the paralysis of fear. That's the thing to do when introduced to a brand new psychedelic substance: just go with it and see where it takes you. This initial phase of depersonalization and physical dissociation lasted a while. Boti went through the same process as me. Although I wanted to treat the newcomers as guests, they ended up treating me like one. I was led to a camping chair and handed a beer. A stick of incense was lit to drive away evil spirits that would confuse me in my impending hallucinatory state.

Our online sources warned that some people do not return from this trip. They get stuck, frozen in perpetual fear and dissociation, and end up in an asylum where doctors can wonder about them. There is a similar risk with most of the drugs I've taken, so I had rolled the dice a long time ago.

I think the trick is not to resist. Let the experience flow

through you, let it bare its teeth, and then eventually you'll move on to another phase.

I was expecting a massively psychoactive substance that causes complete ego death, intense audio-visual experiences, maybe even full blown narrative visions. I guess I was expecting a fancy, even more intense version of DMT. Well, it wasn't that. As the initial phase wore off, the substance showed its true form. There were no visions, but a feeling of strength or power, both physical and mental – it could have come from the most important, most basic effect of the drug: the complete absence of feeling.

My heart had gone cold.

When the state kicked in, I reminded myself to experience that moment as something positive too, even if I had to live these emotions retroactively because I was completely dead inside at that moment. I was dead in a good way, because nothing was getting to me. It was refreshing to be without emotion. Perhaps you can only truly be yourself when you have none; the stream of consciousness shows itself in blinding clarity, to the point where you even see your own self as a machine made of cogs. All you are is cold meat lying on the kitchen table.

When I was freed from the burden of feeling the state of the physical world around me, the objects and the space surrounding them, all the glass, the metal, the concrete, had become empty. Pretentious. Worthless. Devoid of life, in a cosmically definitive way. The feeling of emptiness could have crushed me if I could feel; but I couldn't, so it was actually a great experience!

I did not perceive people any differently. I didn't see people, I saw flesh, transitional material, some electricity, chemicals and decaying organic matter. When they spoke to me, all I could think about was the constant self-deception of human consciousness; lying to themselves in order to be persons, even though they were nobodies in the deepest sense. I too was a nobody. Personhood was a ridiculous construct, but at that moment all I could do was imitate laughter. It sounded like broken glass falling on the hood of a freshly crashed car.

There's an aura around you when you trip on invader flesh. A cool aura, like you are above it all and do not care anymore. You look like a jerk, but a jerk that is strangely interesting or even desirable. You can present yourself however you want – others can perceive you as funny, as dangerous, as sexy, as smart. It's entirely up to you, because it's all mimicry. These states are only in the eye of the beholder. Besides, there are no mental inhibitions or moral issues. You do what you want, but never driven by desire or inner need. Around midnight, I was banging the supposedly lesbian girl in the back seat of her car; not for pleasure or out of infatuation, but because I could. Boti took a guy with dreadlocks to his room, even though I've never known him to be gay. But that didn't matter. Sex has no value of satisfaction in this state; it's an empty act, a sequence of bodily functions without the slightest hint of gratification; yet you can exert fantastic control over your own body and that of your partner. The other person will perceive you as the best lover they've ever had, if you want them to perceive you as such. The small catch is that you perceive the other person as both alive and dead at the same time. You see the transitional state, which is life, and you also see the other state, which is still shrouded by the future. In a way, I was fucking a corpse, but it didn't bother me, which is quite interesting. Another positive experience that was worth living through.

The effects of the meat had worn off by sunrise. I woke up completely refreshed. Breakfast was already prepared. The guys made incredibly tasty avocado sandwiches and some weird plant-based coffee that must have tasted pretty good to people who hate coffee.

I enjoyed my time with our guests. They were foreigners; of course, we were all foreigners here, but they were Western Europeans. Most of them were Dutch, plus a German and a Danish girl, a Portuguese guy and a few others from places where people are not hollowed out by their own country. They came from places that seem really nice from a Hungarian perspective. I was envious of them because they didn't have to choose this one summer to die. Of course, my envy was not overwhelming, nor was it genuine, but rather a reminder of my status in Europe. An anger rose up in me, possibly to compensate for my lack of emotion last night, but my anger was not directed at our guests, but at my own country. Then this anger also faded, because what's the point of dwelling on such thoughts and feelings? There is no need for such negativity; you should just focus on the good things. The day passed peacefully. Afternoon faded into evening and the horizon was still golden, so we took a pill hidden in our guests' Buddha statue and set out to hunt. The pill was a kind of Dutch mixture of poppers. It hit quick and hard.

I was focused, but my thoughts became tight and fierce. My blood pressure skyrocketed. The blood was rushing in my ears and I wanted to do something physical, to move, to lift something. Then I realized I actually wanted to hit someone. I thought about the things that made me decide to die, and I focused on my anger. I wanted to cleanse myself of that anger.

We went to a different part of the shore than the day before. At first we laughed nervously as we made our way to the sea, then we marched in silence. We were all shiny with sweat, a sweat that came from a violent inner heat. Even the girls were tense, ready for destruction. Of course we had weapons with us. Several, to be precise. I carried the pistol we'd been given in my waistband, though I forgot about it for long stretches.

The fish-people came crawling onto the beach just as we arrived. Four or five of them, with the promise of others deeper in the water. There were nine of us. No sooner had the first intruder stood up on its hind legs than we jumped on it. My hunt the day before with Boti now seemed quite ridiculous. We had been scared and had hidden. We had hunted from a distance, but the real fun seemed to be in close combat.

When the monsters crawled out, we would pounce on them and beat them down with baseball bats, chains, axes, and knives.

Our guests came well equipped and provided us with plenty of blunt-force weapons. We struck at the fish-men as hard as we could. Most of them couldn't even get up out of the water before they got hit on the head or arm. I was starting to feel good; I was doing what the pill had prepared me for, and it was a thrill. I was able to externalize all the violence that had been building up inside me.

I screamed and shouted names and words in which I tried to condense my hatred and anger. They meant nothing to the foreigners, but they did to Boti, and he joined in. He screamed the names of those whose heads should be bashed in with a baseball bat, whose bodies should be rocked by the bloody waves, and we screamed our frustration at the corpses lying at our feet. Our guests from the more civilized countries yelled instead with the delight and joy of killing.

When the first wave of obsessive violence was over, we relaxed a little and smiled at each other a lot. Of course, we continued to kill the invaders, but it felt more playful. After a particularly nice hit, we'd cheer, if someone missed hilariously, we'd laugh and tease each other. The wave of attackers thinned as dusk fell. We just casually bashed heads here and there, with a few of them crawling ashore every few minutes. Further down the beach, the locals were also engaged in defence. They were using firearms, mainly hunting rifles and a few submachine guns from army stocks. They shot the intruders in the head as they emerged from the water. One shot, one kill. They smoked calmly and bet on who was the best shot. We raised our bloody tools and shouted our salute to the locals, who raised their rifles above their heads and returned our gesture. It was a cool moment, and the others felt it too. We were connected to these foreigners because we were protecting their land, but also because together we were protecting the entire human race.

They appreciated us, we appreciated them, and wow, what a wave of positive emotion as we stood knee-deep in water stained with blood and guts.

Boti examined the heads meticulously; we even negotiated with the locals so we could open their fish-people too. But we were denied the eyes we were looking for. We cut off about a dozen slices of meat and called it a day.

In the evening, we all ate the meat.

While we waited for the drug to take effect, Boti scoured the internet for new revelations. In the middle of the Pacific Ocean, a city was found that was older than mankind. It had risen from the depths of the sea. An elite team of researchers and a weaponized unit were deployed, but they were never heard from again. They were either killed or lost in the nameless city. Now an army of soldiers had been sent out after them, but there was no news of the success of this rescue operation. The internet went crazy with the idea that this was the capital of the fish-people, but I paid no more attention. I was no longer interested in the news, but focused on the here and now. I felt that our guests, these young foreigners, were becoming important to me; my love for them was exuberant. I'd have died for them, that's how much I loved them at that moment, even though our acquaintance had lasted less than twenty-four hours. I think it was the after-effect of the pill we had taken earlier. Then I got tired and sleepy, but before I could doze off in the corner, the invader meat kicked in.

First came the initial fear-phase I already knew from the day before. I heard someone whispering behind me, and thunder cracked the sky, but I knew it wasn't our sky. It was scary, but I managed. Well, some of the others didn't. Our guests screamed and threw themselves on the ground, as if something from above were threatening them. A girl, whose face was now ashen with terror, tried to burrow herself in the sand in an effort to hide. That was funny. Of course, it wasn't funny for her, but I guessed tomorrow she'd laugh at it too.

After a while we all left the initial phase behind. The real nature of the drug took over and the party got really good. We sat under the lights we had strung up between the caravan and the house, and we felt nothing. Absolutely nothing. It was weird to party like this, being dead inside, but it was incredibly calming and somehow very deep. It was hard to have fun in the traditional sense under the influence of the meat, so we discussed what we should do to make the night memorable. We were only men and women after all, our curiosity sharp as ever even without feelings, so we settled on having an orgy.

We were like insects, a whirlwind of limbs and torsos, masses of meat colliding, robots in heat, imitating life. Meanwhile, we generously gifted each other with absolute bliss, even if it didn't feel like bliss at all. It felt like nothing; just a technicality, a series of incredible orgasms dully noted as passing quakes of the body. Still, a great experience.

After the orgy I fell into a relaxing, deep sleep.

I would have considered it a perfect party, if only we hadn't found in the morning that someone had died during the night. In fact, several people were found dead before breakfast. I guess it was all inevitable.

The girl was found first, her body stuffed under the motorhome. She had been killed by one of the Dutch guys. They slipped away from the orgy to talk and fuck, just the two of them under the influence of the meat, and in the process he broke her neck. When we questioned him about it he said he had no other choice; at the moment he did it, he perfectly understood his reasons and they all made sense, not only to him but to his victim as well. It wasn't murder, he claimed. They had fulfilled a deeper purpose, a necessity that was encoded in him, and without emotions he and the girl saw this predestined need locked within him. That's why he had to break the girl's neck. What he did to her body after killing her, especially to her face and breasts, even he couldn't explain. He stayed silent and shrugged upon inquiry.

The human mind is a strange thing, isn't it? Such nonsense is hidden within it, traps we set for ourselves.

The second victim was the Portuguese guy. We didn't really connect, but I liked him anyway. He put pepper on my avocado sandwich in the morning; I remember that well, such a nice gesture. We found him away from the house, at the foot of a tree. He was naked, in more senses than one. During the night he had retreated to this tree with a Swiss army knife in hand and had disemboweled himself. Or rather, he ultimately disemboweled himself, because he had self-mutilated in several other ways beforehand. He was clutching the knife in one hand; in the other, as much as I understand biology, his heart. It wasn't a pretty sight, but there was something poetic about it. That tree standing there, in its shadow a lonely, broken, battered body, a body now made light by the lack of a soul, grinning eternally for the lack of lips cut away in life. It was shocking, of course; tragic. Yet there was beauty to be found.

I suppose he wanted to know what lay beneath the surface. I understood that effect of the consumed invader flesh; the curiosity to discover how one's own body functioned. There is no pain while you're under the influence; you feel what should be pain, but it's disconnected, just like your orgasms and thoughts. Pain doesn't hurt. Surely he wanted to see how his body operated from within, just as he saw his mind's working. I wonder if he intentionally arranged himself in this position, with knife in one hand, heart in the other. Few people can touch their own heart; and because of that, I hoped that the man, whose name I didn't even know, found a connection with himself in his last moment.

The third victim was the Dutchman who had murdered the girl. He hanged himself in our bathroom while his companions argued about whether it was okay to take the knife from the corpse. Despite the fact that it now had a gruesome history, as it had been used for self-mutilation and suicide, it was an original Swiss Army knife, which represented a considerable monetary value, but also had a personal meaning, as it had been a kind of family gift for one of our guests. After a long argument, they finally took the knife out of the corpse's hand. The Dutchman was dying inside while the drama surrounding the knife unfolded. He did not leave a suicide note, but we suspected his motives.

Boti and I agreed that we should try to stay out of it. Boti thought these guys were amateurs whose minds weren't mature enough for the experiences we were looking for. We didn't really know what we were looking for either, but that didn't matter. He had no sympathy for their grievances and was careful not to make their problem ours. We helped carry the body out of the bathroom and asked them to leave or, if they wanted to call the police, to leave us out of it. Let's just pretend we don't know each other. They agreed to that. Just the day before I had loved them so much, and now I saw them as a nuisance, but there is a time to love and a time to get rid of problems. Still, I wished them the best.

We went for a walk on the beach, Boti and I, to let our guests pack up and leave in peace. I rolled myself a few cigarettes. Down on the beach, the locals were beating some fish-people to death. Boti reported on the latest news and I listened very attentively to take my mind off the morning's events. Then we laughed, because the news was funny, especially the accompanying photos of the old farts in their hoods singing or whatever they were doing at a ruin by the sea. Obviously these old guys in costume were members of the cult or sect we had read about earlier.

They had infiltrated everywhere, from the political to the economic to the religious elite, and they were the ones who started the invasion. The intelligence agencies had already started to smoke them out. It was kind of funny because, man, just look at those pictures, those ridiculous outfits, those pathetic bags of wrinkles barely able to hold their piss calling on elder gods or whatever, but it was also sad. Once again, it was about rich old men fucking up the lives of generations of people. I wished they had been on the beach yesterday so we could have bashed their heads in.

Drawings and paintings of the tentacled, octopus-like gods of the cultists were also unearthed. The gods had the strangest names. These woodcuts and drawings had a certain cool aesthetic. I guess if we all survive this invasion, they will be considered a genre of their own, with exhibitions and art albums all carefully trying to separate the history of the war from the art.

When we felt that enough time had passed, we returned to the house. We were getting hungry.

Our former guests had disappeared. All they had left behind were a few tire tracks, a collection of cigarette butts, a half-read Jack Kerouac paperback in German, a cheap but reliable Bic lighter, and the Swiss Army knife they'd been arguing over earlier. I'd liked them when they were here, but I liked them even more because they had left. Their absence sweetened my memory of them, I think.

They must have dumped the bodies in the sea, hopefully on a beach further down, so they could pin the murders on the fish-people. In the grass we found a single object that linked us to the events of the previous night. We hoped it had been left by mistake and not as a message. It was the Portuguese man's severed penis. He had cut it off himself. Neither of us wanted to touch it; holding a dead, withered, cold penis in our hands that morning was just too much.

We ate a few bites, snorted a few lines of poppers and went back to the beach to kill more fish-people. That evening we ate the flesh of the intruders, and when it kicked in and we were dead inside, it was no problem to dispose of the penis. We flung it in the sea where it belonged.

Still, it made me think.

Night fell and I tried to have a serious conversation. I asked Boti if he really thought it was okay that this summer was the last of my life and also the last of his life, that people had died last night, that we could only connect with our world through drugs, and now we were using another drug to not even feel. I started to have the shadow of a doubt whether it was truly all right.

Boti didn't answer for a long time; he looked at his phone, his face washed out by the eerie glow of the screen. 'The British Prime Minister is a cultist too,' he said, shrugging his shoulders. That was his answer, and I think it was enough to ease my mind.

'We'll find the eyes,' Boti said. 'Once we have them, everything will be fine. Best trip ever, yeah?' he said, smiling. He rarely smiled, although he laughed often.

We knew that finding an eye would herald the end of summer. The thought was tinged with melancholy, because I kind of liked this one summer. It had been such a positive experience. But I wanted those eyes. Every summer comes to an end, so going out on a trip from the eyes seemed like a perfect ending. An extraordinary climax.

Boti said the eyes were probably like radios that high-ranking officers of the invaders could use to receive orders from another world or something like that. I had to laugh when he said that, because it reminded me of the sleeping tentacle-god or whatever the cultist farts worshipped. I imagined the god sitting in the depths of the ocean talking on a walkie-talkie with a giant atlas in front of him, plotting his strategic plans for taking over the world, but whatever he said on the walkie-talkie, however brilliant his plans were, his army just ran to shore like a bunch of idiots to be killed by the Chinese People's Army or the U.S. forces or fucking Croatian villagers. I guess it was obvious, because the high-ranking officials had eyes instead of brains. That thought made me laugh even harder, and eventually I threw up.

I had a feeling this would all be over soon; every object around me seemed to radiate with significance, and I knew we would find the eyes in the next skull we opened.

Guess what: we didn't.

We spent the next ten days on the coast. We killed so many invaders that the Croats should have given us a medal for it, they really should have. The bodies piled up, and I learned the art of cracking open the skulls so we'd be more efficient; we even continued our deal with the locals, so we opened their trophies too. As long as we were there, basically nothing that came out of the sea survived with its head intact.

And that's exactly what we found in those heads.

Nothing.

We ate their flesh to get high, but the novelty wore off quickly. We relied on our own supplies to spice up the days, but even Boti's drug reserve was running low. I was getting anxious because in a couple of days the Airbnb lease would be up. I reckoned I'd be dead by the time we had to leave the rental; and yet now I faced the prospect of living homeless on the beach, or worse, returning to Budapest and going back to work on Monday, knowing I'd burnt through all my savings. My fears for the future would come back to me tenfold, a thousandfold even.

I could not let that happen. I only had to look at Boti for him to understand my fears and for me to understand his. He spoke first, and he spoke for both of us.

'We can't go back. We didn't come here to go back, not ever.'

We made a pact. We had enough weapons. Even if we didn't find the eyes, if we had to give the keys back, we could still finish the summer; we might not go out with the climax we wanted, but we would still go out with a bang.

Afterwards, I stayed on the beach to watch the sunset. It was a quiet moment. I was at peace with everything. I was relatively clean; I don't think I had used anything that day. I had my water shoes on, but they were ripped on the side. I guess an urchin I hadn't noticed, or maybe one of our own knives had slashed them. They were my favourite water shoes. Somehow that made me sad, the thought that I was going to leave my water shoes behind when I died: they would lie around somewhere, damaged, never to be worn again and later thrown away because I had abandoned them; then I realized that I was really thinking about my parents, not the shoes, and I started to cry. I had no name for this feeling, which was scalding-hot like pain and salty like tears and bitter from all the things left unsaid, and I had to fight it before it overwhelmed me.

They would be left alone, so what? I'm alone too, we're all alone. Still, I couldn't stop crying. It must have been the exhaustion. When it was over, I felt cleansed, although some of the bitterness remained. I decided to treat it with the last of our cocaine and made my way to the house.

Boti was standing at the corner of the building, striking a strange pose, like someone who wanted to run away and attack at the same time. I thought it was interesting and honestly quite funny, although I hadn't started laughing yet. I walked over to him, but he wasn't looking at me, just straight ahead, and I could not make out what was going on because I was confused not only by his expression, but also by the structure of his face in the particular colours of that dusk. It was a good moment. Then I somehow understood that his expression was a mixture of determination and fear. Yes, that's what confused me.

I had never seen fear on his face before.

That made me look in the direction Boti was looking, and suddenly it all made sense. A fish-man was standing right in front of us. Strange that I hadn't noticed it, but I had been exhausted and worn down; I couldn't even feel fear. We had no weapons, and even though we had already killed so many of them, it's hard to take down such a creature with your bare hands. In fact, people are usually only killed when they have no way to defend themselves, like the situation we were in now.

I thought I should say something, but I couldn't break the spell of the moment. The monster would attack one of us, and I needed to know the choice it would make – which of us radiated death and which radiated life. I reminded myself that if I was to be attacked, I had to die and not just be maimed by those horrible, circular rows of teeth.

Finally, it decided not to attack either of us. Instead, it used its long claws to gouge out its own eyes. This was a completely new behaviour, we had never seen anything like it before, nor had we read about anything similar. It screamed, but the screams became wet as the blood began to flow from its wide open mouth while the claws dug deeper and deeper into its own head. The fish-man burrowed through its brain, and after a few minutes it pulled a couple of eyeballs out of the sockets where its eyes had previously been.

They were eyes like ours, not like the fish-men's. They lay on the palm of the monster's hand, watching us. The fish-man knelt down, held out its arms and offered us the eyes, even though it no longer had a brain. I thought back to my vision of the elder god and his messed-up, brainless army and almost laughed again.

'This is a message,' said Boti. 'A message for us.'

We didn't need to say out loud who we thought the message was from. Tentacles, sleeping and non-sleeping old men at the bottom of the ocean, which isn't really an ocean but space and time, or some other religious nonsense. I guess old Mr. Tentacle wanted to pull us out of the war because we were growing increasingly enthusiastic about wiping out his troops.

Boti took the eyes out of the fish-man's hand. When the offering was gone, the fish-man fell over and was dead for good. Somehow I envied it for how single-minded its life had been; it had a job to do, did it superbly, really, and then died. No fear, no dread of tomorrow, just a single focus and the satisfaction of a job well done, and that was it, now it would rest forever, stretched out on the lawn of this wonderful little Airbnb. What is success if not that?

We left the body there and soon forgot all about it.

We exchanged a few words in the house, but I had the feeling that Boti wasn't really paying attention to me anymore. He was already in the final preparations for this last, great journey into himself, for the encounters that would allow him to destroy himself. Sure, I understood him. You had to prepare yourself mentally before such difficult journeys. Nevertheless, I missed Boti now. He was physically with me in those last moments, but he wasn't really present as he withdrew into himself. I thought about how we are all actually alone, and just as personality is a construct and a lie, so is the idea that you can really share anything with another person.

Bloody hell, I thought, 'I'm ready,' I said. I wanted it to be over at last.

We took the eyeballs at the same time. I bit down on it and it opened with a strange pop. A viscous, gelatinous substance poured out onto my tongue. I swallowed it all without hesitation and tried not to pay attention to the taste.

I needed something to wash the taste of eyeball jelly out of my mouth. I craved a beer or spritzer and scolded myself for not preparing a bottle. I thought I still had time, at least a few minutes. I'll get something cold from the fridge, I told myself, no problem. I took a single step and lo and behold, I collapsed like a sack of shit and fell down, down onto the floor and further, into the depths between the floor tiles. I fell further, beyond the tiles, beyond the atoms that made up the kitchen, into an infinity beyond the continuity of my understanding of space and time.

It was so sudden. Bang, the eyes just kicked in the door without warning, one moment you're going for a beer, the next you're leaving human understanding of perception and reality behind. Funny thing. My first reaction was, of course, surprise. Then it occurred to me that I was going to die now, along with Boti, all alone, though we could have held hands or something to create a scene of heartwarming humanity for those who would eventually find us. What a waste.

After that, the coherent thoughts stopped for a while. The journey had already begun, and I just let myself be taken wherever the drug wanted to take me. I was not going to resist. I was determined, even if thinking was no longer possible, that no matter how heavy this last trip would be, I would look for the positive every step of the way.

I think I can tell you that I now have a good understanding of what this trip is all about and why most people die or at least go irreversibly insane from it.

The main difference between this and all other drugs is that the eyeballs do not create a psychedelic experience by distorting, exaggerating, and visualizing aspects of your ego, memories, desires, and fears. Quite the opposite. Throughout the trip, you understand that what you are seeing and experiencing is objectively real; not simply a series of visions, but cosmic truths. It's a double-edged thing, because what you see during the trip also sees you.

That's pretty much the main difference from regular drugs.

All right, I'll be honest with you. It was a bit disappointing. Maybe it was just the hype, but I was expecting more.

I mean, don't get me wrong, it was really good and all, a unique experience; okay, calling it a good experience is maybe a bit of an exaggeration, but profound, yeah, and definitely interesting, so there's that. That's positive. It was worth it, because you never know unless you've tried it, right? However, it didn't really show anything new; there was a lacking to the experience.

Of course, there are parts that make most people crack up. For example, you see yourself in relation to the universe with such clarity as you've never experienced before. In that frozen moment, you realize with terrifying certainty that you are less than nothing. Your life has no purpose, no meaning, there is no grand plan in which you are a useful cog, however tiny. Your life in its entirety is a by-product of existence. Sawdust scattered in the wind.

Then you see the whole thing, from head to toe. The ends of time and space, though it never really ends; and just as there is no end, there is no center; no meaning, no purpose, no creator guiding this infinite system to some kind of meaning. In this first phase of the journey, you are presented the facts. I'm sure it's hard for others to experience the utter meaninglessness of their own civilization, even their species, in this way, but it was nothing new to me. I guess I'm far too Hungarian for this; insignificance and lack of control have been always been a fact of life for me. Seeing it as a hard, cosmic truth was fine, I guess. It's good to know that every decision I have made or ever will make is essentially meaningless. It takes the pressure off. But I live in Hungary, so that's no big surprise.

If you can carry yourself through the barren landscape of that first phase without losing it, the drug takes you further – to the other end of infinity. There you meet the Big Guy, the sleeping god worshipped by the old, rich farts of our civilization.

Yes, you meet the thing, face to face, so to speak, but the wood carvings and paintings we have seen on the news do not do him justice, if only because he cannot be depicted. His body exists differently than ours, it extends into other dimensions that I don't think we can really understand. Basically, you see it on this journey, but you do not see it with your own eyes, because just as it cannot be painted or drawn or even photographed properly, it cannot be seen either. You have to see with other than human eyes, because you have to see extensions of reality that are off-limits to us. Human eyes are insufficient, because they rely on light, but this god has nothing to do with light.

Anyway, that was perhaps the coolest part of the trip, this new way of seeing, although you get a headache just trying to recall it from memory. But other than that . . .

I mean, listen, this elder god is right in front of you, but he's not really doing anything. He's chilling in an endless black ocean or cosmic ether or whatnot, and sure, this god is huge, to call him big would be an understatement, like calling a billion years a really long time. In a way, this god is infinite, and when you observe him, you get the feeling that his life is somehow infinite too; he's not really alive and so he cannot ever die. I guess that's why they say he sleeps. As you watch it, you can sense the evil emanating from it, or maybe it's not evil at all, but just something so alien to us that we can only perceive it as evil, and so you understand that the thing is not actually sleeping.

The god opens its eyes and looks at you.

I guess whoever survives the first phase gives up the ghost here. That could be pretty intense, I imagine. A god looks directly at you. He not only looks, he really sees, and it's like a dissection. He scans your soul with his tentacles. You don't see them, these tentacles, you just feel them penetrating you. They're looking for your essence, your soul, to tear it out of you, just like we tore the teeth out of all those fish people.

I guess this is where it's easiest to die. That is exactly what I wanted; not just wanted – expected! The tentacles were inside me, I could feel them probing my soul, searching for the root where they could grab it and just rip it out, with a finality that would mean my end. I let them search, without any resistance, and expected every second to be my last. I would feel a little tug inside me and poof, I would go offline, no image, no sound. It would have been perfect, such a pinnacle of experience, and then I'd log out, turn off the computer, leave the room as if I'd never been here. The waiting was the best part; waiting for the tentacles to yank my life out of me; grab everything I was, pull it out like a weed and destroy it! Annihilate it! Let me be no more! This ecstatic ending was what I'd been looking for all summer, and it would have been perfect, so fucking perfect!

I guess that's how the cultists come to be. The tentacles move something in those people. If they survive the ordeal, they are already part of the sleeping god. They become puppets. I was fine with this option too, on the condition that I should cease to exist as a person once I had been turned into a puppet. I was happy to become an empty shell, to be filled with a completely new person, as long as I didn't have to be that new person.

The tentacles penetrated me deeper and deeper, and I let

them, but of course after a while I couldn't help but notice how much time had passed. An eternity, and let me tell you, experiencing eternity as a landscape, as in the first phase of the trip, is one thing, experiencing it as time standing still while tentacles invade you through your orifices is a whole other story, believe me. I was annoyed, and I feared that my annoyance would spoil the rush of dying.

No such luck.

There are two possible explanations.

One is that I really am a snowflake. It could be that my soul is truly divine, elusive and unreachable. One of a kind, really. It could be that the tentacles sought it and found it, but could not grasp it because I am too strong in faith, or too free in spirit, or insert some other narrative of self-deception that makes people like me seem extraordinary and unique.

Or, and I cannot rule out this possibility, the tentacles sought and found nothing. No soul, no center around which life winds itself into a human being. They found emptiness and slippery chaos. They found a tiny mirror reflecting the essence of the universe; the essence of this god himself.

Maybe that's why I didn't collapse dead right away. I am as the universe is, as it was shown to me in the visions the eyes brought; I am without center, I lack compassion or curiosity for others, or even the desire for life. I am already cold and dead inside, unfeeling and unforgiving.

I try to see this as something positive too. Moments of self-discovery like these are important, and you have to be present in them, because you can only accept yourself if you know yourself as you are. Even if what you are is a void.

Eventually, the tentacles retreated from me in disgust. Those fuckers devoured every human in one way or another, but they spat me out. The sleeping god himself spat me out, and I felt his disgust and also some fear as the tentacles retreated. He was afraid because he touched something that resembled him; he found a mirror and shrieked out at what he saw.

That was the end of the journey. I was spat out of the black ether. I became an unwanted guest, an intruder, even if the eyes were an invitation.

It was disappointing, and I could not find an ounce of positivity in it, no matter how hard I tried. I came to on the kitchen floor as if waking from a dream. I was alive, fully alive, without anything having happened to me. I felt betrayed and angry at these supposedly terrible cosmic powers for not even having the guts to finish me off. Screw them, huh? I wasn't just spat out; they were scared of me. Losers.

A huge disappointment, the whole business with the eyes. I had so much hope for them, and now this. I did everything I could not to live, and it wasn't enough.

I peeled a banana and rolled a cigarette. I had smoked it about halfway when I remembered my best friend and dealer Boti. I searched the rooms and called out his name, but he was no longer in the house.

His footprints were visible in the sand and he had cut himself on the stones, leaving a fine trail of blood behind. He was obviously on his way to the beach, and over time other prints joined his. These other footprints were clearly not human, so I immediately concluded that the fish-people were after him. I could have been worried, but why? If they killed him, that was fine with Boti. We had the same goal.

I saw him in the distance. He was standing in the sea, the waves crashing against his knees. His eyes were red, tears of blood running down his cheeks. He looked at me from afar, but did not recognize me. I, however, recognized him – or rather, the web of tentacles that filled Boti, so that he no longer needed to exist. I was envious of him.

Fish-people surrounded him, and he made his way into the deep water with them. He did not even hesitate as the waves crashed over his head. I watched him until he disappeared and I felt no sadness. He had made it. He was returning home now.

But where should I go now? Where was my home?

It was the last night in the Airbnb. After that I would have to move out and do something with my so-called life, and I no longer had a dealer. The only solution that made sense in this context was to put an end to this horrible comedy. I still had the semi-automatic with me; it would be enough to bury the barrel in my mouth and shoot. From one end of infinity to the other, fast as a bullet.

Of course I did not do it. Not after what I had just experienced. Nothing had really changed, but even though I already had the oily taste of the gun on my tongue and felt the metal near my throat, the thought of suicide just didn't vibe with me right at that moment. I put the gun back in the box, even put the ribbon back on top, and gathered what was left of Boti's supplies. Not much. We had stored some invader meat in the freezer. I put it in a cooler with cold packs to keep it frozen and loaded everything in the car. I left the keys on the counter, sent a thank-you note to the landlords and left the beach for good. I heard gunshots in the distance; the war was still raging, but I was no longer part of it. I was already thinking of having to go back to the office at 9 o'clock sharp next Monday.

When I crossed the border, I was in a better mood. After all, the universe is so big, and we are so insignificant in it; and I am as empty on the inside as the world is on the outside, and I can see that as a good thing. I felt a wave of positivity in my chest. After all, there are no wrong decisions, only decisions that don't change anything at all.

And the summer isn't over yet. It's still warm, and if I push myself and give it my all, I might still die. If not, that's fine too. Que Será, and so on.

If I should feel bad, I will eat some of the meat, and enjoy not feeling anything at all.

This'll Make Things a Little Easier

For the longest time, Petra had felt that she was far from wealthy, but she managed to make ends meet. Others always seemed to be worse off. She read about them in the papers or saw them on the news, especially when winter froze the streets and people were reminded to watch out for the homeless and call an ambulance if they saw them lying on the sidewalk, or when this or that charity was handing out free food to those in need. Of course, she was also afraid of the poor. She tried to avoid the homeless, because they smelled unpleasant and had something about them that gave Petra a suffocating dread, followed immediately by a feeling of guilt. They were people too, only they did not have a roof over their heads; they were like her, only destitute. So Petra could not call herself poor, because she had a house, a bank account into which money flowed from time to time, and a job she could rely on.

Nevertheless, the money always ran out by the last few days of the month. She laughed about it the first time. There was enough pasta and canned food in the pantry to tide her over the few days until the next month's salary arrived. Her salary had not gone up for years, but prices had, so the deprivation at the end of the month became regular, even predictable. She could count on the money running out, she could expect it. The thought made her feel terrible and useless, and she berated herself relentlessly. If she knew she was going to run out of money every month, why not do something about it? For example, she could save up in advance! After all, one has to manage one's own security; politicians even said on the news that hard times were coming and that everyone was only worth as much as they earned. So you have to be careful not to live extravagantly, not to buy the best food for yourself and the children, not to buy brand-name clothes, to turn off the heating in the house, switch off the TV and the internet, stop buying books. You have to make sure that you only spend money on what's absolutely needed for survival, and then the money should be enough. In fact, you could even save for bigger and prettier things once you have done without big and pretty things. Everything we don't consume now is an investment for the future, although the future is also a luxury.

One evening her son Bence asked her if they were poor. At school, he noticed the stark contrast between himself and the other children. They simply had so much more, and Bence felt that he fell into a caste reserved for disadvantaged children. Petra suddenly didn't know what to answer, all she could feel was a paralyzing horror that made her stomach ache. Bence asked the question, but her daughter Juli was also watching her with wide eyes. Juli was already in the gravitational pull of growing up, and with her grew her needs, which Petra simply couldn't finance.

It's just hard for us at the moment. It's hard now, but we are not poor. Others are having a hard time too, but soon we will all get out of it. She smiled as she said these things. Later she vomited in the bathroom and her children pretended not to hear.

This'll make things a little easier, the woman said with a smile, and Petra wanted so much to believe her. Yes, if only things were a little easier. If only she had a little less to worry about. Her heart throbbed with hope.

The woman was a stranger in this environment; a sense of serenity surrounded her, a calm that came from material security. The event took place in the town hall. The few people present were families and lonely women like Petra herself. The public invitation to the event was rather vague; it talked about money and self-sufficiency, and Petra couldn't even guess what it was all about. The posters and announcements promised the same thing the woman was doing now: that it would make everything easier.

As the woman spoke, saplings were lined up along the wall, their roots carefully wrapped in gray cloth. The woman spoke about these trees. The goal was to reforest the environment as quickly and comprehensively as possible, because that was the only way humanity could escape the ecological disasters that neither Petra nor the other families attending the presentation cared about. What did it matter what was going to happen to the ice caps years from now when the bills had to be paid tomorrow?

But that was the main motivation for this government program. People wouldn't plant these trees because they cared about nature or biodiversity. No, the only thing they had to think about was their own well-being. The trees would be planted for their own benefit, with the welcome side-effect of helping nature. That was the best thing about it. The woman, who was so clearly better, cleaner, and richer than those present in the town hall, reconciled these two aspects. She even said it out loud, so often that it stuck in Petra's head for days: if we help nature, we help ourselves.

What was there to lose? Petra signed the necessary papers, submitted photocopies of her identity card and tax documents, and then received the tree.

She planted it in the garden that very evening. The night was cold, but the work warmed her up. She had already got used to doing everything on her own. According to Hungarian law, a family strictly consisted of a father, a mother, and their children, but the father of this family had first sought pleasure with another mother and then solace in another country, leaving Petra, Bence, and Juli behind. He sent some money the first few months after his departure, but nothing in the last couple of years. As far as Petra knew, he might well have died in the meantime. Her family had been broken up by his absence, but the mortgage on the house had to be paid, even if she paid it alone.

Juli came out to help. She had smoked a cigarette, Petra could tell. She didn't have the strength to scold her for it, and she felt she was losing control of her daughter's upbringing. Juli helped with the digging and put the little tree in the hole. That was enough for Petra to overlook the smoking. Just this once she would let it pass, she promised herself.

Once the sapling was safely in the ground, Juli asked the only question that mattered. When will it start working? Her voice lacked the curiosity of a child; it was flat and pragmatic like an adult's. Petra looked at her daughter in the cold LED glow of the streetlights and her heart sank. When had her daughter grown up so much? When did she start asking such serious questions in such a serious tone? She was still supposed to be a child!

She answered Juli as best she could. They had promised that it would grow quickly. A few weeks at most.

It only needs watering a few times a day.

So they watered it; at first Petra did it alone, but Juli wanted to help, and eventually Petra let her. One morning it was Juli's turn to cut her hand and let her blood drip onto the base of the sapling. Bence wanted to join in, but Petra and Juli forbade him. Bence threw a tantrum, of course, and it was easier to give in. They allowed him to prick one of his fingers with a needle. Just a drop of blood so he wouldn't feel left out; even the smallest amount counted. They stood over the sapling and watered it with their blood, and Petra felt their family ties strengthen.

The tree grew overnight. Petra had been warned about it, but it was still terrifying. At midnight, they all awoke to the sound of the tree. In the morning, the ground was churned up by the abruptly growing roots and the thickened trunk. What had looked like a sapling less than twenty-four hours ago was now a large tree of considerable age. Fresh leaves hung from the branches. Petra smiled as her children stood in amazement in the shade of the newly grown tree.

It's done, she said, and the smile disappeared from her face. The end of the month was approaching and she expected to run out of money again, especially as Bence needed a new pair of shoes. Petra had always been a pragmatic person, so she could not believe what they were saying about the tree. Still, she had to believe now, because it was the only way to feed her children until payday.

That's what the woman had said at the presentation before handing out the seedlings. It's not a question of faith, because once you've tried it you will see that it works, no matter your beliefs.

Petra ordered her children to go back inside, and for the first time that week, the two children obeyed without question.

The hollow inside the tree trunk was dark. Just big enough for Petra to hide in. She skimmed through the brochure again to make sure she had done everything right. But using the tree seemed so simple, and isn't simplicity the basic principle of nature? So why should this thing be complicated? Petra undressed in the cold so that her clothes wouldn't get dirty. She tore about half a dozen leaves off the branches; she didn't count them. She followed her instinct; it felt right to put so many leaves in her mouth.

The leaves had a bitter taste; the edges caused tiny cuts on her tongue. The cuts stung. Like a squirrel, she thought, I am like a squirrel, stuffing my cheeks as I crawl into my hiding hole. She wanted to laugh, but she just shivered in the cold.

She had forgotten the knife and quickly ran back to the kitchen to get it; the soles of her bare feet were dirty, now she would have to mop the floor again. She grabbed the knife she thought was the sharpest and hurried back into the yard and into the tree. The leaves scratched at her throat; she mustn't swallow them, the instructions had made that clear.

She crawled inside. If she curled up she just fit, even had

some space to move around. There wasn't any comfort to be found, though; the tree scratched her knees and back when she tried to position herself. She was on her knees, like in a temple. She was about to say an ancient prayer, an offering older than words.

She had already decided in advance where she would inflict the first wound; she had decided in the town hall while listening to the wealthy woman's pitch presentation. On her thigh. A wound there wouldn't bother her so much when she went to work. She didn't hesitate; after all, it was just a small wound, a fleeting moment of pain, really. No need to make a big deal out of it.

She drew the blade across her left thigh. Worried that the pain wasn't severe enough and wouldn't reach the expected level, she pressed the knife harder to deepen the wound. She bit down on the leaves to keep from screaming; what would the neighbors think of her and her family if she screamed. As the blood ran down her thigh, she felt the taste of the leaves in her mouth give way to another scent: that of ink, the smell that lingers on the finger when bills are counted and cash handed over.

She reached into her mouth and pulled out money instead of leaves: 70,000 Hungarian forints. She squeezed the money, damp with her spit, and cried with joy because the woman had been right; it would actually be a little easier this way. They could buy that pair of shoes for Bence, and there would be enough left over for another grocery run and some Betadine for the wound.

The state was lenient. Those who participated in the tree-planting program had to declare 25% of the income they earned in the tree. There was barely any paperwork. The income had to be declared at the town hall, where the government tax was paid out either in cash or by bank transfer. Some refused to declare the money they earned. That was a mistake, because the state wanted its share. They overlooked minor discrepancies because working in the hollow was a lonely job; if you skimmed off a little money by declaring a slightly smaller amount than you actually earned, that was acceptable. However, if you tried to evade taxation, your tree would be cut down by the forest administration and the tax authority would impose a fine of up to one million forints.

That's why Petra carefully separated the state's money from her own from the very beginning. She wanted to sleep peacefully; it was only a quarter of the money – if she handed it over, the state would leave her alone and she could do what she wanted with the rest. She had no problem with that. She could always crawl back into the hollow to get more money. It really did make things easier; the tree helped them through the dreaded end-of-the-month stretch and allowed for some new things for the children. She even bought herself a new coat to replace the old torn one. There were a few weeks when she went to work with a smile on her face because she felt as light as a feather.

Petra had never heard of triple inflation, but it soon became a problem that wiped the morning smile off her face.

Petra knew the first type of inflation because it was mentioned at the first presentation and in the instructions that came with the sapling. This was the inflation of pain. Pain was the engine of the process that turned the leaves into banknotes, but the tree would not accept any pain that was less intense than the previous one. When Petra wanted a little money after her first time, it was no longer enough to cut her thigh. The tree offered her less money for the same pain, or perhaps none at all. She needed a place on her body that would give her more pain with the same method, or a more painful method. She was smart enough to think ahead; it was best to start with less pain, and if the cuts did not produce any more results, she could switch to burning. That should give enough pain to last a while if she did it smartly.

After that, she would probably use the old hammer. The

nails would grow back quickly anyway; she could live with a few broken toes. But she hoped it wouldn't come to that. She figured she'd only crawl into the hollow when they were in a pinch or unexpected expenses arose, and of course around Christmastime, because nothing says love like a few well-chosen presents.

However, Juli was smarter than her; much smarter, and she saw their situation with such clarity. Petra loved her daughter so much; she was so proud of her sharp mind, which Juli had certainly not inherited from her, and her heart ached as she realized how quickly the years had flown by. She feared that Juli might not have gotten enough from her, not enough care, love, or money for her to become a healthy, resilient adult. And yet now they were sitting at the kitchen table, and Juli spoke with such understanding that Petra could hardly believe it was her daughter.

Her arguments were clear. We can't wait any longer, Mom, she said. We have to take as much money as possible, as quickly as possible from the tree.

At first Petra did not understand what her daughter meant and was prepared for a counter-argument because she thought Juli was spoiled and wanted expensive, impossible things, like those silly ski camps her classmates went to, or a new phone when the old one still worked.

Juli, however, explained to her what the problem was.

The tree planting program was a huge success. In their neighborhood everyone already had a tree. The city had never been so green. Even the downtown parking lots had been eliminated so the downtown residents could have their own money trees.

That was the second kind of inflation. If it had gotten a little easier for everyone, it also meant that it was getting a lot harder. Petra had already noticed the first signs, but she did not want to associate them with the trees. As everyone had more money to spend, prices began to skyrocket. The same goods were almost twice as expensive in the grocery store as they had been a few months ago. However, the trees were not following the inflation of money. The trees were only interested in the inflation of pain, and slowly the whole country echoed with the moans and cries of moneymaking.

So it's best to take out as much as we can now, said Juli. We need to earn as much as we can while money is still worth something. If we wait, the inflation of the currency will make our earnings worthless, or the pain required to earn enough would be inhumane.

This played into the third type of inflation. That is, the value of the Hungarian forint had deteriorated in relation to foreign currencies. Since most goods had to be imported, this also contributed to the increase in prices. Unfortunately, the tree was state-calibrated in Hungarian forints; how much easier everything would have been if the price of pain could be redeemed in euros or U.S. dollars.

Juli was right, and Petra reached the hammer stage just one week later.

She still had to go to work, and the pain from her broken toes made her life difficult; she limped badly, and it caused her back to hurt too. At least they had saved a little money, but that that didn't last – prices rose to such heights within a few weeks that the money they had saved was quickly burnt up. Petra felt the same trepidation in her stomach that she had felt before the tree brought her relief; she was anxious, even terrified, when she thought about the end of the month. Her salary was barely enough for a few weeks anymore. How much more pain could she bear, and how much money would that pain be worth?

During her breaks from work, she watched educational YouTube videos; tips and advice on how to inflict pain on the female body in new and different ways. At the end of some of these videos, Petra felt faint at the thought that she would soon have to endure these things for the sake of her children, if nothing else. She made a list of possible methods and felt cold sweat dripping from her armpits. She stole a stapler from the office, just in case.

Juli was once again smarter than her mother.

All three of us watered the tree with our blood, Juli said, so we can all use the tree. I could start the process all over again. I could earn more money with less pain.

Petra refused, of course; she already knew pain and didn't want to expose her children to it. Still, she was filled with a strange pride. How had her children developed into such nice, good people, even without a father? This thought brought tears to her eyes. It was tempting to agree, as it had all become so difficult lately. Her wounds burned and ached, and the Betadine was getting more expensive by the day.

Still, her answer was a resounding no.

Juli was smarter than all of them. Much smarter, and Petra loved her for it. Just as she was saying no, Juli defiantly slammed a hundred thousand forints on the kitchen table and lifted her skirt. A fresh cut sliced open her thigh. Petra couldn't hold back her own tears, she fell to her knees and kissed Juli's wound. She felt like her heart was being ripped out of her body, and now Bence was crying too, because he didn't understand why everyone was so sad.

But despite Juli's help, Petra climbed back into the hollow of the tree the next evening. She had to do it. The mortgage on the house was in foreign currency. The installments were getting more and more expensive as the forint was in free fall, and they were already three months behind. They needed the money as soon as possible. She stripped naked and crawled into the tree, a pair of pliers in one hand, a nail still dripping with alcohol in the other. It was a new method she had seen in one of the videos that were becoming increasingly popular.

She took a few deep breaths; her body and mind were tired from the pain. She was about to leave when Juli sat down at the foot of the tree so that her mother could see her but not reach her. Petra half-turned to send the girl into the house, to warn her of the cold, though she herself was shivering. She could not speak. Her mouth was full of leaves.

Juli began to speak instead; again in that flat, all-too-grown-up tone that made Petra's heart ache.

You know, Mom, I've been thinking and I'm in a pretty difficult situation. I'm here with you, locked up in this house. I know I should love you because you're my mother. But how could I love you, Mom? Have you ever thought about that? Do you remember Kriszta, from class? Sometimes I go to their house and I see a family, you know? A real family. There's a father and a mother, and they're doing really well. They don't struggle like we do, they're not as bitter as we are. And that made me think, you know? Because it's your fault, isn't it? You weren't good enough for Dad. You couldn't keep him, probably because of your penny-pinching sourness. If you'd been better and he'd really loved you, then we could have been like Kriszta's family. Happy. So, what can I say? I really wish Dad had taken me with him, so I wouldn't have to live with you.

The pliers slipped from Petra's trembling hand, but her tears didn't flow; it was too big a thing for mere tears. This pain was black, buried deep in her chest, like a bone stuck in her soul. A wound she had hidden for so long in the hope that no one would ever poke at it, but now Juli was pricking it open with such precision that Petra felt her own body becoming alien to her, because it was the only way she could survive this pain.

When she opened her mouth, banknotes fell out. Twenty-thousand forint bills, a lot of them, even more than the leaves she had put in her mouth.

Juli fell to the ground as if she had suddenly lost all strength. She screamed and spoke again like the teenager she was, overwhelmed with joy and excitement and the terrible feeling of having done something that could not be forgiven, that could not be repaired. She spoke quickly until the words flowed together in a stream of tears. It worked, Mom, I knew it would work! She crawled into the hollow and took her mother in her arms to hug her, explaining through her snot that she hadn't meant it, she didn't mean any of it! She had made it all up to help, to inflict a different kind of pain on Petra so she wouldn't have to mutilate herself; and Petra ended up crying too, not just with relief, but because she understood how much her daughter loved her; only a love so genuine could hurt this much.

Despite all the money Petra earned that night, the situation got much worse; the economy continued to go down the drain. On TV, the representatives of the state claimed that this was actually a good thing and showed figures saying that everyone in Hungary was living much better than a year ago. Well, if they said it on TV, you had to believe it. Petra was fired, and a week later even the company went bankrupt and was dissolved. The agreed severance pay was never paid to her.

So her only source of income remained the tree; at least until she found a new job. Fat chance, considering that most of the stores had closed down and the shopping district in the city center had become a monument to bankruptcy.

Still, she had her house. They could not lose the house, that was the only certainty in their lives. They had to keep the house, whatever the cost.

They couldn't exploit the emotional pain all the time, so Juli was now using the hammer on her body and Petra could barely walk anymore. But the money was still not enough.

So Juli took matters into her own hands again. She tried to look calm as she told her mother, but her forehead was glistening with sweat.

Mom, you stay in the hollow now. Don't move, no matter what. Don't even lift a finger until it's over, okay? Trust me, Mom. You have to trust me!

What choice did she have but to trust? They had already received the foreclosure notice. If they did not pay by the end of the month, the bank would foreclose on the house.

Petra nodded. She didn't move, but how could she? Her whole life had been built on immobility and helplessness, her whole life was a cramped den, a mouth squeezed shut so that others wouldn't hear the screams.

This was the first time Bence got involved. He wanted to help, and Juli had an idea of how he could do it. They discussed it, of course, the two of them. She wouldn't do anything to him that her brother hadn't agreed to.

When Petra had settled in the tree, Juli sat the boy down on the grass where Petra could see him clearly; then she put a plastic bag over the child's head and tied it around his neck. Petra trusted her daughter, trusted her endlessly, even when Bence struggled and kicked and moaned as he was running out of air. Juli only tore the bag off Bence's head when his kicking got too weak, and Petra's mouth was finally flowing with banknotes.

They hugged each other under the tree, knelt on the cold ground, and cried. They were like a traditional family again, because every family on the street, in the city, in the country was like this. Broken and bent and cold and full of tears.

Petra woke up on a Sunday morning to a sense of incredible lightness. The sun was shining through the curtains and she felt light as a feather, though she had no reason to feel so good. Things had not gotten any easier; on the contrary. Nevertheless, she almost laughed; then she let herself and laughed, first quietly, then loudly and resoundingly, a true laugh as if she had become ten years younger. Juli and Bence came into her room and watched their laughing mother, asking her what was so funny, but then they started laughing too. They crawled into bed next to Petra, still laughing, and threw pillows at each other.

Petra then made them pancakes.

She spared no effort and mumbled happily to herself. When the first pancakes slipped off the pan, even Juli allowed herself to be a child again.

After the pancakes, they watched TV. Not the news, but a Bud Spencer movie where the bad guys were punched and kicked out of the frame with a loud thud, and where this big, bearded man was always helping the fallen, never needing money, just beans. They laughed at the movie because it was funny, and Petra already knew why her heart felt so light today, and she did not want it to ever get heavy again. A thought occurred to her that she was going crazy, that her thinking was unhealthy, unsound; but who's to say what's healthy and what's not? Perhaps the state? They got a quarter of the price for her pain; that should be enough.

She kissed her children's faces and told them how much she loved them. Then they watched another movie.

In the evening, Juli and Petra went out to the tree. The neighbors' house had already been seized by the bank. Their house was next.

Now it was Juli's turn to crawl into the trunk. She stuffed her mouth full of leaves and curled up in the hollow.

Now you have to trust me, said Petra. Trust me and do not move, okay? Juli nodded and shivered, not just because of the cold, but because she knew she was about to experience a new method of pain.

Petra took a step back, away from the tree. Juli watched her mother and knew that whatever Petra did, it would be an act born of love.

Petra smiled and still felt so light inside; everything seemed so far away. The pain could no longer reach her because she knew she wouldn't need any more money ever again.

She picked up the knife from the ground. She clutched the handle, waiting for the fear to take hold of her, but it never did.

I love you, she said, raising the knife to her throat. The last movement was natural, as if she had been always prepared for it.

In the hollow, Juli opened her mouth to scream, but only money poured out, and it poured and poured and never stopped.

www.ingramcontent.com/pod-product-compliance
Lightning Source LLC
LaVergne TN
LVHW091138080826
845145LV00008B/2192

* 9 7 8 1 9 5 4 3 2 1 9 4 6 *